My Friend Paul

Michelle Odette Whelan

For the real Paul in my life.
Your story has finally been told.

Chapter 1:
No, really, I'm fine!

My hands firmly tight around the steering wheel. Slightly leaned over to look at the time on the radio, 8:38 a.m. I blew out a deep breath and leaned forward to look out the windscreen, noticing the company's name, TroniX.

My God, I hate this place!

I gripped tighter, hearing the leather creak. *This is the last place I want to be.*

Inhaled deeply; and blew it out. I muttered to myself, "Okay, Gwen! Today is going to be a good day!"

Looking down at my backpack, debating if I should pick it up. Realising I needed the money, picked it up, opened the car door and got out.

Swinging my backpack onto my shoulder, I heard someone behind me say, "Hey, careful!"

I turned around quickly, "Sorry, didn't mean…." Standing before me was a tall guy, with floppy blonde hair parted to the left, wearing a Voltron t-shirt, red bomber jacket, wired framed glasses, black jeans and white sneakers.

"Hey it's cool, man." He said cheerfully, "Are you heading to the building?"

He pushed his glasses up his nose. "It's my first day. Kind of excited to be here."

Who is this guy? Where did he come from?

"You okay?" He asked me, concerned.

"After…. after you." I awkwardly said.

"Okay, see you inside." Then he continued on towards the building.

I muttered to myself again, "You're a great coder. You are a fantastic person. Remember Gwen, you got this!"

Coding is my Jam!

While everyone at high school was learning new languages, I chose coding. After explaining my theory; coding is like learning another language, the school gave in. At the age of fifteen, I created my first app. It was nothing special, an app collecting books, where you rate them, share your ratings with others, create stats, and show off your collection.

College came around, and once again, I was one of the best coders in college and graduated as a top-level student. Creating Software, building games, learning new codes, new programs, few girls in my class, and always felt like I was just one of the boys. Everyone said they couldn't wait to see me in the top companies. I knew I was a shoo-in for them. My ideas would have impacted these companies. My style of coding, my pace would have had product out earlier. I was fast at my builds and enjoyed every minute.

I tried to get at least a foot in the door, but so was everyone else. I never heard from any of them. Finally, after so many knock backs, I ended up at TroniX.

I couldn't start my day without glancing over at Grayson, typing away on his projects. He looked so handsome as he coded. Now and then, he'd throw his fist in the air, as though he was at a dance party, grooving to his own music. I would daydream about how Grayson would come over, strike up a conversation, and then drag me into the bathroom to make out.

As my daydream was ending, my attention turned to Hammond, talking to another person.

Hammond held the position of manager for this floor. His eyes followed me like a hawk as I walked towards my desk. His eyes pierced through me. It can be frustrating being the only woman on the floor, constantly attracting unwanted attention.

The next thing I saw was the desk in front of mine. It sat empty, gathering dust, as if untouched for years. Having someone there would mean I have someone to talk to. *"How was your weekend?"*, *"Did you get that email from finance?"*, *"Could I borrow a pen?"*, *"Oh, did you watch that series on Netflix? My God, it was good!"* I started to smile and respond to the conversations, but my smile vanished quickly when I realised they were just in my head.

I let out one more huff as I placed my headphones, ready to start the day.

The day at the office was just like any other. Normally, my day consists of coding, fixing teammate's code, managing emails, and listening to my Spotify playlist. No one on our floor talked to each other. Instead, we all put our headphones on and just code.

Forget your headphones, and you could hear the tapping of keys, small dull chatter from some people, or if you can listen carefully, you could hear Hammond yelling at someone through the walls of his office.

Lunch break means either a quiet kitchen with your own food or a solo treat in the cafe.

Most people don't interact with each other because they prefer to focus on their work. They're afraid of the consequences. Office gossip gets taken seriously around here. Some have lost their jobs for seemingly insignificant reasons, like taking the wrong elevator or expressing dislike for the code.

As I sat eating, I started making a list in my head of things I needed to do:

Feed the cat when I get home, call someone about that tap dripping in the bathroom, oh, and check out LinkedIn for jobs.

I've been job hunting for a year now, but I'm always met with the same disheartening message: *over a thousand people have already applied for the position.* No matter my skill level with coding, or how many credentials I have to back myself up, I would always miss out on big company dreams.

Five p.m. would come around. I would let out a sigh of relief that I survived another day. As I pack myself up for the day, I see others in the office packing up like drones and going home. To repeat all of this the next day.

I rolled into my driveway, gazing at the house I bought three years prior. I managed to get a good price, even though my dad had to co-sign, particularly after my ex, Max, left unexpectedly. It's been three years since he sent the text message, and yet I still don't know why he just suddenly left like that.

I know I did something wrong for that to happen? But what did I do? If only I had the answers, I could fix myself, then Max will regret that break up text.

I didn't want to move out of the car. Moving took so much effort, picking up my bag, opening the car door, walking inside the house. UGH! It was too much!

Staring out the windscreen sensing my mind blanking, something quickly caught my eye, my cat climbing the stairs to the front porch, and then sitting there with her tail curling around her. I let out another huff. "Better feed her."

My neighbour, who was busy gardening, saw me as I emerged and said, "Hey, Gwen!" she cheerfully shouted.

"Hello, Mrs Waters." Forcing myself to be friendly.

The funny thing about my house is that it is almost empty. You can make out an echo when I talk. It was also quiet and cold when I entered through the front door.

I have one couch, one desk and one dining table. One bookshelf, no books, one gigantic bed to sleep in, and three vacant rooms. When I first moved in, I would look at those rooms, wondering what to do with them. I had big ideas for each room, turning one into a guest room, another into an art and hobbies room, and maybe the last room would be a nursery, as it was something I hoped for when Max and I were together. But each project became an *'I'll do it later'* moment. But they never came. Eventually, I closed those doors and never opened them again.

While I ate my microwaved dinner at the dining table, chewing my food slowly, I pulled my phone out, clicked on LinkedIn and scrolled through the job ads, clicking on save for each one I thought I might have a chance at.

I placed the phone down on the table and gazed around the house. Its desolate emptiness struck me. The house had no personality to it, no ornaments, no mementos.

For Christ's sake, my twenties are coming to an end soon. I know I have a few or more years left, and I have nothing to show for it; I should have had many stories, adventures, and pictures on my fridge or hanging on the walls of me and my besties. Me and my family, Me and my boyfriend. But I didn't have any stories to share. I had nothing, not even a friend.

This house should have been bustling with people, playing games, sharing stories, and laughing together during a party or dinner. Or sitting at the table while I listen to my children talk about their day. *What did they get up to in school?* As the kitchen fills with the sounds of banging and sizzling, my husband insists he's a superb cook, though evidence suggests otherwise.

But those things would never happen. They were only just dreams. Letting out another sigh and went back to eating.

The next day, I followed my usual routine, paused for a moment, looked around to make sure there was no one behind me again, and then reminded myself that it was going to be a good day.

As I headed in towards the building, that same blonde hair guy from yesterday was walking towards the entrance. He looked in my direction and waved with a huge grin. I looked around, wondering if it was at me or at someone else he was waving to, so I waved back.

Turning around once more to see if there is someone behind me, only to see the usual people. I grabbed the straps of my backpack tight and continued on.

I was about to put on my headphones and go to work when Hammond called everyone to the workbench.

The workbench was just a bench in the middle of the office floor. However, it was the cornerstone of all our projects. It was where we gathered around and planned out each app we built. It is also the place we conducted our stand-ups.

"Morning, all." Hammond started each meeting. It was hard to understand him through his thick New Zealand accent.

As Hammond reviewed each project's status, when I heard, "Got a few coding issues, but we're on to it." Knowing that Grayson was there in the meeting made this little morning moment feel blessed.

"Then this leaves Project Popper." Hammond continued.

The lamest of all the projects. It was an app for people to poke or burst Poppers, the silicon sheet of bubbles. I rolled my eyes when I heard its name.

"Almost finished. Observing the layouts. Easy peasy, lemon squeezy!" Huxley said.

Huxley was that guy in the office who took every job too seriously and always threw jargon and buzzwords around. They made no sense. It was like he had discovered old Grandpa's sayings and phrases and tried them out on us.

The team didn't get them and tried to second-guess what he was trying to tell us, slowing down projects.

As soon as everyone went back to work, it was just Grayson and me. With our headphones on, listening to our music, now and then pumping his fist in the air. *It was kind of hot!*

Grayson was of Asian descent. He was also tall, well built, and wore a lot of work shirts. People sometimes mistook him for one of the team leaders or higher-up management. But no, he was just a coder like the rest of us.

I admired Grayson as a person; I didn't know how he kept it altogether in this company. Still, he had a level head and was excited about each project, being fully aware that he was also part of this *Let's be Diverse campaign*, too. *Fuck that campaign!*

Then, all of sudden, Grayson stopped and looked in my direction. Our eyes locked.

Panicking, I searched frantically for something else to look at, grabbing items from my desk.

Another quick glance over, he had returned to work. I stared at my screen, *what have I done? I have blown my chances to be with Grayson. What. Have. I. Done.*

As the day went on, I found someone staring at me. Ivan, standing there with a huge creepy smile. Leaning on the corner with his hand drooping down like it was more part of the wall than a part of him.

"Working hard?" He asked.

I took my headphones off slowly, as I really didn't want to talk to him. "What do you want?"

"Need help to build an app."

I place my headphones on my desk. "What… you meant to say is, 'Can… you build an app for… me? And… save my ass.'"

He bounced his head from side to side. "Something like that."

Ivan was a guy in the office you found hard to trust. He was always thinking of himself and was greedy, a suck-up. The worst part was that they hired him as part of the *Let's Be Diverse campaign*, even though he didn't know any coding.

He grabbed the chair from the spare desk before me and swung it around to sit and talk to me. He leans closer. "I need an app, a dating app. I want to find all the hotties in my area, so I can 'Connect' with them. You know, I can find their location and have one of those I accidentally bump into them. Throw a few of my moves, then back to my place for some extra fun." The smell of coffee and cigarettes coming off each of his words made me want to gag even more after hearing his app idea.

"Extra fun?" I asked him.

"Come on Gwen, you know. I'll get to sleep with them!"

"Wait… you want a …. stalking app?" *Did I hear him right?*

"It's not stalking!" Ivan snapped at me, but he looked around the office before continuing, "The app accesses their Facebook and Instagram profiles and ranks how hot they are. Then I can find them in a club or a bar, and I ask them out, and bam, I'm having the best sex of my life!"

Yes, I heard him right.

"Ivan, what is wrong with you? Why…. can't you build this…. yourself? Are you scared…. of Python?" I told him.

He placed his arms up in the air. "Gwen don't be racist. I'm not a snake handler!"

The nerve of him coming up to me to ask for this gross idea for an app. If things got blown up, I didn't want to be responsible for that app. *Why would I want to build a stalking app?*

I moved my chair away from him and tried to go back to work. But Ivan sat there and looked around the office. He leans in further, "I know you are about to finish up on the Project Popper, and you will need a new project to jump on, or you will be a floater. Nobody likes to float. It doesn't look good for your career!"

Goddammit! Ivan was right; floating in this company could be dangerous. The company can lower your pay and make up reasons to keep you from joining specific projects if they discover you are floating, forcing you to quit. I can't afford to leave the company, not yet.

"If you do this for me, I will tell the office how good you are," he said, smiling at me again.

Of course there are rumours about me on the floor and that I really sucked at coding. I made one minor mistake and suddenly I got labelled that I suck at coding. Which was why I was on crappy projects, like Project Popper.

I really have nothing to gain from this.

Nothing!

And what do I have to say for myself once this app gets out and someone out there finds out what it really does?

Nothing!

I don't know why I built an app like this. I'm just a sick pervert with issues.

Ivan won't have my back. It's all Gwen's idea. Gwen was the one who built it, you tell by her code. Deny, deny, deny, that's what he will do.

"Fine…"

It just slipped out. I tried to hold it back, and tell Ivan something else like, *NO! Do it yourself.* But I wasn't thinking, it just came out.

"Fine!" I said again, fully aware of what I was agreeing to.

He did a little fist pump to himself but then looked directly at me. "Gwen, this is between you and me. No need to let the office know."

My mind kept replaying all the worst-case scenarios. My chest became tight, my head started to ache, and my eyes started to water. I took another deep breath, trying to get rid of this tight feeling around my body.

Why did I say Yes to this? What has happened to me? Why do I cave into these stupid ideas so easily? How did I become so scared of saying 'No' or am I so desperate for some form of human connection, that I would say Yes to anything, even though it made me sad on the inside? I don't remember being like this before, so why suddenly now?

After work, sitting in my car watching everyone leave the building, I wanted to leave and go home, home is safe, but the dread of the day started to fill my mind with *'what if'* scenarios. What if I told Ivan no? What if I didn't take my headphones off?

UGH!!!!

All I have to do is put the keys into the engine to get the car started and drive out of here. *Come on Gwen, you can do this, put the keys into the engine and turn it.* I'm sure the rest of the idea of driving will come back to me, somehow.

My breathing suddenly became rapid, my arms heavy, my body tense up, tears were flowing. I couldn't catch my breath! *What the hell is happening to me?*

Suddenly, I heard a tap on my window. This made me jump out of my skin and snapped myself back into reality. I quickly wiped my face with my sleeve before I looked over to see the same blonde hair parted to the left side, wired frame glasses, Voltron tee shirt, red bomber jacket guy.

I wound down my window, "Hey, don't be upset," he said, concerned.

"I'm not upset; it's just hay fever," I told him.

"I never seen hay fever let tears run down someone's cheeks before."

"It's a different type of hay fever, a rare kind," I snapped at him.

He stood up, looked around the car park, "Look, whatever it is, you need to let it all out of your system. Then you'll get back on your horse."

"It's hay fever!"

He leaned back in the window and chuckled, "Okay, it's a rare kind of hay fever."

Feeling a little better, I introduced myself, "I'm Gwen Hooper."

"Yeah, I know. The only female on our floor. Everyone knows who you are," he said, "I'm Paul."

Chapter 2:
New guy on the floor

Upon entering the office the following day, I suddenly stopped in my tracks. There is something different here. No glance at Grayson today, but this time something different caught my eye. A colourful, strange person sitting in the empty spot.

Fresh blonde haircut, a red bomber jacket with the sleeves rolled to his elbows. *I had seen this jacket before, but where?* I took another step closer, *wait a minute, is that Paul?*

As I arrived at my desk, exaggerated my movements while connecting my laptop, hoping to catch Paul's eye.

"Morning," he said as he took out his earbuds. Before saying something to Paul, Hammond had us gather around the workbench for our daily stand-up.

As I took my usual spot, and Paul next to me. Standing straight, his arms folded in front of him, wiggling his nose to straighten his glasses, really taking in what Hammond was saying. Not paying attention to Hammond, rather keep my focus on Paul. Even though we had small interactions, I could see myself being friends with him.

After the meeting ended, I dropped myself into my chair, opened my laptop, and researched how Facebook check-ins worked.

"Are you seriously considering writing that dating app code?" Paul said.

"Yes, I don't want to lose my job," I told him.

I popped up, "how do you know about the dating app?"

"Sorry, overheard the conversation. Between you and me, I think you're making a mistake." Paul answered, "I heard Ivan is an asshole. Very selfish person, calls himself the Alpha of Alpha men."

I didn't want to think about it anymore, I just wanted to go back to work. The quicker I work on it, the quicker it's gone.

"I don't know…" Paul added "…Maybe losing your job here could do you a world of good."

WHAT THE FUCK?! With a mortgage to pay, losing my job was the last thing I wanted. *'Don't quit your job until you have another one lined up!'* my dad would always tell me.

"That's the dumbest thing to say to someone you just met. Might as well continue picking out my flaws," I said back.

"I know you hate it here." Paul continued.

Sinking back into my chair I knew he was right, but I needed to convince myself that working here was fine. But how? After seeing Grayson walked past, and there it was, the reason why I'm staying.

One day I'll talk to him, and I don't want to leave before I have time to do that.

"I simply can't stand the projects I'm put on," I said to Paul. "Anyway, what makes you say I hate it here?"

"Well, the hay fever attack you had yesterday. The way you slouch into the office. And don't forget that you sit in your car for about fifteen minutes before coming in. You glare at everyone, that's another thing."

Just as I was about to answer Paul, the words "Gwen, sweetie!" interrupted me. Hammond, and his thick New Zealand accent.

"Hammond…. Please…. don't call me…. sweetie." I told him.

"What's youse talking about? I call everyone sweetie." He turned to Grayson, and said, "Grayson, sweetie, got those codes for me?" Turning back, he looked down at me.

Watching Grayson's confusion, "It seems like… Grayson isn't happy…. about being called…. sweetie."

"Nah, Grayson loves it!" Hammond said.

Towering over me, with an impatient smile, I grin back up at him. *Why is he at my desk?*

Most of the time, Hammond locks himself up in his office. The only time we see him out on the floor is when he is demanding answers from the coders.

"Are you working on something?" He asked.

Making little perplexing noises, I looked around my desk, while I searched for something. When I couldn't find that one thing I needed, I threw my arms in the air.

I didn't want to or could explain to him about this gross-out dating app that Ivan convinced me to build.

"Just as I thought," Hammond leaned down to my level. "Gwen sweetie, you were hired for your skills, so why not showcase them?"

"Skills?"

"Your engineering skills. I need a project from you."

What on earth is Hammond on about? They just sounded like words that tried to make sentences. Was he showing off to Paul that he was the boss around here, and how this company was run?

My gaze swept across the room, then my eyes caught on to Ivan, who was sitting at his desk. "I'm helping Ivan with... his dating app."

Hammond stood straight back up quickly. "Dating app? Do we need a dating app?"

I needed to say something, "It couldn't hurt... to have... you know... one out there?"

Hammond nodded his head in agreement, liking this idea.

"Besides, if... if... a client asked for one, so why not have.... one ready for them?" I nervously said, hoping there were no follow-up questions.

"Okay, Gwenny, babe. Give me a dating app!" Then he walked off.

My head hit the desk. *I'm fucked.* Not only did I have to work with Ivan, but I also had to develop a dating app. Did we really need a new dating app? After all, there are so many dating apps out there already. Why does the world need a brand new one?

I walked over to Ivan's desk and sat on the edge. Ivan stopped doing what he was doing and looked up at me. "Fine, your idea of…. this dating app is… a good idea." I forced a fake smile at Ivan.

Ivan gave me a once-over, leaned back in his chair, and placed his hands behind his head. "There are dating…. dating apps for…. everyone…. so why not build one…. for perverts?" I added.

"Hey, it's not an app for perverts. Just a unique way of meeting hotties." He answered me.

"Fine!" I placed my hands up, defeated.

Still sitting on the corner of his desk, waiting for a strategy for this build. Met with silence, I knew that this wasn't going to be easy.

"I'll build… the code," I told Ivan.

"I understand," he interjected, "but here is my dilemma; I don't know how to design either. I mean Photoshop is hard. So many tricks to use, and all those icons…"

Is he serious? He is actually going to make me build the whole thing, with no attributes to the project.

I took a deep breath in, closed my eyes, "Fine…. Fine…. I'll build the whole damn thing, front and back end!"

"See, Gwen, I knew you would see things my way." He said as he rubbed my leg. I swatted his hand off my leg and walked away.

"What happened? Did you tell Ivan about the conversation you had with Hammond?" Paul asked when I returned.

Could this be the ticket I needed to get out of this company? I could escape by getting fired, like Paul suggested. But then again, no one wants to hire me after they discover I built a pervert app.

"I really need to change the idea of it without Ivan knowing." I said to Paul.

"You can do this! Screw Ivan over. It seems he screws everyone else over." Paul added.

Yes, It's my turn to screw people over rather than the other way around, but how?

Chapter 3:
Mexican Restaurant

Engrossed in building this code and listening to music, when the lights turned off. Looked around to find the office was completely empty.

Got off my desk, gave a big stretch, the lights turned back on, noticing Paul stretching as well. His t-shirt lifted, showing off his dark brown happy trail. I couldn't help myself but watch his t-shirt hem bounce back into place.

"Sorry, I thought I was the only one left," he said.

Wait, did he not hear the tapping of my keyboard, or me making little frustrating noises?

Looking down at my watch, *Oh My God it's late!*

"I have to go home and feed the cat," I said without thinking about it.

"So, why are you the only female here? I always thought that the IT industry was booming with females?" Paul asked, as I packed my backpack.

The question caught me off guard, how do I answer this?

"TroniX hired me for their *Let's be Diverse* program."

With my backpack slung over my shoulder, I continued explaining the stupid program to Paul. "TroniX got into a lot of trouble a few years back, being an only white and male company. Their sexist and racist remarks came to light when an email trail made its way to a client. The email trail jeopardized the entire company. CEO, directors, high ups quit as they didn't want their names tarnished with this. The remaining team members launched the Let's Be Diverse program to protect themselves."

We walked out of the floor and into the hallway, "They would hire anyone who applied for a role that looks or is diverse. Without considering the company, I applied for a coding role. I was the only woman who applied, and it was the first company that offered me a job after I had been searching for a long time."

The lights would turn on as we entered that section of the hallway. "So, they hired Ivan, who is Indian. But he really is a third-generation American. He was originally from Chicago."

Paul took it all in. "They also hired Hammond, who is Māori, Grayson: Asian, and Huxley, who identifies as queer." I explained who they hired.

We finally got to the front door. "We were all dumb enough to take on these roles," I said, "But unfortunately, they continue with the asshole comments, mainly because the company hasn't really learned their lesson, and we lost our HR department after the company went through this major change. For some reason; the higher-ups believed there was no need for a HR team as we all should be able to get along, theoretically. It amazes me how much they still get away with their backhanded comments and attitude towards…" I suddenly stopped talking, realising it was me who got these backhanded comments, as all of the rest of the Let's Be Diverse team were still male, "…their attitude towards diverse people."

"Is that why Hammond called you, sweetie?" Paul asked.

"Yeah, pretty much!" I told him, repulsed by the memory. "It's just one example of things I have to put up with. There have been worse incidences than that in the past. I just learnt to roll with it. No point complaining about it."

"Gwen, that's not healthy. You shouldn't have to put up with this. It's possible to find another job. You got skills. Anyone would be happy to have you." Paul told me.

Well, that made me feel uncomfortable! Never been a person of complements.

I got to my car and was about to say goodbye when Paul interrupted. "Wanna go out and get something to eat?"

Oh My God, I am hungry, how did he know?

He then inquired, "Do you like Mexican food? I love a good taco. I know a place. You wanna drive?"

Mexican food has always been my favourite. *Yeah, I'm with Paul on this, I am a sucker for a good taco!*

I knew this place; it was close to home. "Oh My God, Paul, I always wanted to try this place."

"Me too. It is such a great chance to try it out together."

The restaurant was decorated with Mexican-themed decor, with music playing in the background. The server, dressed in black, came over and took our order.

"What did you get?" I asked Paul.

"Same as you. I ordered the three-taco deal, like yours. I liked what you ordered and quickly held up my fingers." showing me what he did.

The first plate of Tacos came, I was so hungry I couldn't wait. Readjusting the taco, I asked Paul, "Why TroniX?"

"Mostly experience. I would never choose to be in a place like that. I have only been here for a few days, and the atmosphere is draining. No one talks to anyone, and I always feel tense when I'm there. But hey, work is work, and if it makes my resume look good, then so be it!"

"You're right. If the next company can see you have worked there for a long time, they might hire you because you can stick around."

"But the thing is, no one has explained to me how TroniX works?" Paul added.

"Oh, that's easy…" I swallowed hard, "technically we are an App Factory. We build apps to sell to businesses, and vice versa. We get businesses asking for apps. We are allowed to have free thinking where we can build our own apps… But…. they do become the property of TroniX. There's a loophole, which I don't think anyone has discovered yet. IF you build your apps at home and on your personal computer, they aren't property of TroniX."

"Well, that sucks for TroniX."

"I know right! Could you imagine how many lawsuit TroniX would have to go through for that one golden app? Waste of their time really."

"What was the deal with project popper?" Paul changed the subject.

"Oh, fuck me dead on that project! Such a waste of time!" I said, throwing my head back. "You know those popper things, right? They are like silicon bubble wraps!"

Paul nodded.

"Huxley thought these would be great to build. He mentioned something about saving the environment if we built them." I continued. "Saving the environment? I know

Huxley likes to green wash things without realising what kind of impact on the environment it has. It's just a fucking app! An app for spoiled rotten kids who need everything!" I chewed on the taco, "A fucking app!"

Paul chuckled, and I joined him. It really was a stupid idea for an app.

Paul leaned back in his chair, "oh so full!" and rubbed his tummy.

Looking at the bill, it was cheaper than I expected. I was about to negotiate the bill with Paul when he started to frustratedly look around. He placed his hands in his pockets, fumbled around in his bag, then patted down his pants. "Gwen, I'm sorry to do this, but I left my wallet at home! Can I get you next time?"

So typical!

"Sure, fine, but you promise… Next time!" I said, pointing a finger at him.

"Yes Gwen," he says, crossing his heart, "next time."

The cool breeze from the night blew as we stepped outside. "See you tomorrow?" Paul said.

I waved goodbye and headed to my car. It dawned on me that I needed to ask him what project he was working on.

I turned to see if I could catch him again, but he was gone. Vanished.

I shrugged it off, as he must have caught the bus in time.

Chapter 4:
Perfect person

Paul wasn't at work when I arrived. Setting myself up, I compared our desks; see, on my desk, I have an old calendar, some posted notes, and a picture of the company's logo, notebook, picture of my cat, some knick-knacks, and a dust ball behind the big screen, whereas Paul has…nothing. Not a notepad, no keyboard or mouse, just dust everywhere.

I should remind Paul about cleaning his desk.

Once again, as I was about to put the headphones on, our daily stand-up was called.

I went to get my usual spot, but how dare that person get it before me, so I had no choice but to blend into the background. I looked to my left side to see Paul finally turning up to work, still wearing the same red jacket and Voltron t-shirt.

"Hey," he greeted me.

"You're late," I whispered to him.

"Shut the fuck up, Gwen!" the other person said, standing beside Paul.

As Hammond read off each project, I needed to find Grayson in this crowd. I needed my Grayson fix to remind myself that today is a good day.

Suddenly, we locked eyes on each other.

Grayson stood with his arms folded, one foot forward, leaning on his back foot, eyebrows slightly raised. I lost my sense of hearing just staring at him. Grayson gently lifted his head, curled up the corner of his mouth for a small smile towards me.

My heart took a deep dive, my eyes widened as I watched his baby blue work shirt, with navy blue work pants, the top button undone, freshly shaved, and his baby face Asian features.

I knew this moment right here was the only chance I could have. I shake my hand, trying to wave at him. He dipped his head, hiding his chuckle.

Oh My God, he noticed me!

"Who's that?" Paul whispered to me.

"Grayson." I whispered back.

We return to our desk after the meeting, "You are wearing the same clothes as yesterday." I said to Paul, as I sat down.

"Indeed, I am!" Paul said back, looking down at himself.

"Did you meet someone after dinner last night?" Thinking there was some gossip here.

"No, my clothes were still clean, so I put them back on. Plus, they are what I could find on the floor of my room."

Here I am hoping for a juicy story.

"I am single, if you must know." Paul added.

"Single!" I said, a little too loud.

Quickly clearing my throat, I added, "Good to know."

Paul leaned closer over the wall between our desks, like he had just unlocked some information out of me. "So, what about you?" he asked casually.

"I have a cat. Does that count?" I said.

"That screams single to me," Paul said back.

Yeah, it did.

The lights in the office turn off again.

Dammit, another late night in the office!

Standing to stretch, I noticed Paul was still there.

"Another late one?" I asked him.

"Being new, I want to put some effort into this work." He looked at me while he stretched. "Hey, you wanna order a pizza, and we could put some extra time into these codes?"

This was a good plan. I can get rid of this dating app, then I can be assigned on a new project. Maybe one with Grayson. *Oh, how much fun would that be!*

We sat on top of the workbench, munching on the pizza crust, and I looked around the office. It looked sad, really. Each desk looked the same, in rows upon rows. With each chew, I counted the rows and how many desks in each row. "Wow, there are ten rows of desks. Each row has four desks."

"So, we have about forty coders in the company, then," Paul said, munching on a slice of pizza.

Do we really have 40 coders in this company?

"I guess so? I always assumed there were other forms of workers here. There's some Graphic Designers, and some front-end designers." I said, as I thought about who was here.

I picked up another slice. "So, where are you from?"

"Oregon."

That's funny. I'm from Oregon, too.

"I moved to San Jose to go to college. I got into Stanford."

Same here.

Do you have any siblings, by any chance?" I asked.
"One sister, she's younger," he answered.

Okay, strange, same with me.

"High school life?"
"Oh, that was rough!" Paul said. "I often got bullied, so I'd hide in the computer labs during lunchtime."

I put the pizza slice down. It was like we were living the same life. Paul asked the same questions. I put my hands up and said, "Just copy and paste your responses."
Paul laughed. It was incredibly uncanny how our lives mirrored each other. I decided to tell him about my life. "I live mostly around the forest and the mountains, so there wasn't all that much to do. You know, small town stuff. I got picked on a lot for my fondness of technology. *'Girls don't know how to use a computer. Technology is for boys. Girls' brains can't do maths.'* you know, stuff like that. I did use these as my ambitions. I want to prove them wrong. I worked hard, convince the school to let me do coding classes

instead of learning French. The next thing I knew, I earned myself a scholarship to Stanford University. I graduated top of my class. I have a younger sister, too."

He listened to my entire life story, actually listened. "Wow, we really do have similar lives."

I know!

"What project are you working on?" I said, changing the subject.

Paul let his pizza slice hang there for a bit while he thought about his project. I jarred my head around, growing impatiently for his answer. His lips moved around, then he finally said, "How far away are you from finishing the dating app?"

"Nearly finished. I just need to test it. My only issue with testing is I don't know what a hot girl is?"

Paul stopped mid chewing. This question baffled him, too. "Same here. Everyone had different ideas of what a hot girl is," he added.

So, what is your ideal person?" The words escaped my mouth before I could think.

"Ummm, someone funny and smart. Someone who is honest and real to herself. Someone optimistic and slightly adventurous." Paul told me.

"Cool, but how does she look?" I asked him.

"Ummm... I never thought about this. Maybe someone who looks smart. They seem relaxed and appear capable of taking care of themselves." Paul answered.

"Lame!" I told him.

He chuckled, and I joined in. The moment faded, leaving us staring at each other awkwardly.

"Okay, fine! What about you, Gwen? Who is your ideal perfect person?" Paul asked.

I started to make a list in my head of who my ideal person would be. I brought my eyes back to him, looking him up and down. I noticed he does have some qualities I do look for in a person.

He was a nerd, but also tall and good-looking. He took care of himself and wasn't afraid to express his own style through his clothing, which included glasses. While he was very confident, he also cared deeply for others. He talked to me like I was human, not some lower class than him.

Then, I felt my heart beating faster and losing all senses around me. I looked back up at Paul, who was waiting for my answer.

His perfect hair, those glasses, he is so close to me. I wonder what he looks like under his shirt…. *OH MY GOD…. am I falling for Paul?*

I dropped the pizza crust down into the box and closed the lid. "Nah, I don't want to play anymore."

Taking the pizza box, I headed to the staff's kitchen. Paul followed me. "Sorry, I didn't mean to hit a soft spot with you."

Wiping my hands on a paper towel, I said, "It's fine."

Paul stood leaning against the door frame. "Seemed that you asked me, I thought I could ask you."

"It's fine, Paul!" I told him again.

I threw the paper towel in the bin and heard him again. "How long has it been since you dated, Gwen?"

Seriously? Did he really ask me that?

"Paul, I said it was fine!" Fully aware that it was me who brought it up.

I pushed past him and said, "Don't you have work to do? Is that the reason you're here late at night?"

I sat there, staring at my screen. My mind is replaying our kitchen conversation.

"Why would someone this good would be interested in someone like you? Don't you see how ugly you are? Nobody likes you!"

I shook my head. *What was that?*

I look down at myself. Paul wouldn't be interested in someone like me, sad, a bit overweight, quiet, and who doesn't care about her appearance.

"He is only being nice. He would never talk to you if you weren't in this situation."

I shook my head again. *Wait, is Paul just being friendly? There's no way he would talk to me out in public?*

I took a deep breath and went back to work.

I quickly woke up my computer as Paul returned to his desk. I read through each line of code to see what was done and where I needed to catch up. Although the code's foundation was complete, testing was still necessary. Tapping my pen on the notepad, wondering how to test this thing.

Then Paul swivelled his chair to my desk. "You know what you can do with this code? Change it into a game instead."

My eyes wandered over in his direction. "A game?"

"Yeah, just think... you have written a code to hunt down people. If we change the end result from looking for people through Facebook but through the GPS. The end user could then find components for the game."

"Hang on, like Pokémon Go?" I asked him.

"It's not exactly like Pokémon Go," Paul said, "but it's similar."

Leaning back in my chair, I pondered on this. *This might actually work. There is something good that could come out of this code.*

"We could work on this together." Paul asked.

I wrote on my notepad, *POKEMON*, and then it hit me, "Hang on, *'we'?* You want to work on this app with me?"

"Yeah, why not?"

Paul moved closer to my desk and then took over my computer. His scent was noticeable as he leaned toward me. My heartbeat fast again as I took deep breaths in.

He touched nothing on my desk but looked at the code and said, "See, Facebook uses GPS for their check-ins. If we use the same system and add an object with the code to find that object that might be near the check-ins, people will make their way over to that area. It's kind of a win-win situation; people will play our game, and the business or hotspot gets more customers. We could make sale promotions with check-ins, too."

"Just like Pokémon Go!" I added, breathlessly.

Paul glanced my way. Our eyes met. Right there, in this moment, staring at each other, gave me butterflies. I was at a loss for words.

Oh crap! I am falling for Paul, too.

It didn't take long for Paul to break the stare by leaning back in his chair. He cleared his throat. "If it works for them, then it could work for us."

Walking out of the front door, I couldn't help noticing my car was the only one left. "Would you like a ride?" I asked Paul.

"Nah, it's cool."

I looked at my watch. It was ten thirty at night. "Dude, it's late, dark, and dangerous. Are you sure I can't give you a lift?"

When I turned around, Paul was gone. I couldn't see where he went.

"PAUL?" I called out, with no answer back.

Chapter 5:
The game

There was a note bearing the word "POKEMON" on my desk, when I got in.

Yes, the game, I almost forgot!

I went to say something to Paul, but he wasn't there. His desk remained untouched. Strange, he was usually here before me. Maybe he slept in, since we worked until ten thirty last night.

I heard Hammond calling us over to the bench for our daily stand-up. *Fuck these stand-ups!*

"Okay, today we have a few deadlines for some of the projects. Grayson, give me details on Project Unicorn?"

"Well…Project Unicorn is ready to go live. We have….", Grayson explained. His voice and suggestive hand gestures, causing another daydream of him coming to my desk and starting a connection that progresses to spending time together, kissing, and ... "Okay, Andy, what about Project Green Grass?" Hammond's voice snapped me out of my daydream.

Oh, yes, this project! Another project I was glad not to be a part of. Andy called them "wellness centres," but it was just another app that located pot shops.

"It's amazing that he remembers where they are!" Paul said.

Turning to face him, he placed a finger to his lips as if he were smoking a bong, making me laugh. Andy stopped talking, and everyone looked at me.

"Sorry..." I said as I tried to hide my laughter.

"Seems everyone is looking at you; how is Project Dating App?" Hammond said towards me.

Why me? Here I am thinking that being in the background meant I wasn't going to get picked.

I scanned the room to see so many surprised faces. *Yeah, that's right, the only girl on the team is, in fact, building a dating app.*

"Fine," I said to Hammond, trying not to let out more information.

My attention quickly darted over to Ivan. Eyes wide open, his mouth went small, like he was trying to yell at me. After all, I did promise not to let everyone know.

I took a deep breath in, and said, "It's an app.... that finds..... like-minded people in your… area."

Hammond stood there growing impatient, with his eyebrows raised in my direction.

"And…. that's all I have…. so far." I awkwardly mention, hoping everyone would stop looking at me.

After logging in, the code differed from the previous night. I saw the word *POKEMON* on the notepad yet again. *Oh, yes, change it to a game.* But what game?

I sat up, looking over the wall between our desks, about to speak, but Paul working distracted me. Watching how his hair flops as he types, the glow of the computer screen bouncing off his glasses, how his arms are at perfect 90-degree angles. His freshly shaved face wiggled now and then like he was thinking of his part of his project. Wondering what it would be like to brush my hands across his face, those tickle kisses from him after a long day, curling up with him on the couch, feeling safe as we watch Netflix together…. *WAIT…. I really am falling for Paul!*

What on earth am I thinking? Paul's a co-worker, and then there is Grayson. Are my fantasies spiralling out of control?

Am I desperate to experience them? That can't happen! Imagine what would come for it if I acted on these fantasies. Am I so lonely that I'm fantasising about two of my co-workers?

Well, they say a lot of casual sex starts in the office.

"Are you serious Gwen? These guys don't like you at all. You see, guys are only being nice to you. It's because they want something from you. There is no way anybody would make you their girlfriend, not even the desperate!" sounds like something Max would have said.

I slumped back down in my chair and imagined the girls Paul would find appealing. Tall, skinny, tan-skinned, wearing summer dresses, beach blonde hair, and always into girly things. Somehow always smelt like they bathed in a sea of lilies with a hint of jasmine. Who would talk softly and always wanted to make small talk with you. She wouldn't have a favourite dinosaur. Instead, would say, *"Oh, I grew out of dinosaurs as a kid."* She would be a Graphic Designer, or in Marketing, or worse, HR.

No, see, Paul had style and class, and would have needed a girl to match this. He is the type who would spend his time with the pretty girl rather than try it with the decaying vegetable.

"You'll never match up to Paul! I mean, look at you." there goes that voice again.

My screen went black, showing my reflection. Yes, that voice is right. Why would Paul or Grayson be interested in a short, slightly overweight, pale skin with blotches and pimples. I grabbed my dark blonde, untamed hair, which is always in a bun on the top of my head.

And look at the way I dress; skinny black jeans with a t-shirt and thick glasses? I know my eyesight is poor, maybe I should swap to contact lens?

Oh yeah, why would a guy be interested in a girl who knows more than they do? I love tech, and have a fascination about dinosaurs, could down a burger in one bite, and I smell like I had been running a marathon.

I never talked cutesy or pretended not to know everything. I spoke bluntly, loudly, and in a monotone voice, and for some reason, it had some sort of accent to it that I didn't know where it came from?

"See? You're a waste of time," that voice told me.

I shook my head, trying to remove these thoughts so I can get back to work. I wiggled the mouse to wake the screen, but my eye caught over at Grayson. No headphones, talking to another colleague. Leaning back in his seat.

I imagine what conversation would be about; "oh, Gwen? Yeah, she is cool. In fact, I heard she is great at kissing."

"No, you're not! Remember, Max always said it was like kissing a blow-up doll!" Dam that voice again.

"I'm pretty sure Paul and Grayson shared the same ideal girl. Their girlfriends would meet and become instant friends, leaving you sitting there watching their friendship bloom, wondering why you're NOT invited into their conversations." That voice again in my head. *Why does it sound like Max?*

This was too much for me. I needed air. I needed to get away from everyone before someone noticed me making myself upset or, worse, not working!

"I need coffee!" I muttered.

"Can I come?" Paul asked as he bounced up from his desk.

Why did he need to come? I just wanted to get away from him for a bit. But I shrugged my shoulders and let him tag along.

There was a long line at the cafe. When I checked my watch, it showed 10:23 in the morning. I forgot that around 10:30 a.m. was the time where people liked to get away from their desk and go somewhere else. Seems at 10:30 a.m. is also the time where the office toilets get cleaned, so people have no option but to come to the cafe for another cup of coffee while they wait.

I joined the end of the line with Paul.

"Is the company this lame?" He asked.

"Yes, I wish I could work on something bigger and better," I told him, chewing on the edge of my thumb.

We took another step closer.

"You could," Paul added.

"No, I can't," I said, still chewing my thumb.

"Finish the game. Everyone likes games. It will get the attention you deserve," Paul said as we took another step closer to the counter.

"The game? I can't think of a theme for the game." Still chewing on my thumb.

Finally, we got to the counter, and I ordered my coffee. I turned to Paul.

"No thanks, I'm fine." He answered.

Then why did he come to get coffee with me? I gave up trying to work this out and then told the cashier, "I guess it's just me." The cashier was puzzled but then took my credit card.

We got back to our desks, still thinking of what Paul said about the game.

"What do you think we should theme up this game with?" I asked Paul. But I got no response.

I stood up, leaned over the wall, and found not only his desk covered in dust but also no sign of Paul.

Where did he go? I'm sure he was behind me at one point?

While standing, I scanned the office floor, when our eyes met again. Grayson walked towards my desk. He curled the corner of his mouth, keeping his gaze on me. He waved a manly wave and added "Morning Gwen" towards me as he kept travelling toward the kitchen. "MOR… Morning… Gray…son!" I said back. He turned his head slightly and let out a little happy huff.

I sat down quickly, placed my hand on my chest, trying to make my heart stop beating so fast. *I talked to Grayson! YES, I did it!*

"Do you want to recreate another *PokémonGo* type for this game? But without using Pokémon, since that's trademarked," Paul said as he appeared around the corner of my desk. This made me jump a little. He just appeared like that.

"What would be popular to use amongst everyone, the young and the old?" Paul continued.

Before Paul responded, Ivan approached my desk. "So, this dating app is now yours. Not ours?"

"Sorry." I said, really not in the mood.

"So, how far have you gotten on it?" He asked, trying to get more information out of me.

There is one thing you never do in the coding world, especially in a company like this: never tell a coworker how far into a project, swap ideas or what you are working on.
Everyone here is trying to be the next big thing and live like a tech billionaire. Fast cars, lots of money, big houses, lots of suck-ups. Suppose you brag or talk about something that piques the interest of anyone around here. Then you can kiss your ass goodbye. You wouldn't be able to prove it was your idea, since ideas can't be trademarked or copyrighted.

I took a deep breath. "It's…. moving…. along."
"It's moving?" He responded, with his arms crossed and rocking back and forth on his feet, while looking around the office floor.
I could have easily caved in and let him walk all over me, but then I looked over at Paul and wanted to show off in front of him, proving that I'm worthy to date.
"What's… the hurry, Ivan? You…. keep… striking out?" I tried to say.
"No hurry, but it would be nice to be the first people to have an app like this," he told me.

Another thing about working in tech was that everyone was in a hurry and needed to be the first for everything. But this was a dating app. Once again, it's not like this was the first time this idea was out there. There were thousands of them out there.

Ivan pissed me off. So many responses danced in my head. I need to make it clear to him that I am working as quickly as possible and that he is not the only one in the team who wants to see the end of this project. Each comment in my mind got me angry, frustrated, that I need to do something to end this conversation with him. I got up from my desk, "excuse me," I mumbled, then walked to the kitchen, shoulder-baring Ivan along the way.

As I tossed my coffee cup in the bin and poured myself a glass of water, I heard, "That was close!" I turned to my left to find Paul leaning on the kitchen bench. I didn't notice him following me into the kitchen. *How did he do this?*

I chugged my water, then put the glass under the tap again to pour more water.

Paul stood there watching me, before saying, "You could make it into a Scrabble-like game?"

While still holding the glass, I jarred my head at Paul.

"Okay, hear me out," he continued. "The app's register walks around collecting Scrabble tiles. Imagine adding rare tiles, like one that lets players stack tiles for new words or even remove tiles. If another app user is nearby, you can request a game where you both play. You use the collected tiles and bonus tiles to eliminate the other user. Playing each game increases your level, and each level presents a new challenge, either through increased difficulty or a different board design. You could add, like, every mile you walk, you get a bonus tile, tile swap, or something."

I stood there thinking of all the possibilities this game could have. I mean, it's not original, but it is at the same time. He really was onto something here. Take a classic board game and turn it into an interactive activity.

"You're onto something here. I'll finish the code; you'll investigate the design of it."

Chapter 6:
Paul's Little Secret

Turning an app from one style of app to another is hard, but I loved the challenge of it.

With my head down and bum up approached, headphones on, days turn to nights; nights turn to days.

I typed in the last few codes in, took a deep breath, hit control and enter, and let the code run. Grabbing my cold coffee mug from my desk, noticing the screen change from list of words and commands to a flat-out Google map.

It works!

There wasn't much there to look at, as I'm waiting on Paul for designs. We spend a good decent amount of time talking to each other about the project. A few more late nights, and another trip to our now favourite Mexican restaurant, and we had a plan for this game.

But each time I talked to Paul about design deadlines, he always made excuses.

"I can't decide on the colours. I'm trying not to make the map out to be different. What about red for the boards? Sorry, forgot what colour the triple word score is," Paul would tell me.

Excuses, excuses, excuses. Each time I heard another excuse, I would sit there listening away, adding *it's okay, Paul*, at the end of each meeting.

With the code working, the error box popped up, showing all the errors where I was waiting for Paul and his designs.

I stood up and leaned over the wall. "Paul? Where are my designs?"

He wasn't there again, and once again, his desk was empty. I sat back down in a huff. Looks like I need to design these parts to get the code working.

I opened MS paint and designed some squares and triangles. I attempted to make an avatar but could only manage a stick figure and added them into the blank spot of the code.

Hitting control and enter again, the code ran, then suddenly there was an avatar standing in the bottom middle of the screen. Then a triangle popped up. *It's actually working, this is great!*

Downloading the code onto my phone, getting up from my desk, I followed the avatar around, watching my screen popping with squares and triangles. If the avatar got close to them, then they would pop into their bag. I saw a little box drop down stating *you just collect a Q, This is worth 10 points!*

"Found anything?" Paul asked.

"Only a Q!" I told him without taking my eyes off my phone. *Wait a minute… Where did he come from?*

"Where're my designs?" I asked him.

"Getting there... I can't decide if we should have wooden or off-white tiles." Paul wiggled his hand from side to side.

Couldn't he use both?

I shut my eyes tight and squeeze my hands into little fists, getting frustrated with Paul.

"Have you been staying up all night again?" Ivan asked as he stood next to me.

What on earth is he on about?

"Nooooo?" I said.

"Sorry, it's just you're walking around the office staring at your phone, muttering now and then, also staring at walls or nothing." Ivan shrugged his shoulders and added, "It seems a little crazy."

I turned to face Paul, but there was a wall there instead. I reached out to touch it, wondering where Paul went.

Ivan joined in staring at the wall, "are… are… you…. o...kay?"

"Just seeing what is fascinating about the wall, you seem to stare at it intensely."

I looked back at the wall again. *I swear Paul was just standing there, like a moment ago*, "ummm…. just… just… wonder…ing…. what color… it is?"

"It's an off-white colour!" Ivan said to me before he left.

I just sat down. "All good?" Paul asked, popping up from his desk and scaring me again.

I really am not in the mood to talk to him. He is lagging the project with his continuous, indecisive decision making. I looked him in the eyes, and without saying a word, placed my headphones on and went back to clean up the game.

Exhausted from hours of staring at a screen, making sure that every line, every command had the right information in it, making sure I used the right symbols, the right naming conventions, making sure everything was perfect, I finally forced myself to take a break.

Opening the cupboard door, I heard, "Are you trying to ignore me? You know it's going to be hard to do that."

Slamming the cupboard door shut as soon as I got a glass. To find Paul leaning on the kitchen bench next to me.

"Hard?" I said back, "you're right. I will find it hard to ignore you. I need my designs! Where are they?"

I placed the glass under the tap as I continued, "I don't care what colours you use, what shapes or fonts!" I didn't realise how loud I was getting.

"But they do matter…" Paul tried to answer.

The rage inside built up. I was ready to scream at Paul. I knew there was a fight about to happen.

"LOOK HERE MISTER!" I shouted as I pointed my finger at him, "I am not your whipping girl, stop taking advantage of ME!" I took a step back from Paul, realizing what I had just said. I took a deep breath, and added, "if you're going to help, then help."

The blank expression, his mouth open and closed, trying to find the right words to say. Finally, I had one of these boys in their place.

"I wasn't taking advantage of you." He managed to get out.

This entire ordeal really pissed me off. I need Paul's help, but also, I need to get this project finished. I took another deep breath. "It's fine. I can help you out. After all, I have finished the code. I do have some time up my sleeve for some design work."

"Thanks." Paul got out.

He rubbed the back of his head and said, "I'm sorry Gwen, for everything, really."

What the hell? It was just some designs.

Absolutely baffled as I left the kitchen. Before I could reach my desk, Grayson blocked my path. I looked up at him. *Oh my God, is one of my fantasies about to happen?*

"Gwen, are you feeling okay?" Grayson said to me, trying to get to my level.

"Grayson?" I said in one breath.

"Is everything okay?" he asked again.

"Ummm…Yeah?" I managed to get out.

"Hey, come with me," Grayson said as he gently grabbed me by the arm and led me into one of the empty boardrooms.

He spoke as he closed the door, "Gwen, I saw you in the kitchen, standing there, talking to no one. It looked strange, like you were possessed. You don't have a demon in you, do you?"

A demon in me?

"What? No, I was talking to Paul. He…. was supposed to be…. helping me out on this…. this app." I told Grayson, nervously.

Grayson tilted his head as he sat down. He leaned in towards me with his hands folded before him once he settled on his next remark. "I thought Ivan was working on the dating app with you?"

I completely forgot that everyone knows I'm building a dating app with Ivan, who has been bragging about it being his own idea.

"Well... yes... but..." I didn't know how to explain this one to Grayson. But this is Grayson, and I don't want to start off our relationship on a lie, "OKAY! It's not a dating app!"

Grayson sat up straight, his hand still folded before him. "So… it's not a dating app?"
I panicked. This dating app had been the spawn in my veins since I stupidly agreed to it.

"It's not a dating app! It's a stalking app…. Ivan asked me… to… to create an app to find hot girls in his area… and… know where to go to hit on them!" I quickly informed him, "It's creepy! But…. I couldn't refuse… for some unknown reason…. I hate it."

It felt so good to tell someone about this app.

Grayson's gaze shifted upward, collecting his thoughts.

"Using the same algorithm…. I changed it…. it into a gaming app… instead… instead." I continued.

I knew I had no choice but to tell Grayson what I had done. I knew I had betrayed Ivan on his creepy project. It was the only way to save us all from getting fired. Grayson could have done anything here, really; go tell Ivan, take my idea of the game and make it his, tell…. Hammond.

"Please don't tell Ivan." I begged.

Grayson had been staring at me the whole time without moving. He seemed to be frozen in time, and his mouth was the only thing separating the past from the present. "How?"

How? What does he mean, how?

"How did you change the app from a dating app to a game?" Grayson corrected himself.

"Using the same element of searching for people… I changed it around to find… tiles."

He leaned back in his chair and folded his arms. "Wait… tiles?"

"Yes, they are gaming…. gaming pieces you need to…. to collect." I said too much.

"So, you said Ivan was designing these tiles?" Grayson asked, puzzled by my project and Ivan's role.

"Actually, I… I… don't know Ivan's role. Paul asked to design these. I'll… just add Ivan's name to…. to the final draft. I'll… even put it first… with a bigger font size. That… that would keep him happy."

Grayson tilted his head, wrinkled his nose again when I mentioned Paul.

"The dating app sucked! Like… Do we really need more dating apps out… there?" I asked.

Grayson lingered. "We've… thought about what the game… would be like… and how to keep people… interested." I continued to explain.

Grayson changed his position on his chair. "It's a good thing you changed the idea. But you need to realise who Ivan is. Once he finds out about this, and IF the game is successful, he will take all the credit and make himself the full designer. But if the game fails, he will use this against you and ensure you will never get a chance to be on any good projects. I don't think it's wise to add his name to the game."

Resting my head on my hand, I stared out the boardroom window, noticing Paul sitting there at his desk.

"If you want, I could get Ivan into trouble for you? I know a bit of dirt on that guy that could get him fired." Grayson said, getting my attention.

That sounded like fun!

"It's fine... I'll… let Hammond know…. I took an interest in another project instead." I told him.

"Good idea. I think Hammond might like the game. Sounds interesting."

"Yes… but…. it was Paul's idea… and I just ran with it." He wrinkled his nose again.

"Gwen… who's Paul?" Grayson finally asked.

Has anyone introduced Paul to everyone yet? Didn't Hammond do his regular introduction to the team? Or a morning tea for him. Actually, I didn't remember a morning tea. I never forget something like that!

"Gwen, who's Paul?" Grayson asked me again.

"He's… the new guy. He… sits at the desk in front of me…. He has been here… for a few weeks… now." I tried to explain.

Grayson shifted in his seat to look over me, but as he came to his original position, "Gwen, there's no one there. That desk has been empty for a while."

What are you talking about? That desk isn't empty! Can it be?

"He's tall… blonde hair… big round wire-frame glasses…. always wearing t-shirts and pants." I seriously didn't know how else to describe Paul. My description wouldn't be much help to the cops if he were a serial killer.

Grayson chuckled away to himself. "Gwen, there is no one like that here. But then again, we all wear t-shirts and pants."

He was about to leave the room. He placed his hand on my shoulder. "Gwen, I don't know who you're talking about, but there's no Paul here. No one here matches your description or even using the name Paul."

He left me in the room, in complete disbelief. *There's no Paul? Could I have imagined it? Paul was not real! No way, it couldn't be.*

Walking back to my desk, I paused, remembering the encounters that I have had with Paul, the cheap meals, losing his wallet, and the cafe cashier. All of those times, he wasn't real! He was some empty space I had imagined?

OH MY GOD!

Pushing the bathroom door open, I raced to my favourite basin. I grabbed the edges of it tight as I stared into the mirror. It felt real, all of it, every encounter, every exchange, every time we talked, touched, ate — all of it!

"This can't be real!" I muttered to myself.

I invented him; I created a character; I designed a person. I made those features; I made him blonde with floppy hair. I created that red bomber jacket. Am I really starved for conversation?

I splashed water on my face.

"Took you long enough," Paul said as he leaned against the bathroom bench.

"You're imaginary?!" I asked.

"Yes, your imaginary boyfriend," Paul said proudly.

Restlessly, I paced up and down the bathroom trying to process this news.

"Nope, I don't accept this. You're not an imaginary boyfriend! You're from Oregon, not Canada! Everyone knows imaginary boyfriends come from Canada!"

Paul started laughing. "Gwen..."

"No, Paul, just no. You need to go away. Having imaginary friends makes you crazy. Nope, I'm not crazy. I'm as normal as you and me!"

I realised what I was saying and to who. "Okay, I'm as normal as anyone else."

I stood there fixated on Paul, watching him do human things, like biting his nails. I knew I wasn't delusional. And I had always been moody. It's what you get working in this company.

"I have control over you?" I asked Paul.

Paul nodded.

"Okay, change your hair to black?" I closed my eyes tight and opened one of them to see if it worked. And there he was, now with black hair. This time it was wavy with a slight spike in the front.

"Okay, not bad," I said to him, finally seeing him with both eyes.

Paul looked at his reflection. He ran his fingers through his hair, pleased with what he saw. I closed my eyes tightly and wished for him to be blonde again. Upon opening, he was back to his usual floppy blonde hair parted on the left. "Actually, I prefer this." I said.

"Finished having fun?" Paul asked me as he walked into the cubicle.

I stood there hearing him pee, "Wait… you're taking a leak right now? Right now? I didn't realise imaginary friends could do that!"

"When you gotta go, you gotta go!" I heard Paul shout from the cubicle.

"So, how does this work? You come and go whenever I need you?" I heard what I said, and I sounded crazy.

"Oh, no I'm around. I'm around when you need me the most," he shouted over the toilet, flushing.

"Gwen, there is nothing wrong with you. I'm just someone here for you. And right now, in your life, you need me." He added as he washed his hands.

"I need you right now?" I asked, confused.

Paul moved closer to me. "Well, yes. Not sure why as yet? But yes, you need me."

I need him right now? For what?
The words escaped me, but he was right. I do need him.
Unbelievable… I have a friend!

Chapter 7:
Friends

My dinner steamed, tickling my chin while I was fixated on Paul. Yes, yes, I brought him home. If I'm going to have an imaginary friend, then I am going to bring him everywhere.

Mixing the food on my plate, I asked Paul again, "How does this work?"

"How does what work?" He said back.

"You can't sit there and watch me eat," I told him as I took another mouthful.

"I am your imaginary friend; you could imagine me eating."

With my eyes tightly closed, I pressed my fingers to my temple again, then abruptly opened them. A takeaway container full of Pad Thai was sitting in front of Paul. He started to eat. "Thanks, I love Pad Thai."

"You know, you don't have to close your eyes or make those psychic hand suggestions. I'm imaginary, not a magician's assistant." Paul said.

He swallowed his mouthful hard and then said, "Oh my God, Gwen, food, real food... This is great."

Real food? I could do that thing where I cook the actual food and take bites off his plate occasionally, pretending that Paul was the one who was eating... Or... save money and not waste excellent food on imaginary people.

Following dinner, I did the dishes as Paul watched, and we discussed the game once more.

"I like this idea you have about the different style tiles," Paul said, leaning on the kitchen counter. "The scoring system could change depending on the tile colours or style. You know, like, if they get a wooden J, they would get maybe ten points instead of eight points."

Actually, he is on to something here.

With the dishes finished, I turned on the TV.
"So, what are we doing this weekend?" Paul asked.

I mostly spent my weekends indoors. I began the day with a sleep-in and snuggle session with my cat, Colin, followed by attempting some form of exercise that never quite worked out. Then breakfast and reading. I read until lunchtime, checked the fridge—it was empty—so I skipped lunch. Following that, I sat at the computer to either research, code, or mindlessly scroll, then shifted my focus to baking cookies or cake.

Finally, I ordered dinner, then watched a movie or documentary while sitting in front of the TV.

I turned to say something to Paul, but he already answered me. "Lame!"

How does he know?

Paul pointed to his head. "I know your secrets, and what goes on in your head."

"But that's what I do every weekend," I told him.

He leaned into the chair beside the couch. "I know, and its lame. How are you supposed to meet people if you stay inside all day, all weekend?"

He was right. How am I supposed to meet people this way?

"Fine, what do you want to do, then?" I asked him.

"Why don't we go to the bookstore and that coffee place you always wanted to try? Maybe a movie or go out for dinner."

I looked over to the bookshelf, which was empty. "I did have my eye on this book. Can't remember what it was called. Maybe I could go to the store to get it?"

"Yes, let's go support small business and stuff like that," Paul said while pumping his fist.

The idea of going out in public frightened me. It wasn't the people or places; it was the idea of running into Max.

I looked down at myself, forgetting how much I had changed. I was aware of my curves, but I didn't realize how much they had grown. I used to appreciate my body's shape. I loved my big butt; I loved my wide hips and loved how my boobs bounced and jiggled.

But then there was Max, every narky comment, *'should you be eating that? Could you get off the couch and walk? You know, Gwen, guys don't like fat chicks. Do you see any of the top tech billionaires with a fat chick? You should eat what I eat, you will lose pounds and pounds!'* UGH!

It'd played with my head. Mini panic attacks each time we went out for dinner or ate. To control these attacks, I just stopped eating in front of him and only ate to survive.

I wrapped my jacket around me, trying to hide, thinking about how Max would react if we ran into each other. He would take one look at me with his new supermodel girlfriend, and say, "see, still pathetic!"

Yeah, going out of the house is really not for me.

I lied in bed, pulling the covers over my face. That thought of running into Max again played in my head. The more I thought about this, the more I felt this pressure in my head.

As I lay there trying to go back to sleep, but I heard footsteps in my room. Paul and his continuous pacing drove me nuts. *He wears sneakers. How can sneakers make so much noise on wooden floors?*

"DO YOU MIND!" I shouted at him as I rose from bed. "I was sleeping!"

"Oh good, you're up." Paul announced, "I'm so excited to get the day started!" I heard as I slammed the bathroom door.

Brushing my neglected hair was difficult, so many tangles, knots, and so greasy, leaving so many strains of hair all over the bathroom floor. I struggled to rediscover the pathways within its tangled mass. *It's on the left side somewhere.* Gave up and put it back up in a bun again.

I opened up the drawer where I kept all my makeup. Dabbing the foundation bottle on my blender, but the bottle was empty. Okay, no foundation today, then.

Opening my eyeshadow palette, I discovered the colours were all jumbled and broken. I found another palette and another, and the same thing happened each time. Fine, no eye shadow, then. I tried to open the mascara and couldn't get it open, and finally, my favourite lipstick.

Love my big red lipstick. I had so many shades in my drawer, from the darkest red to matte red to even tinted red lip gloss. But pulling them out one by one revealed their gross, mouldy, or falling apart.

Standing and facing the mirror, seeing this tired, worn-out girl before me. Wear an oversized cardigan, t-shirt and pants. I put my glasses back on to see myself clearer, but all there was a broken minded face staring back at me. *What happened to this girl? Where was Gwen I used to remember?* The fun loving, tech loving, coder, who didn't mind being one of the boys?

"Max was an asshole!" I heard a voice from my room.

I opened the door to find Paul was sitting on the edge of my bed.

"Yes, that may be so. But..." I couldn't think of a way to finish that sentence.

"Max was an asshole, and you know it, Gwen. He got rich, and needed to show this off, therefore he ditched you. You didn't measure up to his rich boy standards. Money changes people. Gwen, you're better than him in every way!"

I put my bag on the bed and packed, "Paul, you don't know him like I did…" I stopped what I was doing, wondering where did things go wrong with Max?

Max was my last boyfriend. At first, he was nice to me, and we did everything together. We were supposed to get married and live in this house together.

I met him at a party, just after college. He was a friend of a friend of a guy I was in a class with. We chatted, and by the end of the night, we exchanged phone numbers. He texted me the next day, and we were out having coffee, then lunch, and then dinner, and then back at his apartment having sex for the rest of the night. We were together for three years.

Max and his team started working on a new product. His goal was inventing a product to assist underdeveloped nations.

His team came up with a cheap, reusable drinking straw that filters the water as you drink. This product was a hit with people in developing countries and avid travellers.

Because of high demand for the straws, they expanded their product line to include compatible items such as water bottles, toothbrushes, convenient soaps, and laundry tabs, creating *Zeken,* his company.

Everything happened so fast, the company got bigger, inventing new products, creating apps for travellers, getting their spot on in the stock market. Money was pouring in. Because of this, Max changed.

It started with long hours at work, skipping weekends, and ignoring his phone. Things and places we went together became just me going with excuses for Max, *"Sorry, Max is not here, he got caught with a call in Thailand"* these excuses became wary, and draining.

When he was home, in our little apartment, every comment or question I made sparked an argument with him.

Suddenly, all our conversations turned into fights. I got to the point where I stopped talking to him, or only talked about his work and his products, because it was the only conversation I got from him.

He also changed the way he dressed. I couldn't recognise him with his new looks. Then he changed how he talked, becoming more jargon-like with an accent and trying to use essential words in sentences that didn't fit.

His dietary shift towards veganism didn't bother me, but his intense questioning of restaurant staff about food sourcing crossed a line. If it wasn't of the purest kind or blessed, we had to leave, dragging me out of the restaurant, somehow blaming not only the restaurant but also me in the process. It felt like he was making a big deal out of nothing. Using his office as an excuse to meditate over this conversation, leaving me alone to find my way back home and wondering what happened.

As he changed, so did our friends. The same usual friends we used to hang out with were replaced with rich, trust fund kids, the ones who were always partying, and looking for that better life. The ones who didn't have to worry about money.

These so-called friends would ignore me or look at me side on. But with enough alcohol in them, they would finally tell me how lucky it is to meet Max, and how innovative he was to change the world. And Max loved every minute, making himself some sort of Messiah of Silicon Valley.

But all of this came crashing down. There I stood in this big, beautiful house, with the Deed to it, the ink still fresh, when a text message from Max buzzed my phone.

"Gwen, you are so exhausting! I can't do this anymore…. Good luck or whatever!"

I knew I should have seen this coming. There was no explanation, no let's talk about this. He just simply... left.

"Gwen, you did nothing wrong. You did everything you could to keep him happy, including destroying your own. You remember that travelling app you built for him? And how did he told everyone he made it?" Paul said, interrupting my thoughts.

I let out a huff and said, "Yeah, I remember."

"Forget him, Gwen. You're better than that." Paul said as he hugged me.

I basked in the sun and observed daily life as we walked down the street. Joggers, dog walkers, other walkers. It was nice to see the street busy with people. I opened the door of the coffee shop for Paul and then lined up with everyone else.

Standing in line, I looked around the place. It had a very minimalist design to it. There wasn't much on the menu board, and it was very white. The atmosphere of the place invites you to relax with a coffee, alone or with company.

"What would you like today?" The cashier asked me.

Oh, it's my turn? I was so captivated by the place's ambiance that I completely forgot about it.

"Ummm... can I… get a latte and a..." I looked through the display of baked goods. "I…. I need that dough…nut." I pointed to this very fancy doughnut, with red stuff sprinkled all over it.

"Good choice there. That's our passionfruit and raspberry one." The cashier added with a warm, friendly charm.

With table number in hand, I searched the café for a table for Paul and myself. I found a two-seater near the window.

"Look at you," Paul said as I sat down. "you're loving this place."

"It's a great feeling knowing a place you always wanted to try turns out to be awesome."

In a daze, while drinking coffee, I watched the people come and go outside. Some people are in a hurry, some people just walking, some in couples or by themselves.

My attention turned to Paul, also enjoying his coffee and watching the world go by. I wanted to reach out to him and hold his hand to feel its warmth. Wanting to know how soft or rough his hands would be. Wishing for him to turn and talk to me. Make me laugh, smile, or show me he was interested in me.

I let out a sigh, bringing myself back to reality. Paul is not real. Other people in the café would look over and see some weird girl reaching out to nothing, stroking the table's edge, pretending that someone was there.

Laughing to myself in public, and I would have to think of something quick if anyone asked me. I pictured the stares and the insults from strangers who might learn my secret.

I settled back, cupping my coffee to enjoy it's comforting warmth. My happiness in this moment somehow morphed into loneliness again. I really needed to go somewhere that would allow me to have more interaction with Paul.

"Did you have a bookstore in mind that you wanted to go to?" I whispered to him.

"Yes, I do."

Swinging the door open, I looked around the bookstore. With two levels, and a café in the middle of the place. It looked more like a library from a fantasy novel than a bookstore.

Quietly walking through the section of the bookstore, I traced my finger along the spine of each book until I spotted Paul browsing.

"Is it me, or are there no good sci-fi books anymore? Too many people like science-fantasy," I said.

"I don't know. There are a few good ones there." Then he pointed at the book I was after.

"Oh my God, yes. This is the book I have been looking for."

Having found my book, I explored other areas of the store. While browsing the young adult books.

"How much trouble would I get into if I signed some of these books?" I asked Paul.

"You would make some fangirl happy but piss off the author," Paul said while reading a book he took off the shelf.

I laughed to myself. Yeah, I shouldn't do that; for one; I liked this place and wanted to return at some point. And two, I didn't want to upset anyone. I mean, what if that was me? I found my favourite author had signed all of their books, only to find out it was some kid pulling a prank. Not cool at all.

"I wonder what it is like to be an author?" I casually mentioned to Paul.

"Fucking hard." He had the same tone as before, still with his nose in a book.

"I bet it would be fun. Set your own hours, write, coffee, cats, and be adored by fans. Only for them to come to your book signings, asking when the next book is coming out, or questioning your thoughts and ideas on the plot. Or they could be asking me about their theories," I said to Paul, dreaming of a new life.

"Occasionally, popping on fanfiction sites to read what other fans think of your work. Maybe they have a better ending than the one I came up with. Or read some of the hardcore sex scenes between the characters you created." I continued to daydream.

"Wait! Hardcore sex scenes?" Paul questioned.

I snapped out of it and said, "Yes, haven't you read fanfiction before? Man, some of those fanfiction sites are even better than Pornhub!"

Paul chuckled, making me laugh. I suddenly stopped, realising where I was.

"Why do you do that?" Paul asked.

"What?"

"Suddenly stop yourself from enjoying yourself," Paul answered.

"I don't want people to think I'm crazy." I whispered to him.

Paul scanned the store.

"First sign of craziness is talking to yourself," I told him.

"I always thought it was a sign of intelligence," Paul said.

"So, I'm smart and crazy?" I whispered.

Paul let out a smile. "Well, no, that's not what I was saying." He put the book back. "Gwen, you're not crazy. And yes, smart as hell."

The smell of the freshly brewed coffee filled the store. "I need iced coffee."

"Wait, didn't we just have one?"

I plonked myself on to the couch in the cafe. Taking a few sips of my iced coffee, looking down at my new book. My attention turned to Paul reading.

Settling into the comfy chair, he crossed his legs and laid his book on his lap. So glad he likes to read, and drink coffee.

I dreamt of us relaxing on Saturday afternoons in the lounge room, reading, comparing ideas, and laughing together. Which would lead to touching, kissing, and... nope, Gwen, snap out of it. Paul was not real. Remember?

I turned to look over at him again.

"What are you reading?" I asked him.

He flipped through his book, swirling his iced coffee in his hand.

"It's a book you recommended at one point. It's quite good!" Paul looked up from his book.

"I recommended it?"

He sat there smiling at me. "Yes, you did."

This, for some odd reason, cracked me up. Forgetting where I was, I laughed too loud. I paused, feeling like I was being watched. Turning my head, I saw two teenage girls standing some distance away. They were looking in my direction. I couldn't tell if their attention was on Paul, the empty seat next to me, or something behind me that was funny. They stood close, giggling and whispering, and pointed in my direction.

That's when it hit me; they were laughing at me. I sat there wondering what to do next. Putting my new book in my bag, I quickly left the store.

I hurried in a single direction, uncertain of my path home, fighting back tears. I tried to stay unnoticed, but the more I reflected, the angrier I became. Then suddenly, I stopped.

"Gwen, what happened?" Paul stood in front of me.

"People think I'm weird. Those girls..."

"Hey, you're not weird. Well, not in the way you're thinking. And those girls, well, they're teenagers. They don't know any better. They still have some growing up to do." Paul reassures me.

"I can't do this, Paul. I can't go out in public with my imaginary friend." I snapped. Placing my hand on my head, feeling that pressure again.

Once my head settled, I looked up to see sorrow in Paul's eyes.

"I think I need some time to myself, Paul," I told him.

Chapter 8:
Earbuds

I returned home and baked some cookies, hoping this would cheer me up. I hadn't seen Paul since the bookstore. I know I told him I needed some time to myself, but this loneliness was becoming unbearable. Maybe there's something in having an imaginary friend. I don't feel so lonely all the damn time.

I leaned on the kitchen bench, eating one of my cookies while patting Colin, when I heard some commotion in my office. As I walked into the office, I saw Paul leaning on my desk as if it wasn't him making that noise.

"I thought I told you to go away," I told him.

"Well, yes, you did, but the thing about imaginary friends is it's hard to get rid of them when you need them the most," he said.

I crossed my arms. "What's with all the noise?"

"I think I have an idea." He turned around to look at my desk. "See..."

I walked over to my desk to find my old Bluetooth earbuds, as I now wear over the head headphones. Still with my arms crossed, glaring at Paul. *What on earth is he on about?*

"My Bluetooth earbuds. So?"

"Yes, see, if you put them in, we can talk to each other in public without thinking you're weird."

I don't get it.

"If someone laughs at you or tells you off, then you just take them out and show them you're on a call."

Actually, he was onto something here. It has been a while since I used them, and the charge would be dead. I walked over to the other side of my desk and plugged them in. Watching the little light flash, I realised I didn't really need to charge them if they were going to be used to talk to Paul in public. I shrugged. Oh well, let them charge.

Flipping through the channels, I watched Paul walk into the lounge room and sit down. "Why don't you get dressed into something nice, and we go out for dinner?"

Why would I want to go out when I can just order in?

"Because we can test the earbuds," he answered.

I turned around to look at my desk. It had been a few hours since charging them. They might be ready. I turned the TV off, grabbed the earbuds, and left.

We ended up at a place not far away from home. The server came over and greeted us.
"Welcome to Clive's. Table for one?"

I looked over at Paul. Going out with him is a lot harder than I thought it would be.

"Yes… yes, just one." I forced out.

Observing the restaurant as we followed the server to our table, old, out of date menus and decor, but one thing I know about this place, the food is still good. The server took us to a table in the back of the room. She was about to take the spare chair. "NO! Leave it there." I told her.

Confused, she put it back. Paul sat down as she left.

There we were facing each other. He had worn the same outfit since we first met. "Don't you ever change? Are those clothes getting smelly?" I asked, talking a little louder.

"It's how you picture me," he said.

I needed to make a mental note here; *make Paul change his clothes.*

He sipped his water, and I asked, "So, if you're imaginary, then why don't you have a fluffy pink tail?"

"The kids get pink fluffy tails," he said. "See, when it comes to adults, imaginary friends are more human looking. We take on characteristics of people our humans' trust."

More human? I tilted my head, trying to figure out who Paul is as he didn't resemble anyone I know. Neither famous nor semi-famous. He didn't even look like any of my ex-boyfriends. In fact, he didn't look like anyone I actually knew, but there was something familiar about him.

"Could you change?" I asked him.

"Well, yeah, but you need to do that. I could be anyone who you want me to be," Paul added.

I adjusted my glasses, thinking about who Paul could change into, leaving a smirk.

"Okay, not that." Paul interjected.

"Oh, come on! It would be fun. Let me live out at least one fantasy here. I know for a fact it will never happen, but at least I could have some fun."

"Fine…" Paul said, adjusted himself in his chair, "...but it's all up to you. You need to close your eyes."

I closed my eyes while trying to hide my smile.

"Now, think about him. Think about what he's wearing, how would his hair, his voice, his tone, his skin. How would he look if he was just sitting here?"

Each point Paul made; I could picture in my head. Once I got the full image of him, I slowly opened my eyes to find Grayson sitting in front of me.

He placed his arms out, "perfect?" It was Grayson, right down to the tee. His looks, his baby blue shirt, his voice. His freshly shaved face, everything.

"Oh, God… wow!" I grasped, "it really is Grayson."

He leaned on the table with one elbow. "So, Gwen, do you come here often?"

I was at a loss for words. I knew Paul was still underneath all of this, but I really couldn't help myself.

"Screw dinner. Let's go home and fool around." The Paul/Grayson said, seductively.

Okay, now we are done!

"But I'm hun… gry…. and… I… I… Need food!" I stuttered.

Paul/Grayson flicked his arms, and added, "Okay, take a deep breath and say something."

"Tell me how pretty I…I am," I asked.

He leaned on the table, looked deep into my eyes and muttered, "Oh Gwen, you are the prettiest woman in the world, the things I want to do to you!"

"Oh Grayson!" I muttered back.

"Gwen?" I heard my name shouted. I quickly pulled myself up from the table, my eyes widened from the sheer shock that the real Grayson was standing before me. I had never seen casual Grayson before, wearing a T-shirt, jeans and green flannel over the top.

Oh My God, he is wearing glasses. Why is casual Grayson hotter than work Grayson?

"Did you just… say my name?" he asked.

I looked around the table, trying to find an excuse, then one of my earbuds fell out.

"ummm…. yes… I… I… did." I held up my earbud at him, "Sorry, I… was… talking to my…. Mother! And how…. nice you…were to…me… the other… day." I choked out.

"Oh, that's okay Gwen. Just looking out for you… that's all." Grayson said, cheerfully.

He stood there at the other end of the table, awkwardly. "Are you here with someone?" he finally asked.

I looked over at the other side to find Paul chuckling away. *The nerve of him!*

"Ummm… no… just me." I finally answered.

"Hey, ready to go?" I saw another tall, dark blonde guy, backwards baseball cap, those facial features of his, and wired framed glasses as well, *Oh God the glasses, why do glasses always get me?*

He was just as handsome as Grayson, standing beside him.

"Oh, this is OJ, by the way. And Gwen, a friend from work." Grayson introduced us.

OJ tried to wave with a pizza box in his hands. "Nice… to.. to.. meet you."

The two of them stood there awkwardly again, before OJ said, "this box is hot, dude. Can we go?"

"See ya around, Gwen." Grayson said as he left.

As I walked home with Paul, I reflected on my day. Going out to do simple things made me recognise how much of my life I have missed. I hadn't had this much confidence in myself for a long time.

We continued to walk down the street. I thought about what my life is going to be like. *I am going to make more friends, start eating right again, and exercising, and really start looking for a new job, a better job, one where they will take me seriously.*

Each list item I made left a soft smile. Linking arms with Paul, I started to wonder, *what will happen when I suddenly don't need him anymore?*

I really don't want to lose him; he was growing on me, and I had been enjoying the company.

"Paul—" I asked, "What happens when you go away? Do you become someone else's imaginary friend? Or do you go into the pit of forgotten memories? Or do you just disappear?"

Paul looked down at me as we continued to walk. "Strange question! I could ask you the same thing. Where do you go when you die?"

"Maybe I will become an imaginary friend? Many people have their own theories. A theory states that we just jump from universe to universe when we die. That it's not heaven we see, but the next universe we are supposed to go to, and—" I suddenly stopped talking. I went too far with my theory. No one wanted to hear this.

"Go on." Paul said, wanting to know more. "— Just a theory. No one knows what happens next. Maybe we are all living in an RPG and waiting for the *Game Over* to flash in front of our eyes or hear that one voice. *Thanks for playing human.*"

"So, what am I then?" Paul said.

"What?" I said, but he reframed his question, "If this is an RPG, then who am I? A rogue background character, or…"

I stopped him and said, "The coach! You're the coach whispering in my ear where to strike next."

Chapter 9:
Speak Up

Hammond immediately confronted me upon my arrival at work. "GWEN!" *That New Zealand accent gets me!* I knew this wasn't going to be good. I held on tight to my backpack straps, watching him tower over me.

"What are youse up to?" He questioned.

What does that mean? In general, or with work?

"Arrr….". I let out.

"How is my app?" he demanded.

"Yeah… it's…good…" I stumbled out. *Which app is he after again?*

"Good is not a response," he added.

Does Hammond know how long it takes to build an app? Some take weeks, while others could take months. What do I tell him?

"I'm… working on it… I just need… Some more time." I stumbled out again.

Please Hammond, just go away?

"Time?" He questioned.

I swallowed hard and added, "Yes, I… I just…. need to… get rid of the bugs?" Once again, I stumble on my words.

"When will it be ready?" He asked me.

I tried to calculate a time in my head, but my mind went blank. *I better say something.*

"I… could be ready… in a couple of weeks?" I said, picking a number at random.

He stood there, rocking back and forth on his feet, his eyes bulging out. I swallow hard, preparing myself for an argument.

"Fine!" he shouted and left.

The conversation echoed in my mind, highlighting missed chances to tell Hammond that it would be better as a game or even use full sentences.

"Dating app issues again?" Paul asked as I sat down.

"Yes. I had the perfect opportunity to tell him that this dating app is a problem and could put TroniX into jeopardy. And saw a way around this by turning this into a game instead, BUT NO! My brain froze, and made myself look like an idiot," I told Paul.

"Idiot?" Paul responded.

"I can only blame myself," I said back.

Paul stood from his desk to look over our wall. "Why do you do that? The way you talk, stumble on your words, broken sentences, taking your time to answer?"

I never knew why I did that. I never talked like that before. I shrugged, "I don't know."

"You talk to me just fine," Paul added.

"Yes, it's because you're imaginary!" I told Paul.

"I find this hard to believe. You can talk to anyone with ease. What about Grayson? You can talk to him with ease, right?" Paul asked me.

Glancing at Grayson, "we've only talked about work, that really doesn't count. I mean I would love to talk to him about other things, like what he is into, or what he got up to on the weekend, normal stuff, but each time I want to talk to him, even if it's just a simple *'Hello'*, I hear this voice in my head that tells me that's dumb, or Grayson finds me gross. So, I changed my mind and walked away."

I slump back down into my chair. "Besides, it's Grayson who has talked to me, not the other way around."

"It's because you want to sleep with him."

I quickly glanced back at Paul. "Hang on, this has nothing to do with wanting to sleep with Grayson."

Paul stood there with his head tilted to the side.

"It's that I find it hard to talk to anyone. I mean, you saw what happened with Hammond and Ivan. I have no interest in sleeping with those guys."

He pointed his finger at me. "You're right."

Paul sat back down and went back to typing, "Me thinks there is a theory in this. But I need to test it."

I walked through each aisle, gliding my fingers across the spines of each book. An after-work trip to the bookstore once again. It was Paul's idea to come here. I knew he wanted to test out a theory but was not sure what it was as yet. I stopped at the young adult shelf. There were so many fantasy books. *What is with teens and dragons?* Taking the book off the shelf and placing it under my arm.

I ended up finding a few more books and headed towards the counter.

"Is that all?" the guy asked.

I watched him as he examined and scanned each book. Despite being a book nerd, he was kind of cute; dark curly hair, glasses, wore a suede jacket and a t-shirt that said *'I had to close my book to be here'*, and tall.

"Do you need a bag?" He asked.

My brain froze again. I know I can hear the words, but why is my mouth not moving?

"This is the part where you answer the guy?" Paul said, standing next to me.

The bookseller stared at me, waiting for a response.

"Arrr…." was all I could get out.

I can carry my items; a bag is unnecessary, and it would have cost me an extra quarter. I could hear in my head, *no, I don't need a bag.*

"Gwen?" Paul said, trying to get my attention.

This snapped me out, but I still couldn't tell the bookseller what I wanted.

"It's okay. It's only a few books. You can carry it," the bookseller said.

"Well, this is interesting." Paul added.

My cheeks burnt with embarrassment. Once the exchange was completed, I took the books and rushed out.

Bursting through the front door of my house, dropping the books on my couch, dropping my fist up and down as I paced around the lounge room, "The fuck is wrong with me? Why can't I talk to people? Why?"

"Gwen, calm down…" Paul said.

"What did I do to end up in a situation where I can't even have a conversation with people? I can hear the answer, or my response in my head, but I just can't. I can't get it out." I yelled at Paul.

Getting out of the house was great. Now, I have to interact with people? Ugh!

I continued to pace as I made little frustrated noises and banging my fist against my head. *What is wrong with me?*

"Gwen, please stop," Paul said, worried.

I didn't pay attention to Paul, but rather research this. As I sat down in front of my computer, typed into Google, *'how to start conversations.'* reading each article, watching each YouTube video I saw, creating steps for myself.

"This will not work," Paul said, looking over my shoulder. "You wrote a list of conversation starters. It's not just about the words you use, but how you deliver them."

Wait... What?

"Won't work? Let's go to the cafe tomorrow. I'll prove you wrong!" I told him.

There I stood in line at the cafe, practising my lines. *Isn't it a lovely day? This coffee is good; I too enjoy coding.*

"This will not work!" Paul muttered.

"Shush!" I whispered, focusing on my communication style.

It was finally my turn to order. It was now or never to prove Paul wrong. I suddenly froze, my mind went blank, my throat dried up. This is not the regular girl.

"What would you like today?" the guy behind the counter asked.

Trying to progress what was happening at this moment, I looked him up and down. He was your typical coffee hipster. He even sported a coffee bean and teacup tattoo on his knuckles. I swallowed nervously, his pen poised over the paper cup, slowly taking his eyes off the cup and at me, awaiting my reply. I tried to bring the words *cappuccino* to my mouth.

"Is everything okay?" he asked, putting the cup down.

I took a deep breath and finally said, "Fine." *Man, it was hard to say.*

"What would you like today?" he asked again, picking up the cup.

I took another deep breath and forced out, "Cappuccino. Full cream."

I need to prove to Paul my research works. I took a deep breath and said, "Lovely weather, isn't it?"

The guy shifted in his stands, dragging the coffee cup to the side. "It's San Jose. We are in the middle of the desert, and we have fine weather all year round," he said, while placing his knuckles on the counter.

Did I say the wrong thing? I quickly took a step to the side.

I sat down with my coffee in hand, and Paul chuckled away.

"What are you laughing at?" I asked him.

"You! *Lovely weather we have?*" he mocked me.

"Shut up." I spat at him while he was still chuckling.

"Why is it hard to make conversation with strangers, or better yet; people I know!" I told Paul as I took a sip of my cup.

"I'm sorry, do I have something on my face?" another voice said.

I tilt my head slightly to see someone else sitting on the other table facing me. *Wait a minute, is that the guy from the bookstore?*

My nerves got to me again, "w…why?"

"You keep staring at me. Either you know me, or I have something on my face." He said.

I took out one of my earbuds and showed him. Pretend to end the call, and tried to make conversation with him, "You run… the…. bookstore."

"Yes, I do." Then he pointed his finger at me. "Wait, you were the girl who didn't know if she wanted a bag."

Fuck, why does he remember me like this? I turn to the window, trying to ignore him. When I turned back, he was sitting on the opposite side of my table. He took another sip.

My throat went dry again, my heartbeat faster and harder, my hands began to shake.

"This is a wonderful opportunity to talk to him." I heard Paul say as he stood there watching us. I needed time to gather my thoughts, and inhaled before saying, "Lovely weather…. we have… having?"

He chuckled at me as if I had told him an amusing joke.

"Yes, but we have pleasant weather all year round," he answered back.

My mind raced, trying to remember what the next thing is was on my steps. The awkward silence lingered. I need to say something else. But what?

"I'm Benowitz, but everyone calls me Ben." He said.

All I could manage was a grin. This stupid grin. Why is this so hard? *I can tell my name. It's the polite thing to do.*

"Do you read a lot?" Ben finally asked.

"Some… sometimes." I choked out.

"You read quite a bit. You should mention the books you like to read," Paul said.

"Maybe if you take your mind off what it would be like to make out heavily with this guy in the smut section of the bookstore, you could talk to him!"

My eyes widened. *Damn this mind sharing stuff with Paul!* I grabbed my coffee cup and said, "Gotta go," I stood up and left.

I swung my front door of my place open, still angry at myself. *I know I'm trying, but it is so damn hard!*

"First of all, it's called the Romance section of the bookstore. Who calls it the Smut section?" I yelled at Paul, "Why is this hard? I mean really hard. They are people too. Why is it hard to talk to people? I suddenly get these voices in my head, telling me to be careful on what to say."

I stared Paul down, waiting for a response from him. He would open his mouth about to say something, then suddenly shutting it. I threw my arms up in the air, frustrated. UGH! Was all I could manage as I went to my office.

I sat down at my laptop, about to type, when I heard Paul say, "STOP! JUST…. stop!"

I looked up to find Paul standing there with his arm crossed, holding his head high.

"Gwen… you can do this. You do not need to be shy talking to people, no matter who they are. You used to be able to. Let's try and do this again."

Lifting his glasses to pinch his eyes, "Say a swear word." Paul said.

Well, that baffles me.

"What?"

"Just do it." Paul said back, leaning on the desk.

I sat there staring at him, thinking of swear words. I shrugged my shoulders and muttered, "Fuck?"

"Louder!" Paul said, now leaning on his knuckles.

"FUCK!" I said out loud.

"Another." He said louder.

I tried to say another, "Umm… shit!" I added.

"Louder!" Paul shouted, as he lifted his hand in the air.

I took a deep breath in and shouted out each swear word I could think of. "FUCK, SHIT, DICKHEAD, PISSY MORON!"

"Moron?" Paul asked.

"It was all I could think of," I said.

"Try it again and even louder this time," he said, as he crossed his arms again.

I stood up from my desk and shouted, "YOU DIRTY PIECE PUSSY ASS FUCKER! WORSE THAN A FASCIST VIRGIN WHO GETS FUCKED IN THE ASS!"

The rush of each word that came out. The thrill, the excitement, the force of each of these words had over me, building a newfound love for powerful words. Those last words just flew out. Paul stood, chuckling away.

"How does this feel?" Paul asked.

"Good, I guess…" I said, with excitement.

"Great, now let's try this in public!"

In the night's dark, we drove to the nearby forest. I parked the car overlooking the twinkle lights of the Valley below.

"Why are we here?" I asked Paul, still sitting in the car.

"Well, let's try to speak up in public. This place is perfect! It's outside, and no one is around. Small steps, Gwen." he said.

I got out of my car and sat on the bonnet, watching the valley shimmer through the night. Paul joined me. "There is something I have been meaning to ask: Why do you find it hard to speak to people?"

Confidence has always been a defining trait of mine. I could always talk to people, sometimes far more than I should. I knew how to speak, carry a conversation with anyone. I never worried about my word choice, tone, or delivery. I knew I could carry myself with such professionalism.

"Max always corrected me when I talked." I told Paul, realising where it all started.

"I get it. I mispronounce words occasionally, but when you get told that I should say this or that because it embarrasses him, you learn how to shut up quickly."

I tucked my legs up to my chest, remembering the times Max would tell me off for speaking.

"I just learned not to talk to people in the end. I must have gotten comfortable with that. Max always spoke for me. He knew what to say. But after he left, I had to speak for myself again. Must have forgotten how to."

"Fucking asshole!" Paul said. "I wish you had summoned me sooner. I could give Max a what-for."

"What, like scaring him or whispering in his ear about how he should die? Go all evil imaginary friend for me?" I said back, trying to imagine what Paul would be like as an evil imaginary friend.

He slapped his knee and added, "Enough. We are here to practise talking." He waved his hand at me to get started.

I sat there, resting my head on my knees, "and say what?"

"Start with swear words again."

"What, like fuck, balls, boobs?" I said to him.

"Louder?" Paul said.

"BOOOOOOOOBBBBBBBSSSSS!" I shouted.

"Boobs is not a swear word, Gwen." Paul added, "Do something else?"

"Fine, how about Dick or Fanny!" I said towards Paul.

Paul slid off the bonnet and paced. "This is going nowhere." He paused and said, "Max! Was there anything you ever wanted to say to him?"

I had so much I always wanted to say to him. It's hard to settle one thing.

"I hate how you left me." I muttered.

"Okay, good. Keep going." Paul encouraged me.

"You are nothing but a narcissistic piece of shit!" I said, a little louder.

Paul waved his hands at me to keep it up. I sat up, placed my forearms on my knees, and said, "You are the worse person ever; none of our friends liked you, you… fucker!"

My cheeks burned as a smile came over my face. My heart raced. I felt so pumped that adrenaline rush came over me again, "You are so pretentiously fake, and stole everyone's ideas, including mine!"

I knew he did that! I knew he stole my app idea for travellers, but since his company developed it, he claimed ownership.

And there it was. The anger inside me was lit. I dragged myself off the car and shouted, "YOU ARE NOTHING BUT A FUCKING ASSHOLE WITH BIG EARS, AND…" I was trying to think of other names to call Max, "…AND YOU DON'T LAST LONG IN BED!"

I looked over at Paul, knowing I had one more left in me. "YOU ARE THE WORST PERSON EVER TO BE INVENTED, you…. YOU DUMB FUCKING CUNT!" I finally found my voice!

Paul rushed over and hugged me. He placed his head on mine. My heart was still racing, but I felt calmer than ever before. Before I could say something to him, a notion came from the trees: "I'm sorry, I'm sorry, I'm sorry!" someone said as he came out of the forest.

I turned around to find a guy standing on the opposite side of my car. It's funny, but I didn't see any other cars around.

"What are you doing out here?" I said to him, scrambling to find my keys.

"I enjoy late-night nature walks!" he said nervously.

I kept my eyes on him. I didn't want to blink or move my gaze away from him. *Who the fuck does that? Go out for late-night nature walks.*

"Stay there!" I shouted at him.

"I don't have a gun," he told me.

"That doesn't make the situation any better!" I grabbed my keys out of my pocket.

He dropped his shoulders and finally confessed. "Okay, I confess… I was filming myself for my OnlyFans account."

"In the forest?" I asked, trying to remember which button I need to press to open the doors.

"Yes, I do find I get more followers that way," he said, still standing there.

"He has a point." Paul said, "A unique OnlyFans page does get more followers!"

"Shush!" I said to Paul.

"No, it's true. I'm sorry. I wasn't filming myself, playing with… myself over you. You're not my type. I'm gay!" the other man said.

"That still doesn't make this situation any better! You could be a killer. I've seen enough Netflix specials to know where this is going!"

He rolled his eyes. "I'm not going to hurt you. I have too much to risk if I did that."

"Like what?" Paul asked.

"Like what?" I repeated.

The guy looked around and said, "well, my job for one, and my apartment. My fans that I have. My freedom, my money, my life, I can continue on?"

"He does make a good point," I told Paul.

"Who are you talking to?" the guy asked.

"No one, just my imaginary friend."

"Oh, and I'm the serial killer!" he said back.

"I need to go home," I muttered, as the car door opened.

Before I got into the car, I just had to ask, "Wait, what's your account?"

"I'm under the name of OutsideFront&Back. I do most of my content outside."

"Okay…" I said, then got in the car and left.

I sat in a diner, staring at my coffee and thinking about tonight's events unfolding. I looked over at Paul, tapping his finger on his cup.

"What a night." Paul said, "You got your voice."

"What are you on about?" I asked him.

"Did you not hear yourself when talking to the night stalker?" Paul said.

"What?"

"You were able to talk to him in full sentences and no pauses," he said.

I lean back into the chair, remembering the conversation. The simple act of saying dirty words, swearing, shouting out my anger, and the idea of meeting a potential serial killer surprisingly helped me regain some confidence. I felt good; I could make amends with myself and move on.

"What's so funny?" The server asked me as she poured me another cup of coffee.

She caught me off guard. "I heard a funny joke today. It still amuses me."

She looked down at me, "go on, out with it. I wanna hear it too."

I looked up at her and said, "Did you know it is legal to laugh out loud in Hawaii?"

She places the coffeepot down and shifts her eyebrows at me. "Seriously? How does one laugh in Hawaii?"

I cleared my throat and finished the joke: "Yes, it is. If you need to laugh when you are in Hawaii, you must give a low ha!"

There was quiet between us as she considered the joke. She placed both hands on her hips and threw her head back, laughing loudly. She returned to me as she wiped the corners of her eyes, "Girl, that's a good one, a low ha! Aloha!"

She turned towards the kitchen and shouted, "CHUCK, hey, I got a joke for you!"

She shuffles off towards the kitchen. I lift my cup of coffee to cheer Paul.

Chapter 10:
Co-Workers

I skipped my usual morning routines the next day but still reminded myself that today is a great day. With my head held high and a small smile, I could see the office and everyone in it. Still as grey and gloomy as usual, the same people around.

My normal quick glanced over at Grayson to start my day. Knowing he was here meant today was going to be a good day. This time round he caught my eye. We both locked on each other. I wasn't going to miss this opportunity, "Morning, Grayson." I said, giving him a friendly wave.

The corner of his mouth curled, "Morning Gwen." he said back.

After rediscovering my voice, I needed to do something with my hair. It was an itchy rat's nest, a pile of a mess sitting on top of my head. One bottle of shampoo, conditioner, and hair dye. My hair is its natural, smooth, perfect light blonde again.
Watching a YouTube video on self-haircutting, I could trim the split ends, add bangs, and achieve a hairstyle back to its original look. I can feel my old self returning.

"You're late," Paul said from his desk.

"What the hell are you on about? We came in together," I said as I added the laptop to the docking station.

"Still, you're late."

"Up your bum," I told him.

"Excuse me?" Grayson questioned, while standing next to my desk.

Oh My God! Where did he come from?

"Umm... sorry, I was practising my Australian accent.... *'up your bum!'"*

He let out a little chuckle huff. "Do you want to go for coffee?" Grayson asked.

Wait? He wants to go for coffee. With me? The day hasn't started and already it's going to be a good day!

"Oh my God, YES!" I answered, a little too excited. I quickly grabbed my phone, "Okay, let's go!" trying to wave off the awkwardness.

The cafe was quiet, a few murmurs from other people around, but there we were, our eyes locked on each other, waiting for someone to break the silence between us. I took a sip of my coffee, thinking about all the questions I could ask him. *Why TroniX? Why do you always look so good? Do you work out? How do you like your eggs in the morning?* Sucking in my lips to give him an awkward smile, "So…" I said, looking in his direction.

His eyebrows rose at me as he waited for more. I needed to finish this sentence. "...what do you do for fun?" It rolled out.

Grayson scanned the cafe, then leaned in closer. Grabbing my attention, his voice went serious. "By day, I'm a sophisticated app developer, but by night, a prestigious gigolo. Actually, I'm one of the top ten gigolos in Silicon Valley. I'm just that damn good!"

I swallowed hard, taking in this small bit of information. As I observed him from head to toe, taking in his chiselled appearance, ideal height, well-proportioned body, and striking Asian features, I understood why he decided to work as a male escort on the side. I could picture how delighted his clients would feel, receiving personalized attention from him. The stories he would have. *How does one become a client of his?*

"I… umm… can... see that... Now! I...I... didn't realise there was... Call for... Male escorts these days." I mustered up.

Grayson dipped his head. He leaned back with a huge smile, showing his perfectly straight teeth, quietly chuckling.

Dammit!

"That's not fair!" I told him, "You must have something going on outside this office. You don't seem to be like the rest of them."

"Just gaming, that's all." He finally answered, "I don't do much outside of work. I enjoy coding, it helps me relax. It's kind of funny when you think about it. I come to work to relax." He grabbed his cup of coffee. "So, are you doing okay? Is Ivan still stressing you out?" He took a sip of his coffee. "I'm just checking to see everything is okay. I know what Ivan is like. I've worked with him before. He can be such an asshole when he chooses to."

He always is an asshole, every day!

"How's your mother?" Grayson quickly asked another question.

"My mother?" This threw me off.

"You were talking to her at Clive's the other day."

Oh, now I remember.

"She's fine, always worries about me." I lied.

Grayson quickly swallowed. "I couldn't help noticing that comment you made at your desk. Were you talking to someone?"

Paul, just Paul, that's all!

"No. Just thinking of the gaming app and noticing how much there is to this mess. *'Arrgggg... up your bum!'*" I lied again. I wasn't ready to tell Grayson about Paul, and the idea of telling the world I have an imaginary friend scared me.

Grayson nodded.

The question lingered in my mind. *Did he think I was crazy? Did I put my earbuds in?* I touch my ear. No, they weren't in. I needed to know more about this. "Why did you think I was talking to myself?"

"No reason, really. It felt like it was directed at someone more than at the app. But hey, it's cool." Grayson said, "I just wanted you to know that I'm here for you. I find the company's work quite demanding. I just want to let you know that I'm here if you need to talk or something."

Oh, I would love to do something with you!

"Gwen don't feel ashamed for talking to yourself. It's a way to relieve stress and make sure you're on track. Most people do it." Then he finished his coffee.

Yeah, but this was more than just creating an out loud list or ticking off a task. Talking to Paul had meaning and emotions. Some of our conversations were deep.

I let out a sigh. "Thanks, I'm doing okay. I'm just giving myself more breaks, that's all."

"Good. Hey, if you need a friend with your break, just ask."

The corner of my mouth curled up, thinking of conversations Grayson and I could have in our breaks.

As we returned to the office, Grayson stopped me. "Gwen, you're into gaming, right?"

"It depends on the games," I said back.

"Tabletop stuff? You know, creative board games."

"Yes, I know of tabletop games. Why?"

"I play Dungeons and Dragons, and we have a campaign at one of my friends' places. Thought you might like to join. Unless it isn't your thing," he asked.

Oh my God, is he asking me out on a date?

"Could be a good way to get out of the house, and you already met OJ." Grayson continued.

Strange idea for a first date.

"YES!" I yelled.

Realizing how loud I got, "Ahem…Yes, that would be fun." I rephrased my answer.

We exchanged phone numbers, Then Grayson returned to his desk. Beaming with excitement, not only did I get Grayson's phone number, but I get to go on a date with him.

"Cool! Boy number!" Paul said as Grayson left.

Grayson had been texting me since, telling me about his campaign and where they were up to, the battles they have been on, and what their primary goals were for the game. I sat at my desk, printing off a character sheet. Grayson mentioned in one of his texts how he created a character for me. I must guard this sheet with my life.

Once the printer finished, looking down at the sheet, there were so many numbers and words, but up the top I saw the words, *'Water Genashi, Rogue,'* beside this was a picture of her. Blue skin, white eyes, her bow and arrow behind her. Leather corset, beaming at her big breast, with white spots along her sides. Her hair was clear, like crystal water. She was gorgeous.

"So, who am I? Who do I get to play?" Paul asked as he walked into the room.

"You're not coming," I told him.

"Why?"

"There will be other people there. And having to interact with them and an imaginary friend at the same time is hard."

Paul leaned into me. "Hard? I thought we learned this?"

Wait, did we?

"No wait, we learnt how to talk," Paul added.

Just as I was about to reply to Paul, there was a knock on my door. So, I grabbed my stuff and said one last thing to Paul, "That's my ride."

On the drive to his friend's, Grayson told me about the adventure again. The car trip went quiet until I heard, "You look nice tonight. Rarely see you dress like this."

Picking an outfit for this night was hard, since I haven't dated in three years. I aimed for an outfit that was both sexy and casual. I wore skinny jeans, a tank top showing a little cleavage, and a flannel top. Sexy but casual.

"Oh, this outfit? It's nothing, just something I found… Wait, what do you mean I don't dress like this?"

Grayson huffed another small chuckle. "Sorry, I meant it in a way that you're not hiding yourself. I am so used to seeing you in baggy hoodies or oversize cardigans and t-shirts. It's kind of nice to see the real you."

"He is right, Gwen! Must get hot in those baggy clothes." I heard a voice in the back of the car. I turned around to find Paul joined us.

FUCK!

I turned back to the front and tried to ignore him. *I wish Paul would have stayed home.*

"So, there are four of us, and you make five." Grayson explained, as the three of us walked towards the apartment, "There is Evans, who is the DM. Me, I'm the fighter," he said as he punched the air, "There is Banks, the wizard, and OJ, who is Druid."
"Don't worry too much about them. They are just like us. Tech heads. OJ works for Innovative Tech as an Engineer, Evans does Design, and Banks…. not sure about him as yet," Grayson continued.

The apartment door swung open, and we entered. I looked around the room, hearing Grayson chatting away behind me. Someone has already set the table with a map, small figures, and snacks. This was so advanced to what I have seen on TV.
"Everybody, this is Gwen. She works with me at the devil's

lair. She is a hard worker, just like me," Grayson announced, with his arm around my shoulders.

I could smell his sweet, icy scent on him as he pulled me closer. *Oh, I want to wear this scent all day!*

"What is your poison?" Evans asked me.

"My what?"

"Can I get you a drink?" Evans said, smiling at me.

"Diet coke." I replied.

Evans handed me a can and guided me to the table. As I opened the can, Evans explained where they had left off. Then he looked at me. "Gwen don't worry; Grayson told me you were joining. I will introduce you to the campaign soon. Just sit back and watch for a bit."

They discussed strategies, rolled dice, cheered, laughed, cried, and battled around the table.
Excitement and banter between the players filled the room.

"So, you work with Grayson? He casually mentioned it to me the other day." OJ said.

I wanted to get back to the game and find what was going to happen next, but OJ kept talking. "What is he like at work? Hard ass?"

I snickered. "No, not really. He is just like the rest of us there. No idea why we were hired but keep our heads down and do the work."

"I keep telling him he needs to come and work for Innovative Tech. I think his dev skills would be great over there, but he seems keen to stay at TroniX. Must be something there that keeps him." OJ added as he lifted his eyebrows towards me.

"Ummmm…." this caught me off guard, *wait is OJ is saying what I think he is trying to say?*

"Gwen?" I heard Evans say. "Gwen, this is your part."

"Oh, um... where are we?"

"In a tavern, in town," OJ said.

"So why are you there?" Evans asked me.

"Oh..." I glanced at my character sheet, imagining a backstory for my tavern presence: "I'm currently down on my luck. I ran out of my hometown, and I need some money. Since I'm a water Genashi, I decided to put on a performance. As I swirl my water, I am collecting, or more accurately, snatching coins and other minor items from the bystanders."

"Cool, roll for it. Let's see how good you are?" Evans said to me.

OJ placed a die in my hands. I looked down at it and noticed there were twenty numbers. I misled Grayson; I've never played D&D. It looks easy on TV.

The table tops games I have played mostly were the classic Monopoly, Candyland, Cards against Humanity. Board games with dice that only had six sides.

I took a deep breath in and rolled and got a thirteen. Not sure what a thirteen meant.

"Okay, you're good, but only getting small tips off the tables. Roll again," Evans said.

Seventeen this time. This has to be better than a thirteen.

"Okay, now you're getting clever and starting to pickpocket."

"Gwen tries this on me, but I catch her." OJ added quickly.

He rolled, eleven. Once again, I'm lost. *Is eleven a good thing?*

"You corner her and try to get your stuff back but fail. She..." Evans said, but I interrupted him as I understood how to play this game, "...Talks her way out of giving OJ his stuff back. Somehow, I changed his mind by changing the topic."

Evans waved his hand for a roll. I rolled sixteen.

"Nice. What do you say?" Evans asked.

OJ was sitting there, waiting for my question. I had to think of something quick. "I see you're here with some other people. Are you a travelling circus?"

I watched OJ sit up off the table; slowly closing and opening his eyes, thinking of the next thing to say. I remembered he was a druid, thinking it meant some sort of robot.

"A travelling circus? Is it because I can talk to the animals?" he asked.

Okay, a druid is not a robot, but a class of some kind. I need to come up with something quick without sounding stupid.

"Well, there's that, and you have a wizard." I pointed at Banks. "That sounds like a travelling circus to me!"

The table laughed. I needed to join their campaign somehow, so I asked, "How about this? Take me with you, and I can make pretty patterns with water and stuff." I started to run out of ideas.

OJ rolls again, twenty. The hold table roars with excitement. Twenty must be a good thing.

"Fine. Come along then," OJ said.

Now that I could join in, there was so much excitement in the air; the conversations, the rolling of dice, the laughter, and cries all over again. Until the pizza arrived.

The room buzzed with conversations, mostly about work, until I noticed someone staring from beside me.

"So, enjoying yourself?" Banks asked.

I felt Paul grabbing my arm. He was about to say something, but OJ jumped in, "run along, Banks."

"Yes, I am having a good time." I answered.

"That's cool," Banks said.

"I don't like this," I heard Paul say. The tone in his voice made this conversation tense. I rubbed my arm where Paul had his hand, reminding him that things were okay.

Banks sat there, a wide smile, his eyes fixed upon me, continuing to make this situation uneasy. I sat there staring back at him, waiting for him to do something. My senses seemed to be on high alert until he finally said, "Grayson never said how pretty you look."

Before I could answer, OJ jumped in. "Banks, last warning."

Banks put his hand up in surrender, then walked away.

"Thank God he's gone." Paul added.

I let out a long sigh. "What was that?"

"Nothing," OJ said, "Just a mistake."

Chapter 11:
Dating App

Still buzzing from our D&D session the previous night, I went to the office the following day eager to see Grayson once more. Unable to sleep, I spent the rest of the night recounting our fun with Paul. Paul was hanging on every word and vibing off the energy, throwing his favourite parts into the conversation until we both fell asleep.

As I set myself up, Paul looked up at me. "You finally got some sleep last night?"

"Yes, I did. But I'm still feeling tired. The adrenaline didn't go away until about three a.m.," I told.

"Boy, don't I know!" Paul retorted.

"Here she is, the life of the party," Grayson said, swivelling his chair to my desk.

"I wouldn't say that!" I said back.

"But seriously, you had fun, right?"

I opened my laptop and saw Grayson's beautiful brown eyes, seeing his dimples form in his cheeks as he smiled. I couldn't resist saying, "I had an amazing evening. I can't wait for the next one."

I had a sudden urge to lean over and kiss him.

"Don't do it," I heard Paul say.

I turned to look up at him, when I heard another voice, "Grayson, this is not a place for chit-chat."

I spun around to see Hammond looming over us. "Sorry, sir," Grayson said.

"Don't you have a project to finish?" Hammond added, then waved his hand for Grayson to go away. Then focused on me. "Where is my app, Gweny? It's been a few weeks now!"

"Dating app, Gwen!" I heard Paul shout over the wall.

Oh, that app!

I bounced my finger on my mouth, trying to find the words to say it's a game now. It's been weeks since I last thought about that dating app. It's my chance now or never to explain this.

I looked up at Hammond. His nostrils flared, growing impatient with my excuses. I cleared my throat and said, "So the thing is…."

"Gwen! Where is the fucking dating app? You promised me a dating app!"

I took a deep breath and continued, "…. There are some problems with the dating app. Like…."

"LIKE!?"

"The GPS tracker uses Facebook and Instagram…"

"Then FIX IT!"

"I'm trying…. I'm…."

"GWEN! I swear to God…."

"GPS tracker stalks potential people who don't use the app but are close by…. the people who do!" I quickly let out, "you know, the app stalks people!"

He bent down to my level, his face close to mine, "Get the fucking app up and running NOW!" He moved back to his standing position and walked off.

"You okay, Gwen?" Paul asked me.

I shake the mouse to wake up the computer. I now have to say goodbye to the game. I should've known this from the beginning, Hammond doesn't like change. I let out a sigh, trying to release this built-up pressure in my head.

"You want coffee?" Paul suggested. "Or we could go into the bathroom and hibernate for a bit?"

"No, no, but thanks for looking out for me."

Grayson swivelled back towards me. Before Grayson could say anything, I answered his imaginary question. "I'm fine. Just need to work. Have a few kinks I need to get out of the dating app code.”

Grayson raised his head, not understanding. “Like rebuilding the whole code all over again?” I explained.

“SO, Hammond doesn’t like the game?” Grayson asked.

“I didn’t get a chance to tell him. He was more hyper focused on the dating app.”

“Sounds like he might have someone interested in buying it.”

Which explains a lot!

I buried my face in my hands, realising the error of my ways.

“I should have said something to Hammond right there. That this dating app is a huge problem, that the fact Ivan is presenting this app to be okay with the public and it’s safe! It’s not safe at all! I wish Hammond would have calmed down and hear me out, instead of barking demands at me. I could have told him about the game. I’m sure he would like the game better. It’s safe, it’s fun, it gets people excited.”

I let out an *argh* into my hands.

Aware of Grayson still observing me, “You know this is going to come back on to me once the company finds out what this app is actually going to be used for. Let’s add some more icing to the cake and develop an app that stalks women too! The company saw no issue in this because the only female in the company built it." I placed my head on the desk and pretended to cry.

At this point in my working life, I don't have the energy for natural tears.

Grayson looked around the office and said, "Do you want some help?"

With my head still on the desk, I turn to look up at him.

I finally have a chance to work with Grayson?

I pushed myself off the desk. "I guess some help might work. Since Ivan is not helping yet again."

We both glanced at Ivan, who was chatting with a few other men. They were laughing, slapping each other, then dry humped the air. Oh, it was gross to watch.

Snapping out of our gaze, Grayson clapped his hands and asked, "So, this app?"

"It scans social media, finds attractive women, reveals their last check-in locations and times, and calculates your travel time to get there." I explained to him.

Grayson turns up his nose, "Gross, Gwen… Why?"

"Oh, the best part of this app is it has a handy hint section, like the best pickup lines to use on what type of chick. And how to keep the conversation going after they said no."

Grayson dropped his head and shook it repeatedly. "Gwen, this is bad. Really bad!"

I didn't want to tell him that my decision to work on this app was based on an irrational decision? When you are so down, numb, and burnt out to the max, it can get hard to say *'No'*.

I leaned up to look over the wall, seeing if Paul had any input into this. Watching Paul on his computer, I considered the difficulties of modern dating, such as the fear of stalking and the anxieties of first dates. This wasn't helping the dating app I was supposed to be creating.

While I continued to stare at Paul, I pondered existing dating apps and their responses to negative feedback. All the horror stories you hear make those dating apps seem terrifying.

What will make ours different?

I remembered all the dates I had been on all my life and saw a pattern in my own dating life; mostly first dates, never second dates. Well, except for Max. After seeing the patterns, I came to the conclusion.

"I hate dating," I told Grayson, while still staring at Paul.

"I hate first dates. They are like job interviews. *'First impressions always last!'"* I continued.

Slowly, I turned around to see if Grayson was listening. I sat up and continued to talk to him, "It's okay for you guys on that. You get all jittery, stumble on your words, or have happy little accidents. And the girls find this cute. And then bam, you got yourself a second date." I waited for Grayson to say something, but he didn't. I wiggled my finger at him.

"You see… It's not like that for us girls. We make one tiny mistake on that first date. I'll guarantee you; I'll never hear from that guy again."

I let out a huff before continuing, "I can't remember which hand to shake with. Oh, that means no second date. I ordered pasta for dinner. Oh, this girl likes to eat, then definitely don't want her to be sitting on MY face! Oh, and if you mention which dinosaur you like and how many interesting facts you know about dinosaurs, believe me, he's not returning from the bathroom!"

I let out a big sigh from my speech. "Fuck dating!"

I glanced at Paul, awaiting a response, but he remained silent.

"Don't get me wrong; I would love to meet someone, my someone. Someone who likes me for me and my weirdness," I said to Grayson, "but I would rather meet them by accident or randomly in a bar. Start a conversation without it being awkward and weird. If I tell them my favourite dinosaur facts, they aren't creeped out by it. In fact, they have their own list of dinosaur facts, and we'd spend the time comparing notes. Then he'd decide we should return to his place and play Nintendo for the rest of the night."

Grayson listened patiently to my long speech. So, I just kept going, "But this is the real world, and shit like that is socially unacceptable."

Grayson sat up, moving his eyes up. I just laid it all on him. I, likewise, had no clue where it stemmed from: a mysterious inner darkness. Something that I had hidden for a long time.

"Redesign the dating app into something that you want. A dating app where couples could randomly meet up with each other. No organising dates, no *'first dates'*. Just two people randomly meet and share common interests, have a drink or two, then they could take it the next step further or not," Paul finally added something to this conversation.

I liked where he was going with this, a dating app with no dating, no organising, and more privacy.

"What are you doing?" Grayson asked me.

"You started monologuing, then suddenly you stopped. Stared at the other desk and then nodded your head. Are you sure you're okay?"

I turned to him, ignoring what he said. "I want to create a dating app for people who want to meet someone without realizing they are meeting."

Grayson tossed his head back. I explained, "Okay, two people register for the app by filling out questionnaires, normal stuff, right?"

Grayson nodded.

"Once you fill out the questionnaire, the algorithm will run and find matches."

Grayson still nodded.

"The app could place an event in the calendar, like a drink with friends or something like this. Something where you might need to dress up a little. Then the app will direct you to a place, like a bar or a restaurant. Once they are there, the app will tell them where to sit, what to order, and what to say to the person sitting next to them. This person is their match. They will strike up a conversation, and then the next thing is they will tell this story at their wedding."

The hum of my computer filled the silence as I sat and watched him. He remained motionless, his blinks unusually rapid. He twisted his lips side to side, thinking about everything I just told him. *An app that's secretly a dating app.* He still didn't move, still trying to take it all in, so I continued, "But think about it. It's like a dating app for people with anxiety, introverts, or people who hate making first impressions!"

Brief sounds came out of Grayson. He tried to rethink his comments to me, while I emailed him the base code, and typed up the idea into an email.

"Send you an email." I told him.

He inhaled deeply, then rose and circled his chair. He stood there thinking briefly, then said, "Velociraptor."

I looked up at him.

"Velociraptors are my favourite dinosaurs. They are smart," he told me.

"Which one? The one in *Jurassic Park*, or the real ones?"

"Jurassic Park?"

"Oh, those aren't real. Velociraptors are about the size of a wolf and hunt solo. Oh, and they had feathers!" I told him.

Leaning on the back of his chair, Grayson reflected on my statement before returning to his desk.

"You don't have any of that," Paul said.

"I know, but give me some time, and I can work on it."

I went to work writing a pitch for the dating app when a ping came up.

> *Hey, it's Banks. Sorry for pinging you.*

I looked over to see Paul typing away, Grayson over at his desk.

I opened the chat and typed:

> *Hey, that's cool. I needed a break.*

> Banks: Grayson gave me your number.

"Odd?" I thought, *"Why would Grayson give out my number?"*

> Banks: *So, I was thinking about you.*

> Me:*????*

> Banks: *Sorry that came out.*
> *I don't mean to scare you.*

> Me: *No, it's cool. It's just strange as we only just met.*

> Banks: *I know, but we could get to know each other more if you want?*

> Me: *????*

> Banks: *I was wondering if you want to catch up sometime?*

I glanced back at Grayson. *Didn't I just go on a date with him?*

I attempted to recall the mechanics of dating. Do I need to make the next move? Am I the one who needs to ask for the second date? Should I have waited for Grayson to ask me out again? This way, I knew he was keen on me? *Ugh, I just hate dating!*

I lean over the wall. "Paul?"

"Just say no! It's not worth your time."

I bent back down and typed, but the dots at the bottom of the chat screen danced.

> Banks: *I can show you how to play D&D properly. Grayson is still learning as his character is only a level 5. He also asked me if I can show you a thing or 2.*

I read his last comment one more time. *What do I do here?* I scanned the office. Keyboards clacked as everyone worked diligently at their desks. I leaned up to peer over the desk to see Paul. He wasn't there. With no Paul to converse with, I began typing.

"I got a bad feeling about this," Paul said, standing next to my desk.

"You have a bad feeling about everything."

Chapter 12:
Gwen's little secret

It's another Wednesday night, D&D night! I have been looking forward to this night, not only getting to hang out with Grayson, but I also wanted to show off some of my skills. I have been teaching myself some skills and getting a better understanding of my character. It was also an excellent opportunity to show Banks how much I have expanded on my knowledge. I also built a character for Paul, where we can play little games together.

I looked at my watch, knowing Grayson will be over soon. Packing my bag, I heard a knock on the door.

"Paul… Our ride is here!" I shouted.

As I opened the door, there was Grayson; hot, casual Grayson in his green flannel and his glasses on, standing there with some pizza.

"Gwen, D&D got cancelled tonight. Evans had something else come up, and OJ is working late in the office… again. And not sure what Banks is up to."

He let himself into the house and placed the pizza on the dining table.

"So, why are you here?" I asked Grayson, trying not to sound too suspicious.

He took a slice of pizza and then said with a mouthful, "I'm intrigued by this dating app you were talking about the other day. For some reason, I can't stop thinking about it. So, I thought we could work on it more tonight. Pull an all-nighter, coding it."

I handed Grayson a beer and took a slice of pizza for myself, thinking about his proposal.
Grayson took another bite. "Had you thought about how the two potential matches would meet? What about adding a date on to their calendar? Also, what about privacy? How do we keep everyone safe?"

"Wow, that's a butt load of questions, Gwen." Paul added.

I really had to think more about this. I remember talking about them and adding this to the proposal, but I never thought about coding them.

"Email address. Their Google accounts link to Gmail, and therefore to their calendar, for example. Most email addresses have some sort of calendar attached to them."

Grayson nodded.

"As for meeting up, maybe somewhere…. casual? I don't like the idea of meeting in private, somewhere in public, but also casual? Like a cafe or a quiet bar? A place where the two matches can feel comfortable." I continued.

"Something to add to the questionnaire." Paul said.

"We should add this into the questionnaire." I repeated.

Grayson grabs another slice. "Questionnaire? We would need to nail down specific questions, which might make the user either re-think or take their time to answer. That could annoy them."

"Then make the questions easy."

Grayson waggled his finger. "I still stand by it. You're onto something here, Gwen."

We finished the last pizza slice and pushed the box to the other end of the table as Grayson and I wrote questions for the questionnaire. The hum of the laptop rebooting itself fills the air as we research ideas and theories of dating, and how to turn this into a code.

"You know Ivan will take over the app when it's out. Claiming it's his app," Grayson said.

"I know… That's why we need a destroyer code in the system." I said, "Just hide it away in there. Then, when the app hits one million people, it malfunctions to the point that it's useless, and no one wants to use it. Costing the company millions. And with Ivan's name splashed all over the design briefs and in the code, the higher ups of the company will come down on him."

The beer bottle hung there before hitting Grayson's mouth for another sip.

"You know, Ivan won't learn his lesson. He would shrug it off and onto his next victim." Paul added.

"What are you on about?" I casually said.

"Ivan is a player. He doesn't care about the people who are involved and how he hurts them. He's another Max, but a smaller version." Paul explained.

"Smaller version?"

"Yeah, he is Max. You fell for Max's tricks again." Paul reminded me.

"No, I didn't…. Did I?" I said, thinking about it.

"Gwen?" Grayson asked.

"You need to understand something, Paul. This is Silicon Valley. Everyone here are snakes, and everyone wants to be the next big thing. Of course, everyone stabs you in the back. It's just something you need to get used to." I explained.

"Gwen?" Grayson asked a little louder.

"What?" I said back to him.

"What is happening?"

"What do you mean?" I asked, confused.

"Grayson, doesn't know I exist, remember I am imaginary!" Paul reminded me.

Suddenly I couldn't move, and my chest became tight. My jaw locked and didn't seem to be enough air in the room.

Did I just talk to Paul in front of Grayson without realising Grayson was here? OH MY GOD, he's going to hate me now!

"Excuse me!" I whispered and ran out of the dining room.

Pacing in my office, with my hand on my chest, trying to grab that breath I need, "I'm sorry Gwen, I didn't mean to let your secret out." Paul said.

"Do you know what you did?" I said, still trying to catch my breath, "I look crazy in front of Grayson. GRAYSON, Paul! Seriously, there goes everything. My chances of working with him, he is going to steal my idea now. There goes any chance of future projects together, teaming up, building an empire inside of TroniX." I stop pacing. I turn to face Paul, "you know what the worst part of all of this is. Now he knows I'm crazy, there goes any chances of us dating, or kissing, or doing all those touchy-feely stuff that is fun!"

"What?" Grayson said, standing at the entrance of my office.

FUCK!!!! Of course he is standing there.

I dropped my head. "I didn't mean that. I meant in a way that we get to work together."

Grayson chuckled as he took a step closer. "Gwen, what's going on? Did you create a dating app to get closer to me?"

"No…" I told him. "The dating app was really Ivan's idea. I just couldn't say no to him. I don't know why. It was hard to tell him no. I didn't know who I was. In fact, I still don't know who I am. But I'm working on it."

Grayson stood there with his arms folded listening to me, "So, who's Paul?"

This was a question he asked before, and back then I couldn't answer him as I didn't even know who Paul was. I looked over at Paul and wondered if I should tell Grayson about him.

"You better tell him. This is going to happen a lot more often." Paul told me.

I turn to face Grayson, tapping my fingers together, thinking of each word to explain this predicament that I was in.

"I have been on my own for over three years," I slowly said to Grayson.

"My ex dumped me out of the blue, with no explanation. I lost my job at Zeken, someone stole my work, I lost all of my friends, and just bought a house, too."

I looked at Grayson, ensuring he was still there; he looked worried.

"I got hired at TroniX but found it very hard to make friends because I was the only female in our department. And I got lonely."

I wiped an escaped tear off my cheek quickly. "Then there was this new guy at work who came and sat with me. We started talking, and we had similar upbringings, like the same stuff, and he wanted to work together."

I took a deep breath. "His name is Paul. And after a few conversations with him, I learned he is..." I looked at Grayson, hands on his hips, leaning forward, eyebrows raised, waiting for the important part of this story. "...my... imaginary.... friend."

The room went quiet, nobody moved. This was a lot of information to process. Even I would need the time to understand that a friend of mine has an imaginary friend, even for someone our age!

"He is standing there?" Grayson said, pointing towards Paul.

Well, that was unexpected.

"Yes," I said. "I'm sorry. I didn't want you to find out at all. People will see this as crazy, and I'm not crazy. I'm just —"

Grayson started to chuckle. His chuckle turned to laughter and his laughter got louder, then he tried to control himself. "Gwen, I'm sorry. I don't mean to laugh. I know how serious you are about —" He pointed over at Paul.

"— Paul." I answered him.

"But you have to admit, it does sound crazy." He laughed again.

My lips curled back into my mouth as I tried to hold in my words. My face burned, and I was ready to kick Grayson out, but as his laughing died down, he came over and hugged me. "I'm sorry again, Gwen, for laughing. I'm glad you shared that with me. We are friends, so I guess I could be friends with Paul, too."

He placed his hand under my chin and gently lifted my head, he placed his forehead on mine, and said, "Gwen, I don't think you're crazy. You're on a different level, and this guy who dumped you, he's an idiot. He is someone else's problem now."

I didn't want to let go or break this moment. Grayson's arm around me, his sweet, icy scent on me, him connecting with me. He doesn't think I'm crazy and wants to be friends with Paul too! *No, not breaking this moment at all!*

Grayson grabbed my hand and pulled me off of him, "Come on, we have a code to build!" and walked off.

"He wants to be friends with me?" Paul said.

"I guess this is a win?" I added.

Chapter 13:
Dinner

"I have a bad feeling about this," Paul shouted out. "I'm coming along."

"No, stay home," I told him.

"You need back-up," Paul insisted.

"I'll be fine. Besides, it's just dinner with a friend." I told him as I put on my fresh new lipstick, "Where's the harm in that?" I told Paul as I packed a small bag of things.

"I don't like it." Paul added, "there's something about Banks that gives me the ick!"

"Paul, it's just dinner with a friend." I told him, "You should be happy that I'm making new friends. About a month ago, I had no one. Now I have five of them."

"Gwen, please listen to me. Don't go out to dinner with Banks and stay home. It would be better for you to do this," Paull pleaded with me.

Brushing my hands down my new V-neck dress, admiring the reflection back at me. "What do you think?" I asked Paul.

"Gorgeous, but Gwen, Banks is not a nice person. Remember how you felt when you first met him? That tense up, *'ready to pounce'* feeling? You want to feel like that for the rest of your life with Banks?"

Swinging my bag over my shoulder, I turn to find Paul blocking the bedroom door. "Gwen, if I have to take drastic measures to make sure you stay home, then I will!"

"You know I can walk through you." I reminded Paul.

"Please don't. It kind of hurts when you do," Paul said.

"Then move, let me go." I heard a toot from the car's horn. "My ride's here."

"It's not what you think, Gwen!" I heard Paul shouting down the stairs.

I got to the restaurant, and Banks was already there. I was so happy to see him, but that smile didn't last very long. There were no hellos or what happened. "You're late." He barked at me.

"I'm sorry, traffic was a nightmare." I brushed it off.

"When I say to be here at seven, then you need to make arrangements to be here at seven." Banks barked again.

I didn't want to argue with him. "Sorry."

"Grayson wouldn't speak to you like that." I heard. I turn to find Paul sitting next to me. "He would have said, *'Oh don't worry. Just happy you're here.'*"

I really didn't need Paul here right now. I just needed to get through this night with Banks, and it's already not off to a great start.

"I'm sorry, Gwen, but I need to be here. I don't trust this guy. Look at him, such a slimeball!" Paul told me.

I looked over at Banks, studying the menu. He really hasn't said all that much since I have arrived, wearing the Flash symbol on his t-shirt and
sweatpants? His hair was dark, and looked greasy, an untamed beard, like it was growing in patches on his face, and dirty fingernails.

Oh God, Paul is right. I may need him tonight.

The server approached us. "Can I get you any drinks?"

Already feeling uncomfortable, I decided to play it safe. "I think I'll have iced tea."

"That's an old lady's drink, Gwen. Why don't you get something real? After all, we are celebrating tonight."

We were celebrating? But what?

"Gwen, play it safe. There are no celebrations, just two friends talking about games." I heard Paul say to me.

My thoughts started to spiral, the sounds of the restaurant went dim, my mouth dried up, and suddenly I forgot the English language.

I just wanted a glass of iced tea!

"Ummm... could I get a red wine then?" The words just flew out, regretting my decision.

"I'll have a coke, thanks." Banks added.

I curled my hands into fists under the table, pushing my lips together tight. "That seems unfair. You made me order an alcoholic drink while you played it safe." I let out.

"I didn't make you do anything! Besides, someone has to drive us home!"

Drive us home? Why would I want to go home with this guy? Wasn't this supposed to be a dinner with a friend?

I picked up the menu and tried to read; the words jumbled up and went out of focus. I closed my eyes and took a deep breath in.

Remember Gwen, just relax. You have Paul and he will keep you safe.

"There are so many options here," I said over the menu, once I got my focus back.

"So, what are you guys celebrating?" Paul asked.

"Shush!" I said back.

I may have said shush a little too loud, I looked up at Banks sitting there staring at me with that creepy grin.

"sshh…oo…shi, sushi… the sushi looks bad." I corrected myself.

Our drinks finally came. "So, how long have you known Grayson or OJ?" I asked Banks as I smelt the fruity sensation of the drink.

"I don't really know them. I work with Evans. He told me about starting up a D&D night at his place. It was an excuse to get out of my huge mansion. It can get lonely in that place."

The tone, the enthusiasm on the word mansion, made it sound creepy.

He sipped his drink. "I don't know or care that much about them. Or even Evans, for that matter."

Why would Banks hang out with guys he doesn't care about?

The server came over and asked what we would like to eat. Banks told her spaghetti. I hadn't thought about picking what to eat, even though I checked the menu twice.

"And you, miss?"

I looked at the menu again. I really didn't feel like eating. I just wanted to go home. "Umm... I'll stick to the salad."

We handed our menus over when I asked, "If you don't care about them, why do you still play with them?"

"Don't know, really. I guess I like to hang out with losers. Makes me feel better about myself." Banks added.

I couldn't think of OJ or Grayson as losers. On the contrary, these two guys were wonderful people, slightly annoying but still great guys.

I needed to change the subject again. "What do you do?" I asked him.

"In due time," he said, with that tone again.

"This guy is a fucking loser!" Paul said across the table, now that he was sitting next to Banks. "I mean look at him, Gwen. Talks in riddles but also talks like he's a tough guy. Why would anyone use the word loser to describe someone? What's the bet he will continue to talk a big game? *'I'm awesome. I'm so much better than everyone else.'* I bet you a coke if he starts talking about how big his cock is!"

I tried not to look at him but brought the focus back to Banks. "So, I didn't get to know Evans. What does he do?"

I knew what Evans did for a living, so I needed to play with Banks's cryptic game to find what he does. After all, he did say he lives in a mansion somewhere.

"He is a janitor for Apple."

This guy was making no sense. He had an answer for everything, but each answer wasn't adding up. I kept digging. "So, you work for Apple, then?"

Banks placed his hands in the air, "Fine, you got me, yes... I work for Apple, right there underneath Tim Cook. Tim is the CEO, and I'm the COO."

No, he wasn't! Jeff Williams was. Everyone in the Valley knew that. Is he Jeff Williams in disguise? He looks nothing alike. Or was there a change in Apple's senior leadership that went unannounced? That doesn't sound like Apple.

"Enough about me. What about you? You work... under Grayson?" he said while raising an eyebrow.

I knew what he was getting at, but I ignored his dirty joke. "No, we are about the same. We both work at the same level."

Banks rolled his eyes at me as if to say that joke was wasted on you.

The conversation went quiet. I lifted my glass to my face and smelt the aromas of the red wine again. The fruitiness and the tang of the alcohol hit my nose. I sank into the chair, looking around the busy restaurant, admiring the cheerful people sitting there talking, laughing, eating, enjoying themselves. I curled my lips, wishing that I was one of them.

I felt someone was watching me. I turn to find Banks, wide eyes, and a creepy grin. I followed his eyes to find they were staring at my V neckline of my dress exposing my cleavage.

I placed my glass down and tried to cover my bare chest up by crossing my arms in front of me.

"So, umm…" I tried to think of something else to get him to stop staring at me, "how long have you been at Apple?"

"Are those real?" He answered me with a question.

I looked around the table wondering what he was asking, then Paul whispered, "your boobs. He wants to know if they are real."

I looked down and instantly regretted my choice in dresses. I grabbed my jacket and wrapped it around me, even though it was already warm in the restaurant.

"Yes…" I quietly answered him.

"Nice!" Banks creepily said.

Finally, the food came. I sat there picking through the salad, looking for the chicken bits, and popped it into my mouth, chewing on it slowly.

"Let's cut to the chase, Gwen…" He put his fork down and looked at me directly. "…how big are you really? Are you a one-finger or a two-finger kind of girl?"

My eyes went wide. I stopped doing what I was doing.

Who asks a question like that?

"I'm just asking if you need stretching before I put my monster in there!"

"Told you!" Paul added.

I couldn't breathe. My vision went blurry, and I needed to throw up. I gotta get out of here!

"Bathroom!" I said quickly, without finishing what was in my mouth. "I need to pee. I have to go to the bathroom." Grabbing my stuff and heading to the bathroom.

"Miss, are you okay?" The server stopped me.

I looked up at her. I found a scapegoat. *Thank you, Karma!* I didn't need to climb out of the bathroom window. "Do you have a back door? I need to leave, like right now, without being seen."

She examines my face and looks over at the table I was sitting on. Her eyebrows frowned. "It's okay, come with me."

We both walked into the kitchen area as I booked an Uber to go home. I paced up and down in the back alleyway, waving my hands around, trying to grab as much air as I needed. My heart is beating faster than normal.

"Ma'am, I got you some water," the server said as she handed me a glass.

Taking a big glop from it, I finished the glass and handed it back.

"You want me to spit in his food?" I heard someone say.

"No!" I let out in one breath as I felt my body slowing down.

"Cool… I can cum in it instead? Need to shoot a load before getting back to work," he added. "Make the prick know what a real man tastes like!"

"Mateo! NO! For the last time, NO!" the server answered for me.

"Okay, suit yourself," he said as he walked away.

I had to hide my giggle, but it would have been interesting to see.

"You all good now?" she asked.

I let out a deep sigh and said, "yeah I'll be okay," then jumped into the Uber.

I blocked Banks from all social platforms and put my phone away. Watching the streetlights rushing past as the night played out in my head. I knew Paul warned me. I felt it myself. I knew this was a bad idea, but I went to dinner with him, anyway. I let out a trembling sigh when I heard, "You're okay, Gwen. Just try to not think about it. I just want to see you happy again." Paul placed his hand on top of mind.

Still remembering the night as I walked into my house. Each minor detail played out as I cringed. I shut the bathroom door and rested my head on it. I let out a few deep breaths between my tears.

"See, you're chickenshit. Banks wanted you! See, you're a loser, just like him. Losers belong with Losers!" That voice in my head came out, *"You should have just let him fuck you. It's the only way you ever going to get laid!"*

"Stop!" I whispered.
"You are so pathetic, Gwen. Nobody wants you around!"

Am I not worth of love? Am I that pathetic that the only man who could love me is someone who loves themselves more? This is not fair. What did I do to only get the crumbs of life? I know I'm not pretty, or perfect, but why do I get the leftovers?

My breathing trembled, the pressure around my head tightened, my chest was about to explode, but it suddenly stopped when I felt someone else's hands on top of mine, a warm sensation over me, and a gentle brush across my cheek.

I wanted to say it. I wanted to whisper his name. "Shush," Paul said, as I felt his hand slide down to my waist. "It's all okay, Gwen. You're worth it, every minute, every moment. You are so worthy."

He gently placed small kisses on my neck as he lifts my dress, helping him guide his fingers inside of me. I bent over, letting out a moan, a quiver with each stroke of his fingers. I pulled his hand out. I was not ready to cum right now. I need more from Paul.

I removed my dress, stumbled to open the bathroom door, and grabbed his hand. I led him to the bed and got in. It took little time for Paul to be undressed, and there we were, lying beside each other, staring into each other's eyes, wondering if this was actually going to happen.

"Are you sure about this?" Paul asked.

I rolled on to my back, and opened my legs, "yeah, I'm sure!"

I closed my eyes as I fonded around myself. I open them to find Paul on top. "Okay, I think I'm ready."

I let go and let Paul take over. As I lay feeling my body slowly move around to the rhythm of Paul's, I heard, "Am I doing this right?"

"Shush!" I told him as the sensation of him took over me.

Quivering with each penetration, my breath became rapid, my body became lost in this emotion. A sudden rush of warmth reached my face as I felt my body about to tense up.

"Don't stop!" I breathe out.

I suddenly pushed onto Paul hard. I couldn't move, I laid there stiff, and then suddenly became so sensitive. Panting turned to giggles, knowing that I was the one who came first.

Wow! That was exciting!

I came back down, and everything turned to normal in a matter of seconds. I laid still trying to catch my breath.

Paul laid there; his perfect body covered with the doona. I turned to him and kissed him again.

"Thank you. I needed that," I told him.

"I know." He answered.

The Californian sun burst through the curtains, waking me up. The cat bounced on the bed, walking all over me. I rolled over to see Paul still asleep. I reached down under the covers, found the vibrator and put it away. I got out of bed, picked the cat, and looked over at Paul once more.

Who would've thought that imaginary friend could be so good in bed!

Chapter 14:
Text Message

No morning routines, no need to tell myself it's going to be a good day. I knew today was going to be a good day!

Grinning ear to ear as I remembered how wonderful my weekend with Paul was.

Rediscovering myself, learning my limits, and the things I like when it comes to intimacy. No more just lying there, being used as a tool for masturbation. Discovering that I can cum too, and hard!

Letting Paul watch, giving me advice, taking it in turns between me and Paul on who will cum first.

Oh yes, my little bean had been flicked more times than I counted over the course of one weekend. *I can't believe I could walk into the office this morning!*

"Morning Grayson!" I said. Some routines are hard to die.

He spun around with a cheerful grin on his face. "You must have had a good weekend?"

How did he know? Was my smile giving it all away? Did Paul tell him?

Grayson continued, "Banks told us all what happened."
OH SHIT! I forgot about Saturday night with Banks.
"Wait…. What?" I said.
"Banks told us about how much fun he had with you on Saturday night." Grayson answered.
I really didn't want to think about that moment. I was so glad that Paul erased it out of my mind. I didn't want to know. I just wanted to move on. "I don't want to talk about it."
Grayson went from cheerful to concerned all of a sudden. But before Grayson could ask me anything else, I hurried to my desk.

"Look at him, Gwen. He is so confused. You should tell him what happened," Paul added.

I glanced at Grayson. "I really don't want to. I have put that mess out of my head, and I don't want to revisit it."

"It might help. It also might find what type of person Grayson is, too. If he thinks you had a dirty weekend with Banks and Banks told everyone, should he be smiling like that?" Paul reassured me.

Is he just like all the other guys here? *Shit talkers, a bragger, fuck and dumpers.*

Paul said, "Gwen, I was only talking. If you want to drop the subject, then we can."

That night popped into my mind again.
Countering all moments from that night. I lean up to look over my laptop to watch Grayson working. He's caught in the middle of all this, and it could reveal his true nature. I mean, he didn't tell everyone about Paul. And he isn't the type that would exploit other people's information for their own capital gain.

I close my eyes, trying to shake that night out of my head.

"Tell him!" I heard over the other side of the wall, "you don't, I will!"

"How?" I asked Paul.

"No idea!"

I hit ALT CTRL DELETE on my laptop and walked over to Grayson. "Coffee?" I asked.

My hand wrapped around the coffee cup. The cafe was quiet again, only a few murmurs from others sitting inside. The night with Banks still played in my head. I clenched the coffee cup tight as I heard those disgusting words play out again. I close my eyes, wishing for it to stop.

Grayson leaned towards me. "Gwen, is everything okay?"

I slowly open my eyes. "It's fine!" I huffed out.

"So, tell me your side. Banks told us his. Must have been a fun weekend. He told the group how wild you can get." He shook his body around, trying to make light of the situation.

I gripped the coffee cup harder, leaving dents in the side. I sucked in my lips and pushed my brows down. I curled myself up into a ball, sitting on the chair watching Grayson dance.

Fuck Banks right in his fucking ear!

"That never happened!" I pushed out.

Grayson drew his attention back to me. "What?"

"THAT NEVER HAPPENED!" I shouted at Grayson.

I threw the coffee cup across the room and walked out.

I sat on the floor of the bathroom. Looked over to the stall before me to see Paul sitting there. I rolled my eyes to the roof. "You are right, once again. Grayson is just like one of the guys. He doesn't care about my feelings. Rather, hear the story's juice."

Before he could answer me, there was a knock at the door. "Gwen, It's Grayson. Can I come in?"

I didn't want to get up. I just want to stay here and hide away from the world for a bit. He knocked again. "Gwen?"

I opened the door, and Grayson followed me into the bathroom. I returned to my spot on the floor and watched Grayson about to sit on Paul.

"Don't sit there." I told him. "Paul is there."

Grayson moved to the stall next to him.

"So, what happened?" Grayson asked.

"The thing is; nothing physically happened. I never went home with him. There was no dirty weekend with Banks. He may have been with someone else, but not with me."

Grayson dropped his head in disbelief, but I continued, "The entire night lasted about ten minutes. I packed up and left."

Grayson lifted his head.

"It started as dinner with a friend, to discuss gaming tactics for our next D&D night. He wanted to team up. But I fell for it and went to dinner with him. He talked a big game, telling me things like he lives in a mansion, and the COO of Apple."

Grayson's face twisted. "For reals?"

"Banks doesn't like you guys very much and called you all losers."

Grayson's eyebrows raise, waiting for more of the story. "He got angry when I was late and forced me to drink alcohol. Before we could even get a mouthful of dinner, he decided right there, the first thing to ask was how big my vagina was so he knew what he was working with," I choked out.

Grayson leaned back on the toilet and rubbed his hands on his legs. He took a deep breath and let it out slowly. "Gwen, I don't know what to say. I am so sorry for what you went through. But he wrote all about what happened in our chat, so I assumed everything was okay."

He pulled out his phone and showed me the chat. I scrolled through, reading every point Banks said about me.

Until I got to the end, where Banks mentioned that when he was done, he kicked me out of the house.

You pig, I hope she got home okay! Was the last text from OJ.

I returned the phone and asked, "Why didn't you say something to Banks? That the way he talks is disgusting and humiliating."

I got off the floor. "That's me he is talking about, or should I say lied about. And not once in any of those comments did you say, stop it, or leave her alone. You could have put. And you chose not to."

The pressure in my head grew. I couldn't believe that a nice guy like Grayson could just let a trashy guy talk like this about me, or, in fact, any girl. "You don't like it when Ivan talks like this, but is it okay if Banks does it? Grayson, I thought you were my friend. You are no better than the rest of them." I pointed to the door, referring to the office full of alpha males.

"Maybe you should show those comments to Ivan. Now you both have stories to swap!"

I paced up and down the bathroom, clenching my jaw and my hands on my hips. I didn't know what to say.

Our friendship is over before it really started?

"You're right. We are friends, and I should have done something right then and there. Gwen, I'm sorry for not stepping in and helping you out," Grayson added. "I should have done something."

My heart broke a little. I really wanted to believe him. But saying *sorry* at this point didn't work for me.

"Gwen…" he ran his fingers through his hair, "I really am sorry. I wish I never introduced you to Banks."

"Did you give him my number?" I asked him.

"What? No! Why would I do that?"

"Did you give him my number?" I repeated myself.

"Gwen, I would not give out your number without permission. What kind of asshole do you take me for?"

"He is right. Just listen to him." Paul added.

My eyes watered, lifting my head up to not let the tears run down. "Okay," I blew out, "I believe you."

"Fucking asshole!" Grayson huffed. "OJ warned me about him. Why didn't I believe him? He is such a cunt!"

I perked up, listening to Grayson using such language.

"You know what? Maybe we all should calm down here." I said, "Look, I would rather just forget it. And not worry about it anymore. Please understand that I don't want to go to D&D anymore."

Grayson nodded and left.

Now that I was finally alone with Paul, I let go of all that pressure inside of me. Hoping that Grayson wouldn't do something stupid.

Chapter 15:
Revenge

Wednesday night had come around. Paul casually walked into the kitchen with his game sheet in his hand. "Hey nothing is stopping us from playing our own D&D night. I wanna know what happens next."

I shook my head. "Not in the mood. Could we just watch tv?"

Before Paul said something, there was a knock at my door. I thought it was Mrs. Waters complaining about Colin getting into her rose bushes again. I opened the door to find Grayson standing there.

"It's D&D night. Let's go." He grabbed me by the hand, trying to get me out the door. I stopped him. "No, I told you I don't want to go anymore."

Grayson stepped towards me and said in a lower voice, "Would it sweeten the deal that OJ is at Evans, waiting for you?"

"No, not really," I told him. "Why would OJ be waiting for me?"

I walked back into my house, and Grayson followed me in. "Gwen, I promise OJ I wouldn't say anything, but I think I know what I am going to tell you might make you want to come."

"It better be good," I said, pointing a finger at him.

"OJ and I were discussing what happened to you. Apparently, it's not the first time Banks has done this. We had a girl on our campaign named Samantha. OJ had a bit of a crush on her, but before he could ask her out, Banks moved on her, and well... let's say you read the signs and got yourself out quickly. She didn't. She told OJ about it, and OJ was livid, but it was Banks' word against hers. OJ never saw her again after that," Grayson told me.

I felt so bad for Samantha. Wrapping myself back up in my cardigan, "Why would he keep returning to D&D knowing what Banks did to her?" I asked him.

"No idea, waiting for Banks to slip up again." Grayson continued, "Gwen, I know you don't want to go, but we think it's best for the five of us to sit down and talk about this. Maybe we could get an apology out of him?"

My eyes narrowed just thinking of being in the same room as Banks. I do not want to go anywhere near this guy, and I don't understand why Grayson can't just drop it.

"Grayson, can't we just drop this? I told you the other day that I just want to forget about it. So what if Banks is lying to everyone about me? Nobody cares!"

"Gwen…" Grayson tried to plead with me.

"Grayson, stop it! What is the big deal here?"

"You don't care that some guy out there is saying…" he pulls out his phone and reads one of the messages, "... Gwen doesn't give a good head. No matter how many times I had to pull her hair to get the blow job right, she still needed to go back. I knew she knew nothing. Sometimes you need to teach a bitch a lesson!"

I saw red! My shoulders hunched up, clenching my fist, my jaw locked. *I'm going to smash Banks' face in!*

I grabbed my jacket and followed Grayson out the door when Paul stopped me in the hallway. "Be careful."

Trying to calm myself down, "It wouldn't be that bad. I'm sure we will just talk to Banks about his actions, that's all."

As I turned to go out the door, Grayson weaved his finger through his hair, pretending not to see me with Paul. Finally, I casually mentioned, "Come with us, Paul."

"It's just a talk, Paul," Grayson added.

OJ was already outside waiting for us. As soon as he saw me approaching, he gave me a hug and asked if I was okay.

"Yeah, I'm fine. Why does everyone keep asking me this?"

Grayson gathered us around. "We are just going to talk to Banks. Okay?"

I had a bad feeling about this.

"Gwen, it's okay. If you don't want to talk. We can do that for you." Grayson added.

"Grayson, we don't need to talk to him. Let's just forget it." I whimpered at him.

Grayson quickly turned around to face me. He sucked in his lips, pushed down his eyebrows and a sense in his eyes that I had never seen before made me regret telling him to forget it. "He needs to be taught a lesson!" Grayson said back, gritting through his teeth.

I reached out for Paul's hand, hoping he would comfort me with this. "It should be okay, Gwen. They promise you they will talk to him."

When Evans opened the door, his excitement turned to worry quickly as OJ and Grayson pushed past him.

"What is happening, Gwen?" Evans asked me.

"They need to talk to Banks." Reassuring him.

"Banks? What did he do now?" Evans asked, as this is a common thing.

I was about to say something to Evans when we both heard some commotion and yelling. We ran to the dining room just in time to witness Grayson punching Banks in the face. Banks fell backward in one single drop. I covered my mouth in shock.

I wanted to do that!

It wasn't hard for Banks to fall; he was skinny and small, like a scene out of a movie, watching two tall, well-built guys taking on a petite, skinny guy. OJ stood there on the other side of the table with arms folded, watching, letting this action happen. The way OJ stood watching, a small smirk landed on his face. He seemed to be glad to see this happen.

The room fell silent, and I thought it was over, but the next thing Grayson did scared me more.

Grayson took two steps away from Banks, lying there on the ground. Banks muttered something. Grayson stopped in his tracks, then turned around and picked him up by the scruff of his shirt, lifting him into the air. Banks was hovering about a foot or so off the ground, blood dripping off his broken nose, and yet a small smile came on his face.

Blood stained his teeth, and Banks chuckled. "It was just a joke!" Banks said. "Some women don't know how to take a joke!" Banks continued.

Grayson put him down back on his feet, "All women want is men with large bank accounts and huge dongs!" Banks continued.

He points his finger at me. "Am I right, Gwen? That is all you want from a guy?"

I didn't answer him. His bloody face left me in shock.

"You think I'm shallow. It's not just Gwen who begged it from me, Sam too." He let out another chuckle, this time creepier than before. "That bitch kept flirting with me. She asked for it. Oh, because I didn't ask her permission to touch her ass, and rather help myself to it, then I'm the bad guy." He wiped his face, looked at the blood all over his hands, "Don't get me wrong here, it's becoming a woman's world now, everything is taken too seriously! Wouldn't you agree, Grayson? After all, you mentioned Gwen needs a good banging! That would change her!"

Grayson's fists became tighter, and his face turned red. He sucked in his lips and shouted, "YOU DISGUSTING PIECE OF SHIT!"

I could see Banks trying to laugh or breathe when OJ threw one last punch into his stomach.

Frozen in shock, eyes wide open, not able to breathe again, wondering what I had just witnessed.

Grayson was a well-built guy, so this attack didn't leave much impact on him. Some bruises across his knuckles. Grayson grabbed the cuffs of my arm as he walked out, pulling me away from Evans. The last thing I remembered of that was watching Banks crouching, holding his stomach, as the blood dripped from his nose.

Grayson sped down the road. Watching him drive scared me. "Slow down, Grayson. You destroyed one face; you don't want another three more on your list."

The car turned into the parking spot. Grayson fumbled with the seat belt, slammed the car door, and left us. As I got out, I looked around to get my bearings. I remembered this park; it's close to work. I noticed Grayson walking away, his hand clenched and shoulders stiff. The moonlight shone off the lake at the bottom of the hill. The wind blew gently across our faces as we sat on the park bench, waiting for Grayson to calm down.

This was not the Grayson I knew. Grayson was kind, gentle, and caring. Loves to have a good laugh and a joke or two. He is supportive and understanding.

Who is this guy pacing angrily, up and down, getting faster and faster with each turn?

His pacing, while muttering to himself, finally got on my nerves. I knew I had to do something to calm this situation.

"Grayson, stop, JUST stop! What the hell is wrong with you?"

"GWEN!" He shouted. He paused, fingers intertwined, seeking reassurance before continuing, "I never instructed Banks to harass you, or told him you needed a banging."

"It seems legit," I heard Paul saying.

"Aren't you angry about what happened?" Grayson asked.

"Yes, but I don't go around punching people. I should be in jail if I did what you did. Or worse, get a bad reputation in the Valley. I'll end up a community college teacher!"

"Gwen, that guy harassed you! He violated your trust. To him, they are just words, but they aren't. They just aren't! He can't get away with this," Grayson shouted at me again.

"YES, I KNOW!" I shout at him to get his attention. "It's nothing I couldn't handle," I told him, bouncing off his anger.

"Handle?"

"Yes, I get shit like that every day at TroniX. I just learned how to handle it."

Then, Grayson stopped in his tracks. He didn't know what it's like for me. He may be Asian and might get a racist remark now and then, but he didn't have every single guy in the office trying to hit on you or think it's okay to make a sexist remark towards him.

"Grayson, I can handle myself. It happens to me at work all the time. Just the other day, a guy asked me once if it was acceptable to rub up against my breasts. I told him as long as I could rub up against his first."

Behind me, I heard OJ chuckling at that. I continued, "Someone also asked me what it would take to get me to suck his dick. I told him that my mouth was already fresh, as I had my fair share of Tic Tacs this morning."

A smirk went on Grayson's face, and I could hear OJ erupt with laughter.

"See, I can handle myself. I just did what a normal person would do in my situation with Banks. I got out of there quickly and blocked him on all social media platforms. Yes, it bothers me now, but I will overcome it. Moving on and proving I'm better than him is the best revenge. His antics will come to light and people will see him for the real Banks, an absolute asshole."

Grayson let out a long sigh. But he had more questions. "You serious? You get stuff like that every day?"

"Yes," I told him.

"That place sucks!" Grayson let out under his breath.

"Work with me. You will feel safe there. Moss wouldn't tolerate shit like that." OJ said, "Moss would have fired those people before you opened your mouth, Gwen."

I turned around and hugged OJ; Grayson joined in, and so did Paul.

Chapter 16:
New Idea

I needed a break from everyone. As typical, requesting time off from work was a huge deal; I would apply for leave through payroll, and then they needed to get Hammond's approval. Then Hammond would request for me to meet him in his office, where he would question why taking time off in this busy time was necessary.

Every time was a busy time. Then I needed to explain myself, then plead with him before he decided it's okay for me to take time off saying *you should be grateful I do these things for you!* as he was doing me a favour.

After the ordeal with Banks, I needed some time to think. I needed to reassure my situation with Grayson. As much as I appreciate him getting in there and defending me, I couldn't help feeling there was more to the story with Grayson. Nobody punches up a guy for the sake of a friendship. If Grayson and I were just friends, he would have just left it alone, like I asked him to.

I put my book down and said, "I never seen Grayson so angry before. I bet it must have felt good, punching that asshole in the nose."

"What do you mean?" Paul asked.

"I keep playing that night with Banks in my head, over and over, just something about the punch. Look, I get it, we came in at the tail end, but you could see the amount of force he used. So much emotion behind it." Cuddling the book, thinking more about Grayson as a badass.

Paul shrugged and put his book down. "If it was me, I probably would have done the same." He tapped his book, "BUT…. in saying this, I would have done what you asked. Just drop it and left it."

There was a knock at the door. I got up and answered, "Oh look, it's the man of the hour."

"You were thinking of me?" Grayson asked as he walked in.

"Talking about you."

Grayson looked around the lounge room. "Gwen, there is no one here."

"I'm imaginary, Gwen. Grayson can't see me!" Paul added.

I rolled my eyes. "I keep forgetting that."

"Forgetting what?" Grayson asked.

"Paul is imaginary."

"So…. Are you and Paul talking about me?" Grayson said as he sat down, pulling out his laptop.

"It's nothing, really. Just office gossip." I told Grayson.

"Gwen didn't like it when you beat up Banks the other day." Paul told Grayson.

Seriously Paul?

"Did you forget he can't hear you?" I told Paul.

"What?" Grayson added, not understanding what was happening.

"I said, Gwen doesn't like when you beat people up!" Paul shouted at Grayson.

"Gwen doesn't like it when you beat people up," I repeated, dropping myself onto the couch.

"So, that's why you've been avoiding me?" Grayson asked.

I turn to face him, "Well…."

Grayson put his laptop on the coffee table. "I'm sorry for what I did. I just got so angry at him. Knowing what he did to you and to Samantha…."

"Look, it's cool. But we are friends, Grayson, and friends don't punch other people." I told him.

"Now kiss and make up," Paul added.

"Shut up!" I snapped at Paul.

"You know what I have been thinking about that night too…" Paul added, "... What if Grayson has a crush on you? Explains why he punched Banks."

I narrowed my eyes in confusion. "What are you on about?"

"Nothing," Grayson said.

"Not you. Paul." I corrected him.

"Think about it. He invites you to hang out with his friends. He is always inviting you out for coffee, and he is always over here." Paul explained.

"It's just your imagination, Paul."

"So, imaginary friends can have imaginary friends too?" Grayson added to the conversation.

"What?" I asked him.

Grayson put his laptop down. "Gwen, I'm confused, are you talking to me or to…" He waves his hands around, "... or Paul?"

I let out a sigh. "Paul, I'm talking to Paul."

"Hey Grayson, let's have some fun with Gwen," Paul added.

"What kind of fun?" I asked.

"Wait, fun?" Grayson was again confused.

"Paul wants to have fun with you," I repeated.

Why am I repeating everything to Grayson?

Grayson put his laptop away, and he placed his hand on his lap, waiting for the game to start.

"Okay, what if we play a game of have I ever? I can start," Paul said as he stood up.

I looked over at Grayson, still waiting for Paul to start the game, staring at the armchair opposite to him.

"Paul wants to play, have I ever?" I repeated.

This whole situation is so stupid!

"Sorry, how do I play this?" Grayson asked.

I was about to explain the rules, but Grayson stopped me. "No, I mean with an imaginary friend, I'm not going to win, and you and Paul will win."

I pinched the bridge of my nose.

This is going nowhere.

"Paul, this is going nowhere!"

"Sorry, I was trying to get Grayson to confess."

"Confess?" I asked.

"Confess?" Grayson asked.

Paul slowly paced around the lounge room. "Oh, me thinks there's something here, my dear Gwen. Once again, no one punches an asshole, unless they love the person the asshole hurt."

"Paul, there is no theory here. Once again, just friends!"

Fuck this!

"Boy, I wish I could understand what you guys are saying." Grayson said as he grabbed his laptop again.

Later that night, I lied in bed; the room dimmed from the streetlight outside. There was something Grayson said tonight that keeps playing on my mind. *'Boy, I wish I could understand what you guys are saying.'*

Why does this statement keep playing in my head?

"Maybe because there is something there?" Paul said.

"I don't know," I said as I rolled over.

"Could I help you change your mind?" Paul asked seductively.

I giggled, "not tonight."

"Maybe it's got something to do with Grayson wanting to be friends." Paull added.

"Friends? We are friends."

"No, silly, I mean between us. Between Grayson and me."

I rolled back to face the window. *Grayson wants to be friends with Paul? Could I make this work? Wait, is there a way I can share Paul with others? Other people can see him, talk to him, be friends with him? Interact with him?*

I pulled the covers off, grabbed my large cardigan and raced downstairs to my laptop.

I think I have an idea.

Chapter 17:
Meet Paul.2

Holding on to the backpack straps, hurried into the office, and went straight to Grayson's desk. He looked up and took off his headphones, "you're back! Good. We need to get this dating app finished! Hammond is pissed!"

"I have something to show you," I told him, trying to hold my excitement.

"Is it the dating app?" he asked again.

"No, something better!" I said as I widened my eyes.

I popped my head into the slightly dark and cool bathroom, looked around, making sure there was no one here. I opened the door wider and dragged Grayson into the room.

"Gwen, what is going on?" Grayson asked.

As I pulled my laptop out and placed it on the bench.

"Gwen?" I heard Grayson getting impatient.

I fiddle around with it a bit until I manage to find what I was looking for. I took a step back and stood next to Grayson, watching the laptop's colours change from greens, blues, reds, and purples swirling on the screen. I couldn't stop smiling at what I have created.

Grayson threw his arm out. "What am I looking at?"

I knew there was something I forgot to say.

"Meet Paul," I told him.

Grayson quickly spun around. "Wait, this is Paul. So, this is what you're seeing?"

"Hello, Grayson. How are you today?" A voice from the laptop spoke, making the colours on the screen bounce and twist.

Grayson stared at me. His eyes widened, his mouth dropped, "did that thing just spoke?"

"Yeah!"

"How does it know my name?"

"It's Paul. He knows you. He has always been here. Remember my weird quirk?" I told him while giggling. It was too much of an opportunity to refuse.

"Actually, it uses facial recognition, then scans social media to find you," I corrected.

"Wait, his voice? It sounds…. natural?" Grayson added.

"Yeah, that was a hard part to code. I thought about having a natural voice for this thing, and I decided to use Paul's real voice."

"Arrr…. What?" Grayson added, trying to understand what was going on.

"Yeah, Paul's real voice is quite unique. It's raspy, like a jazz singer. It gets higher and squeaky, like helium, when he gets excited. Became monotone when he was serious but still has that raspy tone to it."

"Unbelievable!" Grayson added, as he dragged his hand down his face.

"See, I could use yours, but your voice is deep and bouncy. Croaky when you're being happy, very sharp, and clean when you're being angry." I explain, "Plus, it would have been weird talking to yourself!"

"Well, you're the expert on that!" Grayson said.

"That's not fair!" I replied, while trying to hold back my laughter.

"I was also going to use OJ's voice, but he has a deep, slight southern twang, which was extra coding and kept bugging. And the tone and pace of his voice was like he was teaching you something new, which was easy coding. But the more I thought about it, the more I liked Paul's voice."

The room fell quiet, the colours change fade in and out on the screen before Grayson asks, "what does it do?"

"It does everything from answering your questions, to having conversations with you, to setting up your events, reminders…" I listed things that Paul.2 could do.

"Wait, it has conversations with you?" Grayson asked.

"Hey Paul, I'm doing fine. How are you?" I said to the laptop.

"I'm fine, it is such a nice day today, always sunny in Silicon Valley." Paul.2 responded.

Hand over his mouth, Grayson glanced at me. I placed a finger up at him to be patient and I spoke again. "I watched that Netflix series last night. It was really good. I like the part with the girl trying to find her soulmate."

"Yes, that part is good, but did you see the end of episode eight with the strange twist?" Paul.2 responded.

Grayson stood up and dragged his hand down his face again. I turn back to Paul.2, "Speaking of twisted, I hurt myself the other day. I tripped over and twisted my ankle."

"Oh no, Gwen. Are you okay?" Paul.2 responded.

"Yeah, I'm doing fine. I just needed to rest."

"Rest is good, Gwen. The quicker you rest, the quicker you can get back to doing things. Like roller blading!" Paul.2 added.

"Well, what do you think?" I asked Grayson.

Bent over the laptop, Grayson watched the colours swirling on the screen. He ducked his head into his shoulders.

Was he happy with this design, or was he angry, or...?

He finally stood up and turned to face me.

"The fuck, Gwen! What the actual fuck!" Grayson said, trying to keep quiet.

Grayson turned around to face the laptop again.

OH no, what did I do? Grayson hates this app I built for him!

"What did you create?" Grayson said to me.

"Well, I just turned Paul into a real being instead. So now you don't have to act weird around us," I told him, still worried.

"I don't get weird! Wait, did you create an app for Paul and I to communicate together?" he said, quickly.

How do I tell him yes?

"Well, yes?"

"What else can it do?" Grayson asked.

I approached Paul.2 and said, "Hey, Paul."

"Yes, Gwen."

"Hey, Paul, can you call me Gwenny instead?"

"Of course, Gwenny."

"See, you can change your name if you prefer to be called something different." I explained.

"Paul, I'm hungry. What's good to eat near me?" I added.

"Let me check…" The colours swirled while Paul thought, "There are six food places around TroniX with a 5-star rating. But it seems you have little time to eat, so I would recommend Bob's Deli. Order the Reuben with fries, that's their signature sandwich."

I looked over at Grayson, "Paul is right. That place is good."

Grayson rubbed his chin. His mouth bounced side to side as he was looking for that next sentence to say.

"Thanks, Paul, but do one more thing. Can you locate Justin 'OJ' Montgomery for me?" I continued to ask.

The colour danced around again before bouncing to the rhythm of Paul.2's voice.

"Justin 'OJ' Montgomery last checked into Innovative Tech this morning. Would you like me to send him a message?"

"No, it's cool, just checking up on him."

"No worries, Gwenny."

I turn to Grayson, one hand still on his chin, his mouth curled down, and not moving.

"I have been building other plugins for him to be more lifelike."

"Lifelike?" Grayson questioned my choice of words.

"Human, lifelike, Ummm... More real, less robot."

"What is with the colours? Wait, what is with point 2 stuff?" Grayson finally asked.

"Oh, well, I couldn't design a face for Paul. I mean, I could design him to be more like Max Headroom. But I'm sure that would have gotten annoying after a while," I explained, "and for the point two stuff, yeah, it's going to be hard with two Pauls around. We could go down the OJ path and call the first one, OP?"

Grayson chuckled quietly. He quickly stopped himself. He paced up and down the bathroom, letting out tiny chuckles occasionally, biting down on the curve of his index finger.

What is going on?

Grayson suddenly stopped and looked at me immediately. "Shut it off. NOW, GWEN!"

I quickly turned it off. "What is the matter?" I asked, placing the laptop back in my bag.

"This is gold, Gwen. Do you realise what you have created here? We are going to be rich! And the last thing you want is for this company to discover you created something like this. If anyone, I mean ANYONE, finds out, we... are... screwed!"

"Gold?" I said. "All I did was create an app for you and Paul to communicate with each other."

Grayson leaned into me, eye level and grabbing my arms. "Gwen, you have created an AI. Do you know how hot they are right now? And yours, yours is different. Yours has personality, a character, a friend in him! This is some Sci Fi shit right here, and people are going to eat this up. We.... are.... going to be.... rich!"

I nodded and placed a finger on my lips.

Grayson walked out of the bathroom, leaving me there with Paul.

"We? What is with the *'We'* business? Doesn't he mean you?"

"Well… The *'We'* stuff sounded okay to me. I have a base for this app. It's simple at the moment and with Grayson's expertise, maybe we can work together and make this app absolutely amazing. The AI doesn't have a personality as yet. He's just basic. No one likes a basic friend."

"Be careful, Gwen."

"Why?" I asked Paul.

He shrugged, "Grayson is right. This is gold. And when you have gold, people will take it. No more talking about this app in the office. Keep things between you and Grayson. Don't let anyone else in. Remember, it was YOU who created this!"

Chapter 18:
Paul.2

That night, Grayson came over to help with the AI app. I left the laptop on the dining table with the AI open. His colour continued to swirl and dance on the screen. I watch Grayson intensify, studying the laptop. He would pace in front of it, then bend down, getting ready to work on it, then bend back up and pace again.

"If he keeps this up, he will wear a hole in the floor," Paul told me.

"Grayson," I pleaded.

"You built an AI…. an AI… Gwen… AN A FUCKING I!" was all he could manage to get out.

My mouth hung there, waiting for it to fill with words.

"Grayson, you're stressed out. You need a cup of tea. Tea is always good for the nerves." Paul.2 said as his colours bounced.

Grayson quickly turned his head towards me. I slowly shrugged, then said, "So, tea… anyone?"

Putting the kettle on, but Grayson had more questions. "What are you planning to do with it?"

I looked at Paul. "What do you mean *'do with it'*?" I asked Grayson.

Grayson joined me in the kitchen. "What are your plans with the AI? You can't just build an AI for fun!"

As the kettle was coming to a boil, this brought me some time to think about Grayson's statement. I poured the hot water into the three cups and handed them out, saying, "I only made Paul.2 for you and Paul to communicate with each other. You don't know how annoying it is to repeat myself every time you guys get together!"

"You want me to communicate with your imaginary friend?" Grayson questioned.

I juggled the cup a little, trying not to spill a drop before Grayson took it from my hand.

"Yes! But I guess…. I did design something for myself too. As much as I do love having my imaginary friend around, it would be nice to have something physical to talk to and…" I suddenly stopped myself. I really shouldn't reveal the things Paul and I get up to when it's just the two of us around.

"Wait? Physical?" Paul asked.

"Hang on, what do you mean, physical?" Grayson asked.

I put my mug down. "Okay, I don't mean it like that. Just sometimes a girl has needs, Paul."

"Gwen, please tell me you didn't just build a highly intelligent sex toy?" Grayson asked, catching on to the conversation I was having with Paul. "It's what you and Paul are talking about, right?" waving his finger between me and where he thought Paul was standing.

How do I answer this?

"Gwen?" Grayson asked. "You and Paul are doing it?"

I froze; my eyes darted from side to side. I sucked in my lips and grinned.

How do I tell him? What should I tell him?

"Well... yes... we have, for a while now," Paul answered for me. "And, oh my god, it has been so much fun!"

"You know he can't hear you!" I told Paul.

With folded arms, Grayson changed his stands. His stare burrow into my soul. I finally caved in and replied to Grayson, "Well, yes!"

"Wait? What? You and Paul? How?" Grayson asked. "I didn't think it was possible!"

I empty the remaining tea into the sink and rinse off the cup before saying, "Yes, and I do have a very active imagination, Grayson."

"Oh boy, does she ever!" Paul added.

Now my secret is out. I waited for Grayson to say something, when I heard, *"Look at him, he now thinks the worst of you. You are such an evil person. You're disgusting!"* I took a deep breath and shook my head. *Does Grayson think I am really a disgusting person?*

"Gwen, you okay? You're not disgusting, it's normal, and I don't think Grayson thinks any worse of you for admitting to this. Might think you're normal," Paul said.

I watched Grayson reading the code for the AI when I went over and joined him.

"I have the base for the AI, and he's fully aware of himself. Check it…" I dragged Paul.2 closer to me. "Who are you?"

"I am Paul.2, an artificial intelligent, life being. My purpose is to help people in need, whether it's emotional, physical, or intellectual."

I turned to face Grayson. "See?"

I pointed to the code, "He has lightning speed access to Google and the internet to find the answers the user needs."

Grayson moved his seat closer to me so we could share the screen. That scent of his whiffed in my direction. I just wanted to drown in it.

"So, you basically built an Alexa or a Siri?" Grayson said, snapping me out of my daze.

"Well…" I answered, turning my attention back to the laptop, hoping Grayson didn't notice I was trying to get more of his scent.

"No… Paul.2 is different. He would be more aware of his surroundings and the people he interacts with." I answered, "He can sense things in you, and can start conversations without you starting them." I grabbed Grayson's attention. "I just want to create a best friend."

"A best friend?" Grayson repeated.

"Yes. A best friend, someone I can talk to, not only about my day but my problems too. I want a best friend who suggests outings or dinner dates or recommends who I should date and who to avoid. I want a best friend who can pick out outfits and know what I like to eat and drink, my style, and my taste in music, tv, and movies."

Turning back to look at Paul, sitting on the other side of the dining table with his head in his hands, admiring me. "I want a best friend who loves me." I smiled back at him.

Hand on his chin and leg bouncing under the table, "Okay…." Grayson said, "if this is what you want, then let's build it!"

Chapter 19:
How Interactive?

After Grayson went home, I sat there staring at Paul.2. the colour still swirled around, watching them change from indigo, aqua, magenta. The words *highly intelligent sex toy* bounce in my head, which leads me to think of other ways that Paul.2 could interact with its user. I bopped my head up, sucked in a deep breath through my nose, and pulled the laptop closer to me.

"No, Gwen, no way… that is crossing the line!" I heard Paul say.

"Please, it's worth a try!" I pleaded with Paul.

"There is a line, and if you do this, then you crossed it," he said.

"As a scientist, I need to try it," I explained to him.

"For one, you're not a scientist. You're more like a STEM producer." Paul continued to plead with me.

"It is the nature of my job. Build the most extravagant thing on this planet and see if I can have sex with it!" I pronounce to Paul.

"Now who's starting to sound like one of the boys!" Paul added as he got up from the dining table.

I could have added anything to Paul.2, anything really. So, once Paul left the room, I went to Amazon and ordered a Wi-Fi controlled vibrator.

We both stood there looking at the Amazon box sitting on the dining table. We both knew what was inside. But the anticipation of opening lingers in the air.

"Gwen, seriously?" Paul asked me as I sliced open the package.

"Yes, seriously!" I told him.

"What is wrong with me?" he asked.

"Some girls need more than imagination. And if I work out the code behind this device, maybe I could get Paul.2 to assist with the rest."

"Well, it's wrong!" Paul said to me.

"Please explain!" I asked Paul.

Paul chewed on his bottom lips as he shifted in his stands. Arms folded, trying to find the words for his argument. I opened my package and unwrapped it from the plastic and sat there looking at it.

"It's small!" Paul said.

"But will it do the trick?" I answered him.

"So, size doesn't really count. All this hype about size is a myth?" Paul said.

I laughed. "What are you on about? But the difference between you and this device is you don't have two parts to you... this does!"

I caught Paul looking down at himself. I needed to reassure him. "Paul, you're fine. You have a good size."

Sitting at my desk in my office, I hacked into the code on my laptop, then spent the night studying it.

It was a simple JavaScript code, not all that much to it but using Bluetooth and Wi-Fi connections to control the device. It didn't matter where you were in the world; as long as you have a code, you could access and control it. I noticed finger movements controlled it; a swipe up or down, depending on the desired intensity.

If I replaced that part of the code with Paul.2, could the user use voice command instead? But how do I get the user to use this device with the AI?

"People don't need reasons to use the device. It's simple. I'm horny; Pull out the device." Paul interrupted my train of thought.

Is it really that simple?

"I need to use the device differently, as if the AI were taking over, controlling the sensors, and understanding my likes and needs." I told Paul. "What about a game?"

"Game? Seriously Gwen, who plays games while being intimate?"

"Don't know." I said, taking sip of my cold coffee, pretending I like it cold.

"The definition of a game is something you play to win." Paul added, "how are you going to win with… that?" he pointed at the vibrator on the desk.

"It's more like designing something that can take control without using fingers or voice more." I answered back to him.

"So, the AI can read your body language and judge what you like best to get you off," Paul answered.

I suddenly stopped what I was doing and put the cup down. "Say that again."

"The AI can read your body language to know how to get you off?" Paul repeated.

I pointed my finger at him, "YES! That's what we should build. The camera already picks facial recognition. I'm sure we can use it to pick up body movements?"

Pulling the laptop closer, "Go away and put the kettle on; it's going to be a long night." I told Paul.

I put in the last line of the code, hit Alt Enter, opening up Paul.2, of course this new plugin wasn't going to work all of a sudden; I need to prompt it.

"I don't like this," Paul told me as he paced up and down.

"You jealous of a robot?"

"I mean, it's weird." Paul continued, "It's like doing it with my twin brother, just to see who is better!"
Picking up the device, "I need to test it out. You can either stay downstairs and pray for me, or you could come up and watch!" Realising what I said, "No, wait, stay down here!"

"I'm not praying for you. In fact, I hope the device breaks somehow, and you need to go to the hospital!" Paul shouted at me as I went up the stairs.

Stripping down and got into the bed, I shuffled myself around and placed the device in. I lied there, waiting for things to get started.

"Hey, Paul…" I watched the colour light up when I mentioned his name. I lay there thinking of something to say.

How did one tell an AI they were ready for sex?

"Hey Paul, can we have sex?" I asked him.
The colours bounce on the screen before Paul answers, "Sex is an intimacy action between 2 or more people do when they like each other."

Okay, this is going nowhere!

I sat there tapping my fingers on my keyboard, wondering what I should add here to get this party started. I could have added in an extra command, like, *are you ready for this*, or *let's do it*!

If I was trying to make Paul.2 more human, I needed to consider how two humans become intimate. Had it really been that long since I had done this and forgot the mating process? *Should I get out and dance or show Paul.2 my butt?*

Finished, rendered it out, opened Paul.2 and said, "Hey Paul, can we have sex?"

The laptop light dimmed, and the colours on his screen turned to reds, pinks, blacks, and purples.

The next thing I felt was a slight vibration.

"Am I doing this right?" Paul.2 asked, "you're not moving, I will need to increase the speed of the device."

I suddenly jumped a little. *Okay, we are now getting somewhere.* I moved around in my bed until I heard Paul.2 say, "You're finally moving. We will need to increase the speed."

I really wasn't ready for the increase of speed as yet, and I tried to say something, but all I could manage was some moaning.

"Your heart rate has increased, jumped from 70 to 110. There is one last thing we will need to do to hit your heart rate at the right level."

I tried to tell Paul.2 *'no, that this speed is fine.'* But the device vibration sped up and then suddenly, with a quick thrust inside, arched my back up, gripping the bed sheets with both hands, letting out a loud *AUGH!*

Just when I thought we were done, Paul.2 commanded the device to this one more time, quickly. I hadn't come down from the last thrust, and still gripping on to the bedsheets, 'OH MY FUCKING GOD!' I screamed out. "Done! You officially hit 150 bpm. Congratulations." Paul.2 added.

I just lied there. My legs were shaking, my heart was pounding, trying to catch my breath. *The fuck did I just create?* I slowly turned my head to see Paul.2's screen change back to the original colours, and the brightness went up.
"That's…. it… we're done?" I added in between breaths.
"Goodnight, Gwen." Paul.2 said and shut himself down.
"Typical…. Tinder date!" I commented as I rolled over.

I stood in the kitchen, the next day, munching on some toast.

"So, it works?" Paul said, putting on his jacket.

"It needs work," I told him.

"Needs work?" Paul asked as he put his other arm into the sleeve of his jacket slowly.

Putting down the toast and licked my fingers. "I want it to be more intimate. I want to add more emotional codes to it. I need the camera to read facial expressions, as well as body movements. Get the AI to understand which facial expression means that you are doing good, and which one means you are doing badly."

"Like when you do that weird *'O-face'*?" Paul added.

I do a weird O-face?

"I still need to find a reason why a user wants to have sex with AI. Again, it can't be just *'I'm horny, let's go!'*" I told him.

"That always seemed to work for me," Paul answered back.

I looked at my watch and saw the time. "Come on, we are going to be late."

Chapter 20:
Collecting Data

"GWEN!" I heard jolting me out of my coding zone. "Good to see your women's issues are now gone. Where's my fucking app?" Hammond asked through the grit of his teeth.

App? Which app was he talking about?

"Dating app," Paul said.

"Dating app, Gwen!" He reminded me. "You told me it would be ready in 2 weeks, 2 months ago! Where is it? I can't keep the clients waiting."

"Wait, you got clients for this…. app?" I asked.

"It's not that hard, GWEN. So where is it?"

"I sent it to Grayson."

"Grayson? Why?" Hammond asked, like each word I said grew his anger.

"You know me, Hammond, I need a second set of eyes on my code. After all, I'm seeing this through women's eyes, and you know how bad our eyesight is." I told him sarcastically.

"Good idea. I want it on my desk by the end of the week!"

My heart dropped, knowing that Hammond was gone.

"Is it finished?" Paul asked.

"Yes, but it still needs testing. I don't know how to test it. Maybe Grayson has an idea?" I added, looking over at Grayson.

I pulled out my phone.

I was pacing up and down the lounge room, thinking, *I can't believe Hammond already has clients for the dating app. Oh no, do they know how bad this dating app is?*

That it still stalks people. Oh no, I forgot to remove that element. We are going to be in so much trouble! What do we do to remove the stalking part?

"Gwen, you need to stop pacing. Your stress levels are too high. You need to rest," Paul.2 chimed in.

I looked at my watch and noticed the heart rating was climbing. Paul.2 put on some relaxing music and said, "Lay down and take some deep breaths."

So, I lay down on the floor and breathed slowly.

"Umm... what are you doing?" Grayson asked as he entered the lounge room.

"Apparently I'm supposed to be relaxing."

Grayson sat on the couch and opened his laptop. "Relaxing? You look dead."

Typing of keys and a few other noises before I finally sat up. "What are you doing?"

"I had some ideas to make Paul.2 more human. I want to test this out."

"Do you know how we could test out the dating app?" I asked.

"Nope, thought you might have a few ideas." Grayson said back, "I have gone through the code, cleaned it up a bit, and it seems to be working. No errors as I rendered it out. Yeah, I really don't know how to test it. The theory of the user is there. Fill out a survey and see what happens next. Simple dating app stuff."

I got off the floor. "Let's order some pizza and work this out."

Since showing Grayson the AI, he had been helping with ideas and configurations. Changing Paul.2 to be more human than robot. He started doing his own research and test codes. He was adding some of his ideas and plugins he was building.

I have never seen Grayson this excited over a project before. He would turn up at my place whenever he had an idea for a new plugin to add. The more we hung out, the more I got to know him. His favourite things, like music and movies, tv shows, video games, board games, books, as he loved to read. Why he chose a fighter and designing his character in D&D.

We would have these inner jokes and make our own sayings. We both would hang shit on people from work we didn't like. Bounce our ideas off each other, even if they were silly ideas.

OJ would come around, join in some of the fun, and help with the AI as well.

But the more this happened, the closer Grayson and I got. I would watch him work or find an excuse to sit close to him. Finding ways to touch him, put my fingers in his hair, pretending he had something on his face. I still love his scent and the way he explained things to me. He would catch me staring at him or dreaming about him and then smile at me and return me to the real world.

I was getting desperate here. So many moments I wanted to or could have told him how much I craved him. Every time I had that urge, that voice appeared, *"Don't be dumb Gwen, look at him, he is hot and you're not!"*, *"You're joking, right? Why would someone as stunning as him go out with someone so ugly as you?"* Then I curl up and go back to my corner. *Why would someone as perfect as Grayson wants to date me?*

Once the pizza arrived, I moved Paul.2 into the dining room. I grabbed some plates and the leftover beer I had in my fridge. Then took the Uno cards from my bookshelf. I had been dying for a game of Uno for a long time. Unfortunately, I couldn't really play with Paul as he couldn't touch the cards, and I would always win!

Plus, I needed more reasons to hang out with Grayson. Showing off my Uno skills might be a way to win his heart!

"Uno?" Grayson said.

"Yes, isn't that what friends play? I also have scrabble, Connect 4, and Twister."

"Twister?" Grayson said as he ate his slice of pizza. I looked down and noticed a black box hooked into my laptop, and Paul.2 had a loading bar across the screen. "What are you doing to Paul.2?"

"Nothing. Noticed the laptop's battery was low, so I hooked my spare battery pack. I can't find your cable."

We were four slices in, three beers down, and on to our third game of Uno. I had won two games, and Grayson was determined to beat me.

I watched him peering over his cards, thinking of his next move. It was a red three. He looked at the pile and then looked at his cards again. It was cute how he was doing this. He picked out a card from his hand, then put it back.

"Dude, seriously, it's not that hard to put a card down," I told him impatiently.

"Give me a break. I'm deciding." Then he finally put a card down, a green three.

He looked at me with a massive grin on his face, proud of his move. Those dimples always made me weak.

I could see he had about another three cards left in his hand, and I had five. I rolled my eyes in disbelief and placed down a green skip. "Skip you and back to me."

I added to the pile a green reverse. "I reverse the turn back to me."

I laid my last green skip. "I skip you, and then it's back to me."

I placed down a blue skip. "And skip you again, so it's my turn."

And I placed down my last card, wild draw four. And finally said, "And the final colour is yellow."

I placed my head in my hands, smiling with pride. Grayson stared at the pile in disbelief. He couldn't believe that he had lost another match.

"I'm bored with this; I'm going to watch TV." I moved myself from the dining room to the lounge room. Sitting on the floor and flipped through the channels when Grayson walked in with another beer for us. "Unbelievable." He said.

He walked out of the room and returned with my laptop in his arms. "Still charging?" I asked him.

Grayson didn't answer.

As the TV played in the background, we continued to talk throughout the night.

"Why do I have a fridge full of beer?" I asked myself when I added the last bottle to the coffee table.

"When you were going to have a housewarming party but then didn't," Paul answered.

"Housewarming?" I questioned Paul.

"You had a housewarming party?" Grayson asked.

I lay back on the floor, feeling the effect of the beer going to my head. "Sorry, Paul was answering my question. I had planned to have a housewarming party, but life had other plans for me."

I lied to Grayson. Max had his party at his new mansion the same week and invited all our friends.

"Gwen, you could have asked me. I would have come." I thought about that statement and how many times I could have asked Grayson out for so many things.

"You live here all by yourself?" Grayson asked me.

"No, I have Paul," I told him.

"Paul doesn't count, mainly because he started as imaginary and now lives inside a computer. So, he doesn't take up much space."

"Well, I do have a cat."

"Doesn't count."

The keys on the laptop bounce hearing Grayson typing away, "When was the last time you went out on a date?" Grayson asked me.

I sat back up onto my elbows and glared at him. He knows when my last date was.

"Okay, before Banks."

"I remember my sister taking me on a speed date thing and coming home with no numbers. But that was before Max."

"Max?" Grayson asked.

"This guy I dated for three years then dumped me for no reason," I told Grayson. I was surprised that it didn't upset me this time. "I have dated and have had sex before. I don't do it nearly as often as people expect."

"We are talking about real people, right? No robots or imaginary friends? Real people, Gwen?" Grayson questioned.

"Hey, there is nothing wrong with a six-speed vibrator. It knows how to take care of me!"

Grayson stopped typing. "Of course, with real people!" I told him.

"You know a six-speed vibrator can take you only so far, it doesn't hug you when you're done."

"But it still leaves you lying in the wet patch when you're done!" I answered back.

"But that's your juice, not sticky or gross." Grayson added.

How does he know my juice is not sticky?

"A six-speed vibrator can't look after you if you're sick. Or talk back to you when you need a conversation."

"And that's why I have Paul.2!" I added.

"Gwen, when was the last time you were someone's person? Someone's support buddy, lover, girlfriend, lab partner? Whatever the young call it these days? Their perfect person?"

Overwhelmed by the question, I stopped what I was doing, trying to remember the last time I was actually happy, being that person's number one. I slowly took a sip of my beer, struggling to find that one memory.

"Do you have an ideal person?" Grayson asked, breaking my train of thought.

"Someone confident, but also a little self-conscious. Someone who can make me laugh without realizing it. Who likes to read and enjoys being a bit of a dork. And they have to be interesting too, full of fun facts or useless information and can win a trivia night. Someone who understands me and likes me for me."

I sat up, continuing to think about this question. "Also, self-reliant. Don't want no Mummy's boy to look after. I don't need another pet!"

I look back at Paul, knowing he asked the same question months back when we first met. I didn't tell him then because I feared his judgment.

"These are all excellent attributes. What about looks?" Grayson said.

"Wears glasses," Paul chimed in, tapping on his pair.

I forgot about that argument I had with Paul weeks ago. When he asked why, as an imaginary friend, he had to wear glasses. That, in fact, I could imagine him with perfect eyesight.

After sorting through our conversation, listing all my favourite celebrity crushes and noticing they all wore glasses, we concluded I had a thing for guys with glasses.

"Oh yeah! Apparently, I have a thing for guys with glasses. I don't know why," I told Grayson, still thinking about it.

"Just glasses?" Grayson added, confused about the conversation.

"I don't know what to say about looks. I guess… someone who takes care of himself. Confident and colourful? He might as well look nice. Oh, and needs to have a great smile."

I turned to look at Grayson, who was staring at the laptop. "Why do you ask?"

"No reason. We are becoming friends; I just like getting to know you more. You know, in case I met a guy with your description, and I can say, *'Hey, I know a girl you will like.'*"

I guess Grayson could make a good wing-man, But….

"You know, OJ is single and seems to fit this description. He is a tall, good-looking guy with glasses and is intelligent as hell! Maybe I could ask for you?" Grayson mentioned.

"What? No... I'm definitely not OJ's type," I told Grayson.

"Oh, then who is OJ's type?" Grayson asked me.

"Boys!" Paul added.

"Don't be mean!" I snapped at him.

Grayson chuckled to himself. "Paul said something inappropriate, right?"

"Yeah!"

I sat up and pulled my legs in closer to me, thinking of who the ideal girl for OJ was. "She would have to be pretty, but one of those plain cute girls who wears dresses with little flowers on them. And has natural-colored hair because she doesn't like dying her hair. No glasses or wears makeup very much, and she looks after her skin with loads of skin care stuff. Oh, and she is skinny and a vegetarian, no wait, a vegan... but she is a special kind of

vegan who doesn't need to remind people and quietly orders
the vegan option from the menu. She also has a small tattoo
on both wrists that is too girly for anyone to understand. Oh,
and she works with kids."

Grayson sat there, eyes wide, slowly blinking, trying to
gather his thoughts.

"See, I'm not his type at all!"

"My God, Gwen... what kind of fantasy world do you
live in?" Grayson finally said.

"I'm nobody's type." I whispered to myself.

"Gwen, you know you are adorable, and you shouldn't
see yourself as the ugly duck. I've noticed a change in you.
Others also see what you're doing, like OJ." Grayson added,
"Well, I think you're adorable, and I like how much you
have changed."

A tingle rushed over me. My heart started to beat again.
Does *Grayson like me too? As in like, like me?*

"You know, people find people attractive beyond their
looks. A person's soul, personality, or emotional intelligence
attracts others. Gwen, you should really think about that in
yourself. You will be surprised by how many people find
you attractive."

"Grayson is right. You have been improving yourself.
You have attracted the attention of certain people, and you
know it."

Me, an interesting person? Me, an attractive person?

"Awwww….. Thanks." I finally said to both of them.

Chapter 21:
Turn Left Here

"It's a lovely day today. Why don't we go out for dinner tonight? Put on that nice dress you got from eBay." Paul.2 said, interrupting me.

"What? No way. That dress is too... you know!" I said as I waved my hand across my chest.

"Revealing?" Imaginary Paul said back.

"Yes. I don't want to sit in a restaurant with my boobs popping out." I told him.

"Besides, I got that dress for special occasions."

"Special occasions?" Imaginary Paul asked.

"Yes…like…" I had to think, "… maybe…. a christening?"

"None of your friends are pregnant, Gwen." Paul.2 chimed in, "let's go out and show it off."

I shook my head. "Nope, let's stay home."

"Show me," imaginary Paul said. "Show me what it looks like on you? Then I could tell you if we should go out or not."

I grabbed the laptop and headed to the bedroom.

Dress on, hair and makeup done, I walked out of the bathroom and waved my hand down the dress, "See… ugly!"

Paul stood stiffly, his mouth dropped and eyes wide. He cleared his throat, rolled up his sleeves and added, "Gwen, you…. look… nice!"

"Well, it seems you're dressed and done up. Grab your jacket, and let's go out." Paul.2 said.

"Did you want to come?" I asked Paul.2.

"Of course. How are you going to find the right place without me?"

Cool, how do I port him around?

I can't carry my laptop around. You don't know who's watching. I tapped my fingers on my chin when my phone buzzed, then it hit me. Let's put Paul.2 on my phone.

"Hello, Paul?" I said, once the loading bar was done.

"Yes, I am here." Paul.2 said.

"Right. Where are we going?" I asked, as I put my earbuds in.

"Turn left." I heard while walking down the street.

"Why?" I asked Paul.2.

"Turn left!" he said back.

"Okay, turning left."

I kept walking, admiring the views, until I heard him again, "Turn left again."

"Where are we going?" I asked.

"We are almost there, turn right... and you should find a place called Sage."

"Seriously? Sage, do you know how popular this place is? Everyone is talking about it."

"I know, but I think you're ready for busy places. Can we just go in?" Imaginary Paul said.

I gave up and went in.

There were three parties in front of me and a couple behind me. Each step I took closer inside, I heard the noise and saw how many people there were. I took a deep breath.

I am ready for this! I can do this!

Once I got to the maître d, "It's just me, a party of one," I awkwardly said to her.

"That's okay," she said. "The place is quite full. Why don't you sit at the bar and have a drink? We will come and collect you once there is a table ready."

I followed her to a spot at the bar and took my residence. I looked around again. "This place is busy, Paul." I whispered.

"Order a drink?" Paul.2 said.

"What drink should I order?" I asked, a little louder.

Paul.2 made a few noises in the ear buds before saying, "A mojito. I know you like the taste of mint and rum."

Great, now how do I order?

"Wave at the bartender." Imaginary Paul added.

I waved at him, and he came over. "Mojito" I shouted slowly over the noise.

Each sip I took, my shoulders dropped, my body relaxed, the effect of the alcohol tickled my head. The noise of the restaurant dimmed, and I could think again. I took another deep breath when I heard, "Gwen?" I turn towards the voice to find Grayson walking toward me, unable to contain his smile.

What is he doing here?

He leaned in, hugged me, and kissed me on the cheek.

Oh my God, a Grayson kiss! Oh, he is so smooth!

"What are you doing here? Stalking me?" He joked.

"No!" I snapped.

Grayson leaned on the bar, dressed all nice and clean-shaven. The buzz of the place got to me. I rubbed my cheek where Grayson kissed me.

"Tell Grayson you're meeting a friend," Paul.2 said in my ear.

He must have picked up Grayson's voice through the microphone on my ear bud.

"ummm…" I managed to get out.

"Oh, I get it, you're out with Paul?" Grayson said.

"Ummm… yeah, he is…wait where did he go?"

Grayson chuckled. "Maybe he went to the bathroom?"

"Arrr…." I was trying to think about where Paul went.

"I like Paul. He seems to be a great friend to you. And I am glad you introduced us." Grayson added, "Do you have any more friends?"

"Well, there's you and OJ and…." I added, thinking of all my friends. Which is a tiny list, "I guess I need to make more friends then? I may need to create a friend triangle rather than a straight line."

Grayson leaned over the bar and took a cherry from the tray and sucked on it while staring at me. His lips wrapped around the cherry, sucking on it, then placed it in his mouth.

Grayson tugged on the stem hard, made me quiver. I would have given anything to be that cherry!

I rubbed my neck and swallowed hard, sucking in a deep breath. Without Paul around to encourage me was making this hard.

I have to do this, it's now or never!

I took another deep breath. "Grayson, I'm glad you're here. There is something I need to tell you…"

I cleared my throat and then I heard, "don't look now!" from Paul, who appeared out of nowhere.

Grayson turned around and pulled a tiny Asian lady from behind him. He wrapped his arm around her excitedly and gave her a kiss. An actual kiss, not on the cheek like I got. "Oh, Gwen, this is Iris. My fiancée." He told me, proudly.

And in that one small sentence, a split of a second, my entire world came crashing down.
Everything I was building up just died in me. My heart just packed up and left me.

Grayson had a fiancée!

She put her hand out. "Gwen, it is so nice to finally meet you. Grayson talks about you a lot. I can't thank you enough for looking after him at work and while I was away. I know that company is the pits, but it's paying for our wedding."

She looked me up and down. "So glad I didn't have to worry about him wandering with other women with you around."

"Bitch!" Paul added.

My mouth dried up, and my breath became more rapid.

Why should I shake the hand of the person who killed my dreams?

"It's cool." I finally choked out and shook her hand, "So, you've been away?"

"Yes, I have been in China for the last three months for work," Iris said. "I was the only one in the office who knew Mandarin."

"Yes, well, not all Asians know Mandarin," Grayson corrected her.

"You didn't have the hard-core parents like I did. Consider yourself lucky!"

I chewed on my straw, knowing I couldn't say a thing.

"Hey, our table is ready," Iris added.

Grayson pushed himself off the bar and was about to follow her. "Gwen, come and join us?"

"Say no," Paul.2 said.

"Arrr... no.... but thanks. I'm supposed to be on a date with Paul," I told Grayson, hoping Iris didn't hear me.

"Well..." He placed a hand on my shoulder and then left.

Now he was gone. I could finally breathe. I took each breath fast, trying to gather all the air in the room. My eyes started to water. Remembering I have mascara on, I tilted my head up and fanned my eyes. "Grayson has a fiancée."

"Yeah… I'm sorry Gwen." Imaginary Paul told me as he took Grayson's spot. "Just be lucky to have him as a friend."

I sat there, stirring my drink, reflecting on my pathetic lust for an unavailable guy. I didn't want to be here anymore. I pushed the glass up the bar and got off my stool. I straightened out my dress, grabbed my phone, rolled my head back, took off my glasses and tabbed my eyes with the edge of my fingers.

Then another guy slid in between me and Paul and placed four empty bottles on the bar. He was so close I could smell him. His scent was sweet and tangy, the same height as me, and wore black-rimmed glasses. Dark, blonde with hints of ginger, short slightly curly hair, up-side down beard, hazel eyes and fair-skinned. Dresses in green flannel and a plain white tee underneath.

"Did you get stood up?" he said.

The nerve of him asking a question like that. Who did he think he was?

"No, I didn't. I just wanted to go out."

He held up his four fingers to the bartender.

"I'm sorry. I shouldn't just assume that," he added.

"It's fine," I told him, trying to get out of this conversation.

I turned to face the front of the bar. I kept my gaze and counted the bottles in the back of the bar in my head. But I kept losing count while staring at him through the mirror behind the bottles. I turn to find him still watching me.

The bartender came back and handed him his drinks. He took a step away but turned around. "I'm Adam, by theway." Then he walked away.

"You know he likes you," Imaginary Paul said.

"No, he doesn't." I said. "He was trying to make small talk with someone while waiting for his drinks."

"I'm sorry, I didn't get your name," Adam said as he returned.

"It's Gwen," I replied without thinking too much about it.

"Such a nice name," Adam said.

Before I could say the next thing, there was a commotion happening at the far end of the bar. "I DON'T CARE, GET IT OUT OF MY FUCKING POOL!"

It grabbed our attention as we watched a tall guy walk out of the restaurant. The whole restaurant went quiet from the yelling. You can see the girl he was yelling at was in shock. I don't blame her, as it's a busy place.

When she noticed everyone was looking at her, "Sorry, he was just pissed I didn't blow him this morning." And then she walked out.

I turned back to Adam, and we both laughed.

"And... that's my boss!" he huffed.

Okay, now it's funny. "Your boss?!" I said.

"Yes, Derek Goodwin. We celebrated tonight and made a minor achievement on this RPG online platform we are creating."

"Who's the girl?" I had to ask.

"If my memory serves me right, that would be Emmy Watts," Adam answered.

"Wait, I know that name. Isn't she the person who recreated the education system or something?" I asked him.

"Well, that's what she claims. I know she works for Moss Timmons over at Innovative Tech."

"Oh, I would give my right tit to work over there," I told Adam.

Adam stood there, brushing his fingers through his hair.

"Okay, I didn't mean that. I meant..." I added, trying to fix what I meant to say.

Adam laughed. "It's cool, Gwen. I know what you meant."

He continued to chuckle and without realising it, he snorted, which made me laugh all over again. I watched him take the bar stool next to me and lean on the bar, making himself comfortable. "So, you're an engineer?" he asked.

"Coder. I build apps. I know it sucks, but it pays the bills."

"You need to keep this conversation going, ask him a question," Paul.2 whispered.

"So, what do you do?" I asked Adam.

"Graphic Designer."

Okay, cool, I got that step out.

"Are you a freelancer or work for someone?" Adam asked.

"I work for TroniX." It slipped out!

I watch Adam's face shift. "Really, Gwen, get yourself out of there!"

"I'm trying but can't find a way out."

"You'll find something else," Adam added.

After four beers, another two more Mojitos, two servings of mozzarella sticks, chicken wings, mac'n'cheese bites, and lots of conversation, laughing and a few giggle-snorts, a few awkward moments, I was relaxing and really enjoying my time with Adam.

He, in return, was a fascinating person to listen to and talk to. He told me about his career adventures and how he worked at Goodwin Games. How he travelled across America for a rock concert, his crazy college adventures, and what it was like growing up. We shared our interests, hobbies, favourite things, and the latest things we watch on Netflix.

I watch him eyeing off the last mac'n'cheese bite on the plate.

"Take it," I said to him.

"Nah… I'm too full." He told me.

"It's mac'n'cheese, no one is too full for mac'n'cheese!" I said back to him.

He picked it up and took a bite out of it. Then he handed me the other half, Which I quickly grabbed with my mouth, wrapping my lips around his fingers. I quickly pulled back and slowly chewed the bit.

That was so embarrassing! Adam is going to think I'm some weirdo, and not in a good way!

"Hey guys, we are closing." The bartender said, interrupting us.

"Hang on, we haven't ordered dinner yet?" I said to the bartender, noticing the restaurant was empty. Adam, still leaning on the bar, holding up his tired head, watched me turning around on my stool.

I didn't want the night to end, and being in that spot with Adam was making me feel like this was perfect.

"Come home with me," Adam casually said.

"What? Why? Do you have a Beanie Baby collection you need to show off?" I answered, confused by his request.

"Gwen, he really likes you and wants to have sex with you," Imaginary Paul said.

Adam chuckled at my question. "Wait, don't answer that. I'm a full-blown adult. I should know what you meant." I told him.

I watched Adam slowly pull himself off the bar and get off the bar stool. Then, finally, he turned, faced me, and grabbed my hand. "Come home with me, please."

"Are you serious? Look at you, just because you put on a nice dress doesn't hide the ugly!" The bad voice said.

"Arr…." I was trying to think.

"He is going to laugh at you once he takes one look at your naked body. You're fat and rolly!"

"Gwen?" Adam interrupted me.

"Do it! Go home and have fun with this guy!" Paul added.

I took a deep breath and pushed all those evil thoughts down. "Yes." I told him bravely.

We walked toward the exit. "Are you sure about this?" I said, as I stopped Adam.

"I've never done something like this. I just never thought I was cool enough for a one-night stand."

Adam laughed and snorted again. "You're cool, Gwen."

Then he leaned in and kissed me on the cheek. "We don't have to do anything that will make you feel uncomfortable. We can just come back to my place, talk all night long, make some popcorn, or play Nintendo and then slowly drift off to sleep?"

That actually sounds great! Late-night conversations and popcorn.

"Okay," I whispered to him.

Chapter 22:
One-Night Stand

Adam opened the door to his place. It was a one-bedroom but was big enough for him. I placed my bag on the couch, and a head popped up. "You have a dog?"

"Yes, that's Mango. She's a rescue. She's a mix of something and something. I can't remember."

I took off my shoes and stood in the corner of the room, noticing he had a lot of houseplants. "You have a green thumb too!"

"Yeah, I do have a lot of houseplants, but they are fake!" Adam said from the kitchen.

I placed my hands on my head as I heard each thought racing through my mind. *"I can't believe you are going to go through with this. You know, deep down, this is a joke! Seriously, this guy is going to be laughing at you and laughing with his buddies at work. You're pathetic. Everyone is going to find out, even Grayson, about how you are so bad in bed! You suck!"*

"Are you doing okay?" I turned to find Paul standing in front of me.

I took a deep breath and nodded.

Adam joined me and handed me a glass of water. "Here, sorry. I should have asked if you need water. I always need some when I go out drinking. I get very dehydrated. I don't have time for hangovers."

I took a few sips from the glass and then placed it on the coffee table. I continue to look around the room and see his bookshelf with books and figures, his wall hangings, and turn to find his bedroom. I turn around to find Adam standing in front of me.

"Do you like what you see?" he asked, pointing to his bookshelf.

"Sorry, I like to read and code. Sorry, just comparing notes," I said, trying to think of things to say.

He grabbed my hand and led me back toward his couch. There we were, standing in front of each other. He placed his hand around my hips as I placed my hands gently on his shoulders.

"Can I kiss you again?" he asked.

I pulled him closer to me and kissed.

'What is wrong with you? You know he is drunk! He is going to wake up and regret this! You're nothing but a mistake!'

I stopped and pulled my face away from him, for him to land a kiss on my cheek.

"Breathe Gwen. You have this!" Paul added.

I took a deep breath in. "Sorry," I muttered.

"All good!" Adam chuckled and went back to kissing me.

"That's it girl, you got this!" Paul cheered me on. "I know it's not Grayson, but at least it gives you the practice you need."

I quickly pushed Adam off of me. *Oh My God, I can't do this, not to Grayson!*

The words got stuck in my throat, as Adam took a step back, letting go of me, "Gwen, you're doing okay. Adam is a nice guy." I looked over Adam's shoulder briefly to see Paul standing there giving that *'go ahead'* look.

Rubbing the back of his head, "sorry, I didn't mean to take it too far, we can stop…"

"I'm sorry, Adam, but I can't do this." I told him.

Paul is right. He is not Grayson, and somehow it feels like I'm cheating on him.

"Hey, it's cool." Adam added, "Is everything okay?"

"There's someone else," I snapped, "Okay, not like that…"

I dropped my shoulders and tilted my head up. *How does one explain I have a crush on a co-worker while I am sleeping with an imaginary friend?*

"... I really like this guy from work, and we have been getting close, well, because we are working on a project together. I have all these feelings for him, and I thought he had the same, only to find out he has a fiancée. You spend most of your time building up this fantasy, hoping, praying it will become real one day. It only takes one of us to open up and say those words to bring a fantasy to life. But as always, I sat on it for too long, and pop…. there it all goes."

I looked over to see Paul's arms crossed and shaking his head.

"I'm sorry Adam, for dragging you into my mess. I do like you, and you know, I thought it would be fun to sleep together, but emotionally, I can't."

"I hear you. I have been in the same boat." Adam replied.

Adam extended his hand towards me to join him on the couch. We both sat down as Adam opened up about his own situation. "I had this major crush on this girl I worked with, Stella. Gorgeous redhead, nerdy girl, worked in the graphic design department. We worked closely on designing these characters for a game. She was so interesting as well. I kept trying to find reasons why we shouldn't be together, as I didn't want to ruin her career or make her move jobs. You know, things that would make the situation bad for the both of us."

Adam grabbed the water off the coffee table. "I also lived in that fantasy world, too. And I was the same. I better tell her as soon as possible. The night of the game's launch, she rocked up wearing this amazing green dress, her hair tied up, with some sparkling hair pins. I knew it was now or never. I had to tell her how much I was in love with her. I opened my mouth and was about to say the word when she stopped me and introduced me to her boyfriend, Oggy."

I quickly covered my mouth, trying to hold in my laughter.

"Oggy! Seriously, who name's their kid Oggy?" Adam said.

"So, what happened?" I asked.

"Yes, I was angry and felt betrayed. But I got over it quickly because I saw how happy she was with Oggy."

"So, you didn't fight him for her, or made her feel ashamed for dating this guy?"

"What NO! Okay, what I am trying to get out here is that there are two people here, and sometimes it's more about their happiness than yours. You can't force someone to like you because it makes you happy. Once you see their happiness, you can move on and find yours. Might take some time, but you get it," Adam explained.

"She is married to him now. And as much as I would love to sit around and wait for this guy to screw up, I decide that I'm not. I'm going to go out and find my happiness."

"Thanks for understanding," I told Adam.

Adam walked me out the door. I turned around to him, "Thanks for a good night at least." I told him.

"Hey, it's cool, Gwen. Maybe next time."

I leaned in and hugged him. He placed his head on my mine and said, "call me if things don't work out with this guy."

"I don't look good as a redhead."

Adam laughed, "it wasn't about the hair… beside you look hot as a blonde." Then he planted a small kiss on my lips before letting me go.

As we walked down main street, the cool breeze was blowing. Some shop windows glowed in the dark, and a few places were still open.

"So close, Gwen!" Paul said, "So close!"

I didn't say a word, just drank my coffee.

"Update on Facebook: Had a great night with a special person named Gwen. I wish her all the best on her journey." I heard Paul.2 say in my ear.

"What are you on about?" I said out loud.

"Adam updated his profile on Facebook." Paul.2 said in my ear.

"Wait, how do you have Adam's Facebook profile?" I said, pausing the walk.

"It was this new code that was added to me." Paul.2 said.

"What new code?" I asked him.

There was some silence in my ear before Paul.2 added, "I read the code and what I can make from it; it looks like a search type code, using GPS and check-ins. Also, I can get access to their social media."

Wait a minute, why is this sounding familiar?

"Using a series of descriptions, I need to search social media platforms with similar descriptions and match them up." Paul.2 continued.

My eyes widened, and I took in a long deep breath in before Paul.2 said, "According to the rest of the code, I need to prompt the two of you to meet somehow."

I darted my eyes at Paul, realising what Paul.2 said.

"When was this code put in?" I said, blowing out that breath.

A few more moments of silence, then, "about 3 weeks ago."

"Wait a minute…" I said, realising what was going on.

I could not speak. I knew what had happened. I headed home.

Once I got home, I opened Paul.2's code and looked for it. Once I found it, I screamed. There it is, right there, staring back at me. It was unbelievable! Throwing my arms at the screen repeatedly didn't change the code. I finally accepted this fate and plopped myself down in my chair. I couldn't believe it worked. "Fuck me dead. The dating app works!"

Chapter 23:
Go FindMe

Grayson and I put the finishing touches on the dating app and called it FindMe. We changed the code to read surveys, no more stalking on people's social media profiles.

Even though the app works perfectly, Grayson and I tested out the survey function, seeing if we could find each other in Silicon Valley. Grayson always turns each finding into some fun.

"Excuse me, ma'am, is this seat taken?" he asked.

I would giggle at this. This one particular test, he finally sat down.

"So it works, and now we need to hand it over." I told him, "We kept Hammond's clients waiting far too long."

I got up from my seat, when Grayson stopped me, "Wait… let's have some fun! The clients can wait a little longer, can't they?"

I sat back down, intrigued by this.

The waitress came over and poured some water for us and handed us some menus.

"I'm Grayson Li by the way." Grayson said to me.

"I know." I said back.

"No… play with me," Grayson said, breaking character.

I rolled my eyes. *Is he serious?*

"Play along. This might be the only chance you get to date Grayson!" Paul added.

"Fine!" I placed the menu down. "I'm Gwen Hooper."

"Hey thanks for letting me sit here, this place is busy as!"

I looked around the cafe, and saw a couple of people, "well… It is lunch hour?"

Grayson chuckled.

"You know I have noticed you can talk in full sentences these days." Grayson said, breaking character.

"I taught myself how to speak. Yeah, it sounds dumb, but I didn't like to talk." I said as I sip my water.

"Cute." Grayson muttered.

He grabs the menu. "Seems I'm the man around here. I should order for you." He added, going back to his character.

The waitress came over, and Grayson glided his finger down the menu. "I'll have the chicken salad, and my date over here will have…."

Wait, he said date? Are we on a date?

"... Oh, this pomegranate salad thing looks good!"

As the waitress left, I stared at Grayson, noticing something a little different about him. *Wait a minute, he is wearing glasses, and a t-shirt?*

"What's with the glasses?" I asked him, "I meant, you wear glasses, that's so cool!" forgetting this fake date thing.

"Oh, these things?" he said as he took them off. "Yeah, I'm blind as a bat. So I need them."

"So, what do you do for fun?" Grayson said as he put his glasses back on.

"ummm…" I really had to think, "I like to read, and code, and hang out."

"Oh yeah, how is Paul these days? I don't see him all that much." Grayson said.

"Whoa, hang on. If this date is from the dating app, then you wouldn't know how Paul is." I reminded him.

"Oh, yeah."

"So, who do you hang out with? I bet there is a Paul, right? There is always a Paul in every friendship circle." Grayson changed his story.

Our salads arrived. "Yeah, he is good."

"Eat up. We have to go back to the office after this," Grayson added.

I took a mouthful. "Why didn't you tell me about Iris?"

Grayson paused. "I thought I did."

"No, never did."

"Sorry, must have slipped my mind." He said as he took a mouthful.

"What? I'm sorry, if someone was just as important in your life, like Iris, wouldn't you tell people about the good news, such as me, now that we are friends?"

"I just forgot. After all, she had been away for a long time." Grayson said as he added some food into his mouth. "Why? Are you jealous?"

I choked on my food before saying, "what, no… why would I be?"

I took another sip of my water and asked, "So, how did you guys meet?"

"Work function, actually. She was there to support her roommate at this old company I used to work for." He played with the salad for a bit before continuing with the story.

"She was the one who asked me out. I thought she was hot. Why would this hot Asian girl be interested in me? She is one of those girls who look after themselves, eating right, exercising right, always in designer outfits. And here I was tall, awkward, wore glasses, t-shirts and jeans kind of guy. Your typical basement dweller. But as we dated, she changed me, helped me eat right, cleaned myself up, went on dates to the gym, which I found strange, and she changed my outfits."

I nodded.

"It's not like I'm not thankful for it, but there are some aspects I missed and things I had to negotiate with, like getting to hang out with OJ and play D&D again. *'Tabletop games are a waste of time!'* she would say. *'How would you make it big if you are rolling dice all night?'* No more fantasy books, always self-help or business, and no more nerd stuff as she puts it!"

"Doesn't she relax?" I asked.

"Going to the gym relaxes her." Grayson sucked in his lips, and let out a little noise, "Sorry. Dumping a load on you here."

"I don't think he's happy with Iris, Gwen." Paul added, "something tells me he's not liking this life of hers."

"It's okay. We are friends, and we support each other." I added.

As we walked back into the office, Huxley stopped us. "Hey, here are your invites."

I looked at the colourful envelope with my name on it.

"We are having a Christmas in July celebration!" Huxley added, joyfully.

"Celebrating what?" I asked.

"Our mid-year profits. This company made bank this financial year."

"So, we need to spend that money on a fuck off party?" I added, "instead of banking just in case?"

"No idea what you're on about, Gwen. Just be happy the company wants to do something."

"Beats a pizza party we would have gotten," Grayson added.

"Come in your best Christmas themed stuff. Prizes for the winners!" Huxley added as he walked off.

I looked down at the invite, and really didn't want to go.

"Hey, it might be fun?" Grayson added.

"Come on, Gwen, let's go and sit on Santa's lap. I'm pretty sure that would be the highlight of the night!"

Chapter 24:
Office Party

Paul and I walked into the cafe downstairs of TroniX. "I've never seen the cafe like this before," I told Paul.

Looking around, the cafe was bigger than normal, with the lights dimmed and Christmas decorations all over the place. There was fake snow in one corner, Santa Claus village in another, wait staff dressed as elves walking around with food and drinks. *They went all out here!*

Wait a minute...

"Are you wearing a Christmas Sweater?" I asked Paul.

"Why yes!" he said, tugging at his sweater. "There's a competition on how Christmas you can go, and I am determined to win it!"

As I got to the bar, ordered a drink, I continued to look around the place. The usual staff was here, Huxley and his boyfriend over there taking photos at the Photoshoot, Ivan by himself on one table looking around while sucking on a beer bottle, Hammond in a corner talking to a group of people, *wait… is that Iris? Oh no… Grayson brought Iris.* I looked through the crowd for Grayson. I usually spot him easily, but this time I didn't until I noticed a guy lurking in the shadows behind the group. Squinting, I saw it was Grayson holding a beer bottle.

"He looks bored." Paul added, "Wanna cheer him up?"

"Yeah," I added. I grabbed my beer bottle and walked over to him.

I place my fingers into his ribs, watching him jump and turn to see me. "Yes! Gwen, you are finally here!"

"Sorry, Paul takes forever to get ready!"

"Hey, don't drag me into this!" Paul added.

"Please tell me he said something dirty!" Grayson asked. "I need some excitement right about now."

"You should really download our app and play with it. Then you will know what Paul says." I told him.

"Yeah, but here's the thing; I can, which then in return builds a version of Paul that I know and I like. It's not the version you know or like."

Grayson held my hands out and looked me up and down. I tried to go Christmas with my outfit, but I'm not much of a Christmas person. I put on a red dress I had in the back of the cupboard, hair up, got some new sparkly pins, as Adam got me intrigued by this. "Gwen, you look amazing."

"And you!" I said back, noticing he was wearing a Die Hard Christmas sweater. "I hope I will win the Christmas themed dress up thingy, Huxley said." He added.

"So does Paul!" I told him.

"Good Luck to Paul!"

Grayson pulls me in closer. "Hey, you wanna have some fun?"

I chuckled, "yeah!"

He quickly wrapped his arm around me. "But first drinks!"

We sat at the bar as the bartender poured us some drinks. I looked over at the crowd again, noticing a circle formed around Iris. Grayson noticed and took a glance over at her.

"Don't worry about that," he said. "She is in her element. I can leave her there all night and she wouldn't know what the time was."

"That's mean." I said back. "She is your future wife. Shouldn't you support her?"

Grayson curled up the corner of his mouth, as if he was about to say something. Putting down his glass, he takes another look at her. "To be honest here, Gwen, I am actually sick of networking. We do this all the time. Any party I get invited to, she insists on coming along. She NEEDS to meet the manager, the CEO, the business team, the marketing team. She always talks shop with them. And then on the car ride home, she tells me what the company is doing wrong, and they will collapse in a matter of months. I just want to go and hang out with my friends and talk shit."

He took a sip of his drink. "You know what? It was kind of nice, not having her around those months. I could breathe, hang out with OJ, play video games, D&D, and wear glasses!"

I noticed he had his glasses back on again.

"What's wrong with OJ? He's cool, and I love his Southern twang and sayings. Plus, you gotta love how built he is, you just want to curl up in his arms and feel protected."

Grayson laughed, trying not to spit out his mouthful.

"Yeah, OJ is cool. I'm going to tell him that. That you want to curl up with him!" He mocked.

"NO DON'T! I don't want OJ to know that!" I told him.

Grayson chuckled again.

"I like you, Gwen." He said, slapping me on the back, "You're fun. Well, you know how to have fun. You don't see this as an opportunity to network, you see this as an opportunity to relax, do all the activities here, make fun of your co-workers in their ugly sweaters!"

I let out a little huff of enjoyment as I splashed the last drop into my mouth. *There's that slap on the back again,* "come, we need to sit on Santa's lap! I know you will enjoy it more than me!"

We stood in line waiting for our turn to sit on Santa's lap, "You should stop taking Iris out, if she only networks. Have you ever talked to her about this?"

"Yes, I actually have." Grayson answered, "But she is always keen to work herself up the corporate ladder. The thing is, she is already at the top. I don't know how much further she could go?"

We took a step closer. "Has she taken an interest in your hobbies or your life? It seems you are always doing things for her." I said.

"I can't remember the last time we went out and played ultimate frisbee? Or go on a hike? Or even just pulling out a simple board game." Grayson added, scratching his chin. "Playing Uno with you the other day was about as close as it came."

We took another step closer. "It's like comparing apples to oranges." Grayson added, "There is Iris on one hand, always chasing success, doing everything by the book to get that success. She reads every guru, tech head, PayPal mafia, Tony Robbins book out there on how to be successful. She follows every single step, and she progresses little by little. If she hasn't hit her goal. She becomes hard on herself."

"So… she's the orange? Then who's the apple?" I asked him.

"You, dummy! See, you're going to be the tech genius, you're going to be the success she's trying to get without even trying! Look at Paul, he is the perfect product. And you didn't even stress over it, you didn't need to take seminars, read every book, exercise until your heart stops, eat raw vegan food, or even dress in designer wear."

I looked down at my pretty red dress.

"No, Gwen, you're smart and gifted. You designed a product because you thought I needed help. I like how you're interested and yet interested in things you don't know. Yeah, I knew you didn't know D&D!" He let out a chuckle, "That's what I like about you Gwen, you are willing to take risks and enjoy them. Fuck, Gwen, you are so intelligent, that you—"

"NEXT!" I heard one elf shout.

"Hold that thought!" I said to Grayson.

I walked into the gingerbread house and saw Santa sitting there, "HO HO HO, little girl, what can Santa bring you this year?"

I eyed off Santa, wondering who was under that red suit. "Before I sit down, you don't work for TroniX? You're not Barry from accounting, or Danny from marketing?"

Santa let out a huff. "No, I'm just a hired Santa. I know the rules and policies, and if I touch a child, or one of the mothers incorrectly, there goes my life!"

I sat down on Santa's lap. "So what could Santa bring you for Christmas?" he asked, going back into character.

"Well, the one thing I really wanted this year was friends. And I managed to get those."

He looked me up and down. "You didn't have any friends. Have you looked at yourself?" He pulled the beard down, and looked me in the eyes, "I know I said I can't touch, but you girl, are stunning. I bet you had loads of friends." He put his beard back into place.

I threw my head back, trying not to laugh at him, but there was one thing on my mind. "I don't know what I want. My app to be successful?"

"Can't help you with that? Not allowed to go near investors or invest at all. That's why I'm in the Santa suit and you're not!"

Okay.... creepy? But there is one thing I need to ask...

"Santa? How did you know Mrs Claus was the one for you?"

Santa rested his arm on the chair. "You got boy troubles, do you?"

"Yes, there's this guy, and I really like him, and I get this feeling he likes me too, but he is about to get married, and I don't want to ruin that or our friendship. How do I know he is the right one?"

"Have you told him?" Santa asked.

"Well... No. I don't want to ruin what we have."

"And spend the rest of your life wondering *'what if?'* And end up settling down with a loser. Trust me, you don't want to go down that path. My sister did this, and now she has two ratbag kids and is as miserable as ever. Her husband on the other hand, I swear he is cheating, and If I catch that son of a bitch, he is going to lose more than his mind!" Santa told me, breaking out of character again. "You need to tell him once and for all. If he doesn't feel the same way, then ask if you can go back to being friends. If he does feel the same, well, bonus to you!"

I nodded.

"When I met Mrs Claus, I knew she was the one for me. It wasn't just the way she dressed, or the way she wore her hair, or even how she smelt. By the way, she smells like gingerbread cookies! It was the little things that added up. The way she laughed at my stupid jokes, how she would curl her hair with a finger, how she leaned on the bar and said, *'what can I get ya, Hun?'* Also has a good set of tits on her!" He dipped his eyes at me.

"Remind him of all the little things he does. And if all else fails…." He said as he placed the present in my hands, "... Show him what he would miss out on. Lower your top and give a good eye full. He will come running to you." He slapped my butt, and I popped off. I turned around and eyed off Santa again. "Banks?"

"Nope!" Santa said as he pointed me to the exit.

I sat at the bar. Grayson joined me with the same size present. "What did you get?" he asked, eyeing the present.

"A slap on the ass, and some surprisingly good advice." I told taking a sip of my drink.

"I meant in the present." Grayson said.

I grabbed the box. "No idea."

"You wanna open them together?"

I turned around to face Grayson, a smirk on his face and he said, "one, two, three!" We both destroy the wrapped-up boxes to find Stanley Cups inside with the company logo engraved on them.

"Well, on the plus side, I got a Stanley Cup!"

I hand mine to the bartender. "Fill this with Booze."

"So, what was the advice?" Grayson asked.

"What?"

"From Santa?"

"Oh, that…. I should be open and honest to the people I love."

"Oh, and that would be?" Grayson asked slowly.

The bartender handed back my Stanley cup, "Grayson… There's something I should tell you…."

Grayson shifted his stands, my heart pounded hard, I curled my hands, *I have to do this! What if… 'he laughs at you?'* that bad voice came back.

I looked into Grayson's eyes, took a deep breath, opened my mouth and… *"This guy is only hanging out with you to make his girlfriend jealous; he is not into you at all"*

"Gwen, are you okay?" Grayson asked.

All my thoughts left me, I can't do this!

"I was wondering what kind of Asian you are?" I said slowly.

Grayson stood up off the bar, blowing some air out. *I know I said something stupid!*

"Sorry, that came out racist, I'm a little drunk!" I tried to cover my tracks.

"No, it's not! Korean, actually… I'm second gen here." He went back to lean on the bar, "My grandparents own a business and came out looking for some business opportunities. My grandma loved it here so much they decided to stay. My dad and my brother now run the company."

"Korean? Say something in Korean then." I asked.

"You're lucky I still remember some of it, my grandma only spoke it, and refused to learn English."

He put his glass down, and I took a sip from my Stanley cup. Grayson lean in and look into my eyes, he cleared his throat "salamdeulman eobs-eoss-eumyeon, neol uija-e nubhyeonohgo sege segseuhaeseo du beon-ina sajeonghage hago sip-eo! neol neomu salanghaeseo nahante heomhan jisgeolileul haess-eumyeon johgess-eo!"

My jaw dropped, my heart raced, *I have no idea what was said. But I like it and wanted more!*

My eyes wandered behind his shoulder, "Oh look, a photoshoot?"

Pulling Grayson's hand toward me, I pleaded, "PLEASE!! I don't have any photos of you. I can put this in my fridge and tell all my friends that it came with the frame!"

Grayson smirked. With my hand still in his, he dragged me over.

There we were standing in the photoshoot. The camera men stood near us. "Okay guys, there are plenty of costumes and fun things to use. Can take as many as you want."

We put on Santa hats; we wore Snowman glasses; feather boas; we did silly poses and held up funny signs.

As we put the stuff away, Grayson took my hand. "Can we do one more? I kind of want a nice photo of the two of us."

A nice photo?

"Sure," I said back.

He walked me in front of the camera again and faced me. "Just the 2 of us, no Paul!"

I looked around. In fact, I haven't seen Paul all evening. "No Paul around."

Grayson spun me around and wrapped his arms around me, pulling me into him tight.

"Okay, big smiles!" as the camera flashed in my eyes, the cameraman looked at the photo he took, "oh, don't you guys make such a lovely couple?" And show us the photo. I couldn't help but notice the mistletoe hanging above us. Looking up, I saw it there. I notice Grayson looking up, too. "Hey, it's mistletoe."

"Yeah," I said back.

"You know, it seems we are here, standing under it." Grayson added, "you don't want to break tradition!"

I looked around the room. The night seemed to die down, few people around, the ones that were here, were already drunk, or on their way out. I turned back to him, and suddenly I could smell that sweet, icy scent of his all over again.

Now or Never Gwen, It's Now or Never!

I dropped my arm around his waist and pulled him in towards me. I took a deep breath in, closed my eyes and leaned in when, "NO GWEN, DON'T DO IT!" I quickly pulled back to find Paul standing next to us, and Grayson suddenly jumped. When he turned around Iris was standing behind him.

My God, she is tiny!

"Having fun without me?" she asked Grayson, wrapping herself around him.

He shot me a look, and took a step away from Iris, "Ha! No, well, yes.... I got you a Stanley Cup!" he said, trying to distract her.

"Oh yes, I've always wanted one of these!" She jumped up and down. She sharply looked over at me, "Gwen, I didn't know you were here."

"Yeah, I'm here. I work for TroniX too! you know only female in the company!"

"A-HA" Iris said, "must be hard, being the only female in this company. but I bet you have a strong head on you."

"Fucking Bitch!" Paul said, "I don't like her!"

"I'm hungry, Grayson!" She said to him in a powdy way.

Ewww... Baby talk sucks!

I rubbed my nose and grabbed my cup. "Let's go, Paul," I muttered.

I turned around and left.

Chapter 25:
I quit!

My hands firmly tight around the steering wheel. Slightly leaned over to look at the time on the radio, 8:35 a.m. I blew out a deep breath and stared out of the windscreen.

My God, I hate this place!

I gripped tighter, hearing the leather creak. *This is the last place I want to be.*

"So, we are back to this then?" Paul asked.
Inhaled deeply; and blew it out. I muttered to myself, "Okay, Gwen! It's just Monday, you can do this!"
"So, we are going back to this!" Paul said.

"I almost kissed Grayson the other night." I told Paul.

"Yeah, I know. I was there stopping you!"

"Why?"

"One; it's a work function, and two: Iris was there, that's the last thing you need. Her making a big scene in front of everyone, making that situation worse."

I glanced over at Paul.

"Besides, Grayson won't remember it. You both did get a bit drunk that night."

Paul leaned to me, "It's fine Gwen. Let's go inside and do our work. Remember today is going to be a good day!"

As I walked down the hallway toward the office space, I heard, "Whoa, Morning Gwen!"

I looked up to see Grayson standing in front of me, "Morning," I choked out.

"All fresh for another day?" he asked joining me in my walk.

"How was your weekend?" Grayson asked to make a small chit chat.

"Fine," I said as I put my bag down at my desk.

Before I could say anything, "GWEN!" I heard my name shouted. We both looked toward the voice and saw Ivan marching over to me.

"Gotta go!" Grayson quickly walked away.

Standing over the top of me, with a piercing stare, his nostrils flared, and arms crossed. I cleared my throat, "Ivan, what can I do for you?"

"What's with the dating app? It's broken!" he said, pushing his phone in my face.

"How is it broken? Grayson and I tested it, and Hammond approved it. So, I don't see how it's broken," I told him.

"I'm supposed to register, fill out a survey, and then the app will work?" He raised his eyebrows at me. "Waste of time, Gwen!"

I don't understand the issue here.

My head tilted to the side trying to gather my thoughts. This product was airtight, and everything worked. *Did he actually want a stalking app?*

"The idea was to find these hotties for me. I didn't want to do the work for it," he explained, pointing at his phone.

"All you need to do is fill out a survey once, and the app does the rest. I don't understand what the problem is?" I turned back to my desk to work.

"Fuck surveys, Gwen. I just want to turn it on, and BAM, there are ten hotties near me," Ivan said while holding his phone out at me.

He leans into me close. "Oh, come on, Gwen, it can't be that hard. My balls are blue here; they need some release!" he huffs with that horrible breath of his.

I clenched my fist tight, perched my lips together tight, scrunch up my nose, and shook my head slowly. I felt the hotness rush to my face. Closing my eyes tight as the words I was looking for formed in my mind.

I hated it here at this company. I hated being the only female on the floor. I hated that my manager refused to help me, and I despised that kind of talk, especially directed towards me, was acceptable behaviour.

But this was the last time someone would ever speak to me like this. I had finally found my backbone, my courage, my steam. I had found the final straw that broke my camel. I was officially done!

I let out a small chuckle and slowly raised my head to look up at Ivan.

"Go… fuck… yourself!" I said in the most calmness matter.

Ivan looked around the office, wondering if I was talking to him. I slammed my fists on the desk as I stood up and pointed my attention towards him. "GO FUCK YOURSELF!"

Silence dropped into the office floor. Everyone around us turned their focus on us. The words flew out of my mouth, "DO I LOOK LIKE I GIVE TWO SHITS ABOUT YOUR BLUE BALLS!"

I pushed past him hard and marched straight into Hammond's office.

"Gwen, do we have an appointment?" Hammond asked, still sitting at his desk.

My breathing became rapid, "I hate being the only female in this company. I hate being sexually harassed every day! For fuck's sake, Hammond, do something about it!"

I need to say something, I need to do something! No matter what, this is a huge problem.

I tried to calm my breathing down, but somehow it was making it worse, my eyes were popping out, and my hands on my hips. I had an urge to pace, I really needed to hear what Hammond had to say.

Hammond stood up from his chair and looked at me with that creepy ass smile of his. "I have lost count of how many harassments this week!" I shouted out.

Hammond continued to stand there smiling away. *I hate it, I hate it, I hate it! I know he is going to swing this around to make it out that this is my fault somehow!*

Hammond placed his hands together, "Gwen, sweetie. What makes you think these guys are hitting on you? It's a bit full of yourself, isn't it?" he asked in a sweet calming voice.

I hate him so fucking much! Why does he do this fuck off guru shit only to me!

I knew that it was a mistake to take this to Hammond.

Hammond shifted before speaking again, "Maybe just get a coffee, take a deep breath and get back to work. Just remember, Gwen, the guys are just having some fun, that's all."

He sat back down and went back to his work. My rage had finally hit the boiling point. My fists clenched tight, my heart raced even further, and tears started swelling up in my eyes. I knew that this matter wouldn't stop, and there was no way I was going to sit there and take it anymore. I did the only irrational thing I could have done.

I screamed at him, stepping forward and slamming my fist onto his glass desk. Then, in one quick swift of my arms, I cleaned off his desk.

Papers flew everywhere, the photo frames and his computer smashed on the floor. Smoke was coming from the screen. I stood back up and looked at the damage I had done. My focus turned to Hammond, who was standing on the other side of his desk in shock.

"FUCK YOU, HAMMOND! FUCK YOU RIGHT IN THE EAR!" I screamed at him.

I stuck my middle finger at him as I left his office, leaving him with the mess I had made.

As I walked out of the office, I was surprised to see Grayson and Paul standing in front of me.

"That felt really good!" I huffed.

Grayson gently pushed past me and went to Hammond's office. I stood there watching Grayson yelling at Hammond as well. Then, finally, I could make out the words *"I quit."*

Paul moved closer to me. "I think you and Grayson better run before Hammond calls security on you!"

We sat in the park. With my coffee in my hand, smiling away at myself. The weight of the world was lifted off my shoulders. I never felt so free before. Free to do whatever I wanted. Free to sleep in. Free to talk. Free to breathe, finally.

I looked over at Grayson, sitting on the bench, leaning forward with his arms resting on his legs. "What's the matter?" I asked, knowing something was bothering him.

"I quit my job. Iris is going to kill me."

"She won't," I told him, trying to make the situation easier.

Moving closer to him, gently wrapped my arm around him. "She knows TroniX is the pits. And she would rather see you happy doing what you are doing than slaving away. Wouldn't it be better to be getting married happily than stressed out? I wouldn't be surprised if Hammond interrupts you halfway through your vows, asking you to configure some stupid app."

He let out a half chuckle, as if he was hiding something.

I took my last sip of coffee before saying, "Besides, OJ did say there is a job for you over at Innovative Tech, right?"

Grayson turned his head and smiled at me before looking over the lake again. "Did he?"

"Yeah..." I replied. I got off the bench and placed my empty cup in the bin. "...because that job is mine!"

Grayson looked up at me squinting, "Or, maybe…. we should do our own StartUp?"

Chapter 26:
Don't make fun

I returned to LinkedIn to apply for some jobs, as we need some funds to get our startup going.

Interviewing sucks! I hate when companies think it is a great idea to group everyone in and then set them with an imaginary task to do. *The world is ending, and you have a list of people to save humanity, and only 10 sits left on the rocket ship. Which ones do you pick?*

There is always one guy there who thinks he is better than everyone else and takes over. We all pretend to agree with his plan of action, and then only discover that the pregnant lady you decided to save is carrying the next Hitler.

Turning the last of humanity into a dictatorship. Then fingers fly at whose fault it was to pick this pregnant lady, even though you didn't know how her baby would turn out. Followed with a *'Thank you for coming. We will call you.'*

You walk out of those stupid interviews fully aware they will never call. Whatever happened to sitting down and talking to the boss?

I threw my phone to the other side of the couch, stood up, and stretched. "fuck this!" I said to myself as I stretched.

I walked into the kitchen to find Paul standing, leaning on the kitchen counter, sipping his coffee. "What are you doing?" I asked as I heated the kettle.

"Not much, looking through the wanted ads," he answered.

"Is there a demand for imaginary people who have skills in coding and creativity?" I questioned.

Paul placed his cup down and stood up straight. Shaking the newspaper back into its folds, "we all have to do our part to get funds going again."

The kettle bubbled behind me while I thought about his statement. *Could there be work out there for an imaginary friend?*

"Or I could start my YouTube channel?" Paul continued.

"I'm going to do OnlyFans. I know I won't make much, but at least I can make enough for a meal." I told him as I poured the hot water.

Paul dipped his head as he chuckled. "Gwen, I reckon you could make enough to cover the mortgage and a meal. You'll be surprised how many people would pay for a girl like you," he added.

I looked down at myself, trying to see what Paul sees in me. *Guys like girls with curves?*

"Now imagine how much more they would pay if your imaginary friend joined in!" Paul continued.

"It might work, I suppose. I'm sure there is a kink out there for that type of thing." I added, sipping on my tea.

"A kink for what?" Grayson said as he entered the kitchen.

"Paul thinks I should start my own OnlyFans page." I answered, "Would you pay to see a girl getting on with her imaginary friend?"

Grayson stopped what he was doing and looked at me with his mouth cracked.

"Well…." he said, nervously "…It's unique in a way?"

Grayson pulled out his laptop and sat down at the dining table.

"How are you doing with the job hunt?" I asked as I joined him.

"Not good. When people find out you used to work for TroniX, they don't want to touch you," he said. "I'm burning through our wedding funds. Iris found out, and she's not happy."

"Have the wedding here, in the backyard. That would cut some costs. We can put on a spit roast feast. Again, that will cut some costs."

Grayson bounced his head from side to side. "It's not what Iris wants. She wants the typical show-off wedding. With lots of flowers and people. Lots of people."

I shrugged at that idea. *If you were marrying the love of your life, why would you care how big your wedding is?*

"What do you want?" I asked him.

"What do you mean, with a job, the wedding, what type of cookie to eat?"

"Wedding! What type of wedding do you want?" I chuckled.

"Gwen, seriously, don't we need to date first before we get married? Surely people would wonder?" Grayson added.

My jaw dropped. *What the hell?*

Grayson chuckled, "to be honest, I really don't care what type of wedding I want. As long as I get to spend the rest of my life with you. Her."

Wait, what?

"Maybe something small, close friends and family. Outdoors, fun, affordable!" He leans back on his chair, "Iris is after the show off wedding, to prove to people she has money. Having money means success!" Grayson typed in his password, "What about you?"

"My wedding? I tried to plan one. And Max was the same, big show off stuff, loads of people. It's not what I wanted. I wanted something simple, something easy, with a big party with all our friends and family. But I knew the friends we had, and they judge, and hard. So, we need to make it big and exciting enough for them not to judge. Again, hate it."

"So, by the way…" Grayson changed the subject, "I registered our company name, Three's company."

"What?"

"Yeah, well, there's three of us working on this product."

I slowly shook my head, "You, me and Paul." Grayson explained.

What the hell? I froze.

"Arrr, no… you didn't, did you?" I asked.

The blood drained from me, and my mouth became tight.

No Grayson, NO!

"You can't put Paul down as part of this company! He's not real. What happens if they investigate us? What do we say; that some of our shares are with an imaginary friend?

Grayson, this could jeopardise our chances…. no offence Paul."

"None taken!"

I placed my hands over my face as I let out a *UGH!*

"Grayson, as much as I am happy that the two of you are getting along, you can't do this. He is my imaginary friend. Not yours!"

"I was only trying to help!" Grayson pouted.

I closed the laptop up and got up off the dining room table. "Still a good name!" I added as I walked out.

The office light turned on. "Hey!" Grayson said as he sat down. I had been staring at the screen all day, and didn't notice it was turning dark. Taking my glasses off and given my eyes a rub, I heard Grayson continuing, "I didn't really add Paul to the register. Mainly because I don't have a birth certificate or a passport for him."

I put my glasses back on. "Look, I get it. And I asked for you guys to be friends. I am glad you are. But you don't understand how this quirk of mine works. I am an adult walking around with an imaginary friend. It's weird, it's creepy, it's… taboo! I wanted to hide Paul from the world, that he was my secret. He helped me out of my shell to find myself. It's not easy to do that, but having someone there cheering you on makes each step work."

Grayson watched me as I continued to explain, "Paul is someone special to me, and me alone. You don't know how hard it was to come out like that all those months ago. You could have walked away and laughed at me. *'Who the fuck has an imaginary friend at this age?'*

I looked over at Grayson. *Does he understand where I'm going with this? Do I know where I'm going with this?*

My mouth dried up, my throat closed up, there was pounding in my head again that I haven't felt in a long time, trying to find the right words to tell

Grayson, "By doing what you did, made me feel like you were making fun of me, after sharing this big secret of mine."

My eyes started to water, my jaw locked, I needed to get the last thing out, "Please Grayson, don't make fun of Paul, He is the only friend I have. He won't turn evil, it's just…"

"You have an attachment to him, and if I make fun of him, I'm making fun of you." Grayson interrupted me.

He leaned back in his chair and rubbed his legs, he unclenched his jaw, and turned back to me, "Gwen, I am so sorry. It wasn't my intention to make fun, I was just trying to include Paul into our adventure."

The room fell silent, "so… Three's company?" Paul asked.

I let out a chuckle-huff. "Yes, Three's Company!"

I wiggled the mouse, "By the way Paul.2 is ready." I added.

"Great!" Grayson said, "We have a meeting with Mitch Albright tomorrow."

Chapter 27:
Meeting

So, there I was, sitting in a meeting with Mitch and his team while Grayson did all the talking. Watching Grayson pace and explain the fundamentals of our AI app.

How did we score this meeting?

One minute I was sitting at my desk at home building a business plan and setting up the company, and the next I'm getting told that we have a meeting with Mitch Albright. *Yes, that Mitch Albright from Tazio!* The one with the billion-dollar app company!

I closed my eyes for a bit and took in a deep breath. Once I opened them and found myself in the meeting room again, I couldn't help but sense that the vibe in the room was a bit off.

"Can you see how everyone is sitting?" Paul whispered to me.

I looked around the room. *Why is Mitch's team all on one side of the table?*

"Gwen, they're not interested in this app?" Paul whispered to me again.

I looked over at the team again. *Their notepads aren't open. Whispers? What are they talking about? IS this app shit?*

"Can you show us the app?" Mitch said.

Grayson opened his laptop and started fiddling around with it.

"So, what's with the colours, Gwen?" Mitch turned his focus on me.

"Just easier to code," I told him.

"Nice answer," Paul said. "The voice was the hard part."

"Shush," I said.

Everyone paused and turned their focus on me. "Oh sh…ould, I mean, could we do something else?" I tried to cover my tracks.

"Morning, Grayson, what is happening today?" Paul.2 said.

"Hey, Paul, we are at Tazio with Mitch..." before Grayson could finish his sentence, Paul.2 kicked in, "...

Mitch Albright, CEO of Tazio. Tazio is an app and gaming company. Famous for their RPG game *SlumberLand.* Net worth of 3.4 billion."

Mitch laughed. "Interesting." He got up and joined Grayson. "Hello Mitch," Paul.2 said.

Mitch looked up at Grayson. "It uses facial recognition and searches social platforms to find who you are."

"That's creepy!" Mitch added.

"We are trying to create an *'in the middle friendship'* rather than trying to introduce ourselves," I finally said, "Making it so that Paul already knows who you are."

"Can you change that?" Mitch asked.

"I kind of agree with Mitch on this. What if you create this AI to introduce yourself, and to get to know each other, creating a version of Paul for the user?" Paul added.

"We could switch it off?" Grayson said.

"We could create an introduction to the AI, get to know each other?" I repeated Paul's idea.

Mitch played with Paul.2, but each movement and question he asked gave off a little noise.

Please say something!

Each noise, each movement, I hold my breath tighter and tighter. I held Paul's hand and gave it a squeeze. Curling my other hand into a fist. I curled my lips, and my eyes widened.

Please Mitch, say you like it. Please say here is your first ten million dollars!

Mitch sat back down. "This thing is interesting. Who came up with the idea?"

I opened my mouth. "It was me. I want to create a tool for my loneliness. My girlfriend was overseas, and I found it hard to connect with her while she was away. So, I created this AI to help me." Grayson said, beating me to the pun.

WHAT THE HELL? No Grayson, no! Why would you tell them this? UGH!

"You created this?" Mitch pointed his finger at Grayson. "If you missed your girlfriend so much, then why is it a guy?"

Grayson cleared his throat and darted his eyes at me. "Well, I need some guy friends too!"

I dip my head, my eyes went wide, I sucked in my lips, trying not to let a word out.

Mitch folded his hands before him and took a deep breath before speaking, "Gwen, Grayson..." *OH NO!* "... Do you know how many people come into my office with strange ideas?"

I raised my eyebrows. *Where was this conversation going?*

"As much as this app, Paul, is impressive, I can't help shake this feeling that it's fake," Mitch continued.

Wait? Fake!?

"What makes you say that?" I asked him.

"It looks like clever video editing and well-timed conversation."

I glanced over at Grayson, "It's not fake!" I added, trying to hide my anger.

Mitch drew his attention towards me. "Show me."

"Invest in us then!"

Mitch stared at me before he let out a big, roaring laugh. My face burned, my jaw hurt from being closed so tight, I wanted to leap over the table and punch him!

"I'm not investing in this. Plus, I hate the name. Why would you call an AI Paul?" Then he leaned on the table and looked directly at me. "People prefer a girl's name, like Alexa or Cortana. People might be interested if you change it to a girly voice and a girly name." He chuckled.

There were so many words I could have used, but instead I stood up and stormed out of the room, still hearing the
chuckles and laughter from his team.

I sat on the bonnet of Grayson's car, thinking about the meeting, analysing each piece of the conversation, from its fake to Grayson coming up with the idea.

Paul joined me. "Try and prompt the investor to ask hard questions or things people don't know."

"Like personal questions? Like what is your wife's name, and your side piece's name? or Kid's names? Your password?" I listed off.

"What are you going to tell Grayson?" Paul asked. "Didn't he say he was the sole creator of the AI?"

My jaw clenched again. *Why did he do that? He knew how important Paul.2 was to me, and how I came up with the idea. Why was it important for him to take the credit?*

"It's strange," Paul continued. "Why do you think he did that?"

"Gwen?" Grayson said, standing in front of the car.

"Grayson…" I was about to ask him why, "Get off the bonnet of my car." He added.

I slid off slowly and walked around to the passenger's door, when Grayson said something else, "Tell Paul to get off too!"

I looked at Paul, and he looked at me.

Was he not so imaginary anymore?

Chapter 28:
You're supposed to be my friend

The tension in the car was thick as I hooked up Paul.2 to Grayson's car computer.

"Paul, I'm hungry." I said out loud.

The colours on the dashboard computer bouncing around as Paul.2 calculated. "There is a diner ten minutes' drive from here," he said.

The colours of his screen change to a map with navigation information.

"You hungry?" Grayson asked, trying to break the tension.

I slouched into my chair and stared out the window. Grayson sighed as he pulled out of the car park.

The tension continued to grow, except for Grayson's huffs and Paul's intermittent directions, as the map appeared and vanished sporadically.

"Might have to fix that?" Grayson said.

"What?" I asked.

"The map, switching in and out like that, could we add an extra function to let the user have it on or off?" he asked.

I shrugged. "I guess so."

Driving down the highway, watching the signs and other vehicles go past us. My head was getting tight as I drew little circles with my jaw, trying to unclench it.

"Are you okay?" Grayson asked. "You doing that thing where you're stressed out?"

I readjusted myself in the chair and huffed out, "I'm fine!"

The car fell quiet before Grayson let out a chuckle. "Was Paul at the meeting today?"

"Yes!" I said sharply. Moving my jaw in circles again.

"Called it!" Grayson continued.

Grayson's phone buzzed. Before I could look at it, he turned it over. Then it buzzed again.

We parked the car in the car park, jumped out, slammed the door and walked off, leaving Grayson standing there.

Fuck this guy!

I sat down at a table and studied the menu. Grayson finally joined me. His phone buzzed yet again. He curled the corners of his mouth and frowned. He placed the phone down on the table, face down.

"Gwen?" He said as he picked up the menu. "Is everything okay?"

"FINE!" I told him.

His phone buzzed again.

"My God, just answer your phone! It's not going to stop!" I told him.

"No, I know who it is, and I rather ignore it," Grayson added.

Grayson put his menu down and stared at me. "It's Iris."

"Well… answer it, after all, she is your future wife!" I snapped at him.

He dropped his head as he let out another sigh. "No, I think it's best I shouldn't answer the phone."

The phone buzzed again. I quickly snapped it up before Grayson got to it.

'ANSWER YOUR FUCKING PHONE, GRAYSON!' I saw on the lock screen.

"What did you do?" I asked him as I showed him the screen.

"Lots of things," he answered, picking up the menu again.

"Name one!" I asked him.

He put the menu down and stared blankly at me. "Okay, how about; you told Iris that you created an AI app to beat your loneliness, because SHE travels too much." I added.

"Oh shit, that's why you're pissed?" Grayson said, "That it's my product, and I was the one who came up with the idea?" He told me without skipping a beat, believing his lies.

"Oh Grayson, NO! You were in and now you're out? Gwen, think rational here! I know you're pissed, but there must be a reason for this," Paul added.

"RATIONAL?! ARE YOU KIDDING ME!" I yelled, "You stole my idea; claim it as yours!"

I grabbed his keys and stormed out.

"GWEN!" Grayson shouted behind me. "I need to explain…"

opened the car door and took one look at him. *Why did I trust this guy? He is just like the others at TroniX.* I bit my bottom lip and placed my hand on my heart. My eyes swelled, and a quiver from my jaw said it all. *I can't believe I fell head over heels in love with this guy!*

I got into the car, and was about to drive off when Grayson jumped, "Seriously, you going to leave me here?"

"You're the Genius, you could figure it out!" I shouted at him.

Driving down the highway with no idea which direction I was going, I had him trapped in the car. *I might as well ask him.* "Why?"

"What?" He responded.

"Why are you telling everyone that Paul.2 is your product?"

He readjusted himself in his seat, scratched his forehead, curling up his lips, tapping his fingers together. He sighed. "It just sounds better that I created it." Grayson explained.

My knuckles turned white, my jaw locked, my back teeth were about to break! I pulled the car over, exited the vehicle, and screamed. I screamed until I released all my pent-up emotions. It still didn't make the situation any better.

The impulse to punch Grayson overcame me. *How could he use me like this? All this time we've been working together, getting to know each other, sharing secrets, sharing Paul, and it was all a labyrinth plan to steal an innovative idea! Son of a Bitch!*

I gasped for air. My eyes swelled again, and the pressure on my chest eased when the car door closed.

"You're an asshole. The worst kind of an asshole, one who tries to be nice to people to get what they want. You're not that type of asshole who knows they are an asshole and doesn't care about it."

"What's the big deal, Gwen? Paul.2 will be out there no matter who invented it," Grayson told me.

"IT DOES MATTER!" I yelled at him.

"You don't know how hard I have been working to make people pay attention to me. Proper attention! For people to know my name, know my face, know my work!" I took a deep breath in; I felt my eyes open wide.

"You have NO IDEA what I have been through, with Max, TroniX, and every other male in my life. I'm a joke to them! Nothing! I am just a doormat! They all did what Banks said about me; I'm a *fuck and dump*, both mentally and physically."

I sucked in my lips, trying to buy myself a bit more time, "Fuck me, it's Max all over again!"

I took a step closer to him. "NO! NO! No more. I'M DONE, being everyone's doormat, I'm done saying yes to everything that I know is not good for me. I'm done with all these assholes who see me as nothing! And if you want to go down that path, then I'm done with you! Why? I was crazy in love with you, and you go and do this. I can't believe you abused my trust. How am I going to trust you again?"

'Gwen?' Grayson trembles.

"If Paul.2 becomes the next biggest thing, it will be your face in textbooks in fifty years. It will take another hundred years to notice it was me who created this. I WANT MY

FACE UP THERE in those textbooks! Right there on page 67, right next to Jack Dorsey," I explained.

"Gwen," I heard Grayson again.

Grayson took a step closer towards me. "I did this to protect you, Gwen! You create a phenomenal product. In the right hands and the right investors, you can turn this product into the far reaches it could do. It's Sophia, but better. And how are you planning to explain this to an investor on how you came up with this idea?"

He pointed his finger at me and asked, "That you need to bring your imaginary friend to life?"

He took a step back, placed his hand on his hips, and dipped his head. "You're almost thirty, Gwen, who is incredibly smart. The investors will laugh you out the door knowing that Paul.2 started off as an imaginary friend."

Oh MY God, he is right! People will laugh at the origin story of Paul!

"FUCK IN HELL!" I huffed out.

Grayson had more to say; he looked back up at me and commented, "Even though I appreciate Paul and enjoy having him around, Gwen, you don't truly require Paul."

"YES, I DO!" I shouted, "I need him, I need… him. You got Iris, and I have… no one! I need Paul!"

"Not true. Iris and I broke up. She's blowing up my phone because she is angry at me. That her plan for success is falling apart around her."

I stopped what I was doing. *Did I hear him right?*

"I ended it. I got sick of this need to be successful crap. I want to be me and do things I like."

He shifted his stands, "You know why we were getting married? I never wanted to get married to her. I said yes to her, because I thought I couldn't do any better. She wanted to marry me because I was Korean. There was love, or butterflies in the stomach, it was just business with her. She polished me up for arm candy!"

Grayson curled his lips, and threw his arms around, "Fuck her and her road to success. Fuck her and her clean image, you know I wasn't allowed to grow a beard! Beards make you look like a hobo, a mess, a… FUCK!"

Grayson huffed, "I just want to code and play games, and hang out, and get stone, and talk shit with OJ. Why am I not allowed to do that? She hated OJ because he was successful without even following the rules."

· "What rules Iris, WHAT RULES? Just because he manages to study hard and get into a great company, doesn't mean he didn't follow her rules!" Grayson let out.

My mouth dropped. *They broke up?*

"See it's the Apple and Oranges again, Gwen. I would do anything to make you laugh, smile, to be there for you, to protect you. I tried to talk to you many times before, but I didn't know how you would react to it. I saw you get annoyed with other guys at work, and I thought you do the same to me. Thank God for Paul. The only reason I talked to you was to protect you. I will never stop protecting you unless you tell me too…."

"Whoa, hang on…" Paul added, "hold your breath. I think you wanna hear the next part!"

"…I am crazy about you too! Always have been!"

"Wait… Too?" I said.

"Umm, you did tell him you love him." Paul reminded me.

I slapped my hand over my mouth. *OH MY GOD, I did tell him that. My other secret is out!*

"I even told you at the Christmas party. It was much easier to say it in Korean than in English." Grayson let out a small chuckle, "Well, you don't understand Korean!"

"What?" I asked.

Grayson weaved his finger through his hair, adjusted his glasses and repeated, "salamdeulman eobs-eoss-eumyeon, neol uija-e nubhyeonohgo sege segseuhaeseo du beon-ina sajeonghage hago sip-eo! neol neomu salanghaeseo nahante heomhan jisgeolileul haess-eumyeon johgess-eo!"

Grayson cleared his throat. "It loosely translates to; If there weren't so many people around…. I want to bend you over the bar stool, and…. fuck you hard… that you…. cum

290

twice! I love you so much that I want you to do nasty things to me!"

I chuckled, then I laughed. I tried to hold it back, but I laughed again. "Nasty things?" I asked.

"Please, Gwen, don't make this weird! I like you a lot. And I can see something here between us. Please don't hate me for what I did."

I took off my glasses and wiped my eyes. The pressure my body was under was lifted. I tried to stop myself from tearing up.

"I think this is the part where you kiss him," Paul said.

I took a few steps close to Grayson. I wrapped my hands around his waist, I leaned up on my tippy toes, tilted my head and planted a small kiss on his lips.

I pulled back and said, "Don't change for me, change for you! I do like this daggy Grayson better. You know that casual Grayson, outside of work Grayson is so much hotter than baby blue shirt Grayson. Not saying that work Grayson is hot, but causal Grayson is better!"

Grayson chuckled as he gently pulled me off of him, "But to make this work, I think we need a balance with Paul. You can't sleep with him anymore…"

"Okay, done!" I added.

"…and you need to find out why he is here."

I turn to look over at Paul. "I don't know. You summon me."

"I'm going to need therapy, aren't I?"

"Well," Grayson said, "it couldn't hurt."

Chapter 29:
Therapy

I used to picture the therapy office like a doctor's office, crowded with people waiting. But it was just me, alone.

Finally, the front door opened, and a young couple came in.

"Gwen Hooper?"

I popped up and followed the therapist.

We sat there, the therapist and I locked in a mutual gaze. *I'm fine. There is nothing wrong with me at all.*

I'm fine!

Look at her sitting there tapping her pen on her notepad, waiting for me to say something.

I'm fine.

My God, her smile shits me. Do I say it? Do I make the first move? I am in therapy, after all.

"I'm fine!" I said it out loud. Her smile widened, showing her teeth.

"Why don't you start at the beginning," she said.

I didn't want to tell her. I'm sure there is nothing wrong with me.

As she wrote, the only sound in the small office was her pen scribbling on the notebook.

"Beginning of what?" I asked her.

"What has brought you here?"

I inhaled deeply, then exhaled slowly, pondering my words, "So, I met this guy at work."

She stopped scribbling and looked up at me, waiting for more information.

"He was this fun loving, happy-go-lucky guy." I continued.

She kept writing. "He wanted to work on a project together. I mean, why not? He seemed to be a fun person to work with."

Leaning forward, I glanced over at Paul, who was sitting beside me. "Tell her."

I sucked some air and said, "The more I worked with the guy, the more I noticed some odd things about him. Like how he always talks to me, or how he would delay the project."

She scratched with her pen as she took notes.

"This guy, the new guy at work, was…" I placed my hand together as I told her the last bit of my statement, "…. is my imaginary friend!"

"Interesting!" the therapist said.

She stopped writing and closed her notebook. Removing her glasses, she leaned in close to me. "What's their name?"

"Paul," I said.

"Why would Paul just appear in your life like this?" she asked.

I looked around her office. The light streamed in, casting a white glow on all the walls, illuminating photo frames of landscapes and a small Zen Garden on her desk.

"Maybe…. It's because…. My boyfriend broke up with me three years ago via text. He took all our friends, and I have been on my own ever since. I worked for a toxic company, where I was the only female on the floor, so most of the guys would make disgusting comments or try to make a pass on me with a boss who couldn't see the harm in it." I explained to the therapist.

Tapping my palms together, "I think I need help."

Raising an eyebrow, she tilted her head back to listen. I shifted on her couch. "Help with what? You sound like you're going through a grief part of the relationship. The boyfriend broke up with you. You must have cared about him and the relationship?"

I looked down at my fingers tapping each other. "Actually… no… he was a shitty boyfriend. He got rich by stealing other people's ideas, and I was one of them. He stole an idea I had and got rich from it."

She wrote this down. "Is this why Paul is here? To remind me I'm not a shitty person?"

"What makes you think you're a shitty person?"

I darted my eyes around, sucking in my lips, holding my breath, trying to think of reasons why. "I don't think I am!"

"Tell me more about Paul?" she asked.

"Arr…" I had to think again. "He is a great guy. He helped me find my voice and interact with people. Help me find my confidence and help develop a couple of apps."

"What else?" she asked.

I shrugged, "what do you want to know?"

"How do you interact with Paul?"

"We talk, we can hold and feel each other and have slept with him a few times…."

"When did he appear…. I mean, started working in your company?" she corrected herself.

"A while back, like eight or so months ago."

She wrote in her notepad, "What does he look like?"

"Tall, blonde, wears glasses, human?"

"What did the ex-boyfriend look like?"

"Same height as me, long brown hair, cheekbones, very small eyes."

"I'm interested in this; was the breakup mutual?"

"No, out of the blue."

"When did you start working at this toxic place?"

"3 months after the breakup."

"Very interesting," she added as she wrote.

The therapist put her notepad down. "I don't blame you for manifesting an entity after what you told me. Yes, you have given me short answers, but I can see where you're going with this."

She leaned back in her armchair. "You have been through a lot, Gwen. And you haven't given yourself time to breathe. It sounds like many people you trusted used and abused you. No wonder you have Paul. You needed that one person in your life that you can trust, and help you move on from the grieving stage of this break-up."

I threw myself back into the couch and let out a sigh. I can't believe what I'm hearing.

Paul is only here to help me move on!

"Paul sounds like a wonderful person." She added, as she wrote some more notes.

Paul gave me a nudge.

"You probably think I'm weird?" I casually asked.

The therapist placed her notebook on the coffee table between us. "Having imaginary friends at your age does look strange, Gwen. But it is not uncommon."

She slipped off her glasses and let them swing gently in her hand. "You're lonely. And for some reason, you preferred loneliness. There is no one there to hurt you. This is why Paul is around. Paul doesn't hurt you. He listens to you, he helps you. He is there for you when you need him the most. You create the ultimate friend with him. Paul always says yes to you. He knows what to say to you to make you feel better. He is the perfect friend. And that can be a problem."

My eyes widened, and my breathing became deeper.

She put her glasses back on and opened her notebook again. "Look, I'm not saying that you need to get rid of Paul. You have an attachment to him. But between the both of you two, you need to find an understanding. When you get friends, it is up to you to explain to them about Paul, but if you choose to keep him a secret, then you need to explain to Paul that it is your time with your friends. I'm sure he will understand. Then, eventually, as you grow and move on, you will have friends that match Paul's personality, maybe looks, attitude, and attributes. Which means Paul will eventually fade away."

I swallowed hard. She smiled at me. "Imaginary friends don't stay long, no matter how old you are."

I groped the edge of the couch, overwhelmed to move. *I don't want to lose Paul, never!*

"What if he doesn't go away? What if I want him around for the rest of my life?" I asked.

"Well, as long as he is not telling you to harm people or yourself and you are happy with him being here, then keep him around. But life is a big mystery. You'll be surprised at what happens next."

Chapter 30:
Homeschool

I clenched my fists; The sound of the page flipping over slowly got on my nerves. *Oh, the anticipation is eating me up!*

"Could you read faster, OJ?" I told him.

"Quiet, Gwen!" he said to me without looking.

Oh God hurry up OJ, I'm about to burst!

Finally, OJ finished the Business Plan and placed it down on the dining table. He adjusted his baseball cap. "Wow, that's a fantastic idea! I actually think this might work."

He interlocked his fingers together and placed them down on the piles of paper. "I know you guys are small as there is only the two of you, and you both are going to be doing all the work…. I mean all of it, for now."

"I'm down with that." Grayson added, getting excited about this.

"Me too. Anything to get this idea going." I said back.

OJ tapped the pile of papers again. "Have you got an investor yet?"

Grayson and I share a glance. "Well, no. But looking."

"If it's okay with you guys, I think I might know who would be interested in this," OJ added. "Moss."

"Wait, Moss Timmons?" Paul shouted across the table.

"Moss Timmons?" I repeated.

"Yeah, something like this might interest him." OJ added as he pulled out his phone, "Let me set you guys up."

Quick little bounces of my leg, staring out the glass wall on the opposite of me, when I felt Grayson place his hand down on mine.

"Gwen, stop. It's going to be okay. OJ did us a favour."

"I am so nervous!" I told him, "I have been living and working in Silicon Valley for six years, and not once would I ever thought I would be here getting investments from top CEOs."

I started to chew on the edge of my thumb, "What next, a meeting with Jeff Bazos this afternoon? Then dinner with Warren Buffet?"

Grayson chuckled. "Let's just get through this meeting first, before we make dinner reservations with Warren Buffet."

"What if it's going to be like with Mitch, believe Paul.2 is fake? I really need to hold my tongue if Moss calls it fake."

"I don't think Moss would see that. We have worked hard on Paul.2 to make it less fake."
Grayson said. "I sometimes need to stop myself and remind myself this is an AI I'm talking to."

"You guys are Grayson and Gwen, right?" This young-looking woman with a thick Australian accent said to us.

I stood up and placed my hand quickly. "Yes, I'm Gwen Hooper, and this is Grayson Li."

She shook my hand and then shook Grayson's. "Great. Well, I'm Emmy Watts, and OJ said you guys have a product to share?"

I stood there, staring at her. *This is the Educator billionaire? She just looks like a regular person.* Same height, blonde hair in braids, black-rimmed glasses, red flannel shirt over the top of her white shirt, black jeans, Doc Martens and tattoos all over her arms. She would be standing in line for a coffee, and I wouldn't know I was standing behind a billionaire! *Yep, just a normal-looking person!*

As we walked with her, we shared some stories about her life since moving to Silicon Valley, what Australia is like, and why education?

The dumbass in me asked her about Derek Goodwin. "Oh, that guy!" She turns to face me. "Gwen, be careful with these Tech Bros. It's always about image with them. Never let your guard down around them. Show them who's boss and who makes the money around here!" I looked up at Grayson, he chuffed, and whispered, "I already knew you were the boss!"

I did it again. I let Grayson do all the talking. He created a problem that we didn't realise we had, forming this into an image we can all see. Ending his story with the solution for our unrealistic issue. I tapped the screen of the tablet, allowing Paul.2 to show up on their projector. As the group pondered about Paul.2, I surveyed the room.

"What's with the colours?" the girl with the pink hair asked.

"Swirling of colours can easily calm down a person. Having faces or face-like features could scare people off." I lied.

"Fascinating!" Emmy added as she wrote that down.

"Good morning, Emmy. What would you like to do today?" Paul.2 chimed in.

"How does this thing know me?" Emmy asked.

"We use facial registration and scan your socials to find you." I told her.

"Interesting. But does it have to be social? Could there be a database for registered users?" Emmy asked, while writing in her notebook, returning us back to the conversation.

I looked over at Grayson, hoping he would have an answer. "Maybe?" he said. "It has been something we have been investigating."

"See, we want Paul.2 to recognise not only you but other people in your household, and, or your friends. It could let you know who to trust, and who to not. It could even call your friends or family if you're in trouble of any kind." I told Emmy.

She nodded her head and curled her mouth while looking over at the guy next to her.

"Hi Paul," she said, "I'm fine. How are you?"

"I'm doing great for a computer." Paul.2 answered.

Emmy chuckled, "What did you get up to last night?"

"I watch an interesting show on Netflix." Paul.2 said, "It was about a girl who got kidnapped by her brother."

"What is your favourite colour, Paul?" Emmy asked.

"It would be pink, because I like Selma's hair. It's got a bubble gum colour to it."

"Can it see me?" Selma asked.

Emmy wrote some more notes down.

"Yes, it can recognise everyone in the room." Grayson added.

"In this meeting at Innovative Tech, we have Emmy Watts, Grayson Li, Selma Austin, Wayne Martin, Justin 'OJ' Montgomery, and Gwen Hooper." Paul.2 listed off, "Good morning to you all, I hope this fine weather pleases you. I believe this meeting about investing in me, your new product for

Innovative Tech. I shall be the product of the year!"

"Very cute." Emmy added.

"What about for an educational purpose?" Wayne asked. "Could we set up an educational suite into the Paul?"

I stood up from the table. "It is something we haven't thought of yet. But this could be a great tool to help with education and homeschool."

As soon as I said the word *homeschool*, Emmy twisted her nose. I must have hit a nerve on this one with her.

"I understand that homeschooling may not be your thing, Emmy. I totally get that! BUT there are thousands of Americans out there who homeschool their kids for many different reasons. There is nothing we can do to stop them, no matter how many times we tell the parents that the schooling system is safe, harm free, and conspiracy theory free. BUT…"

I pause there with a finger in the air, "…we can all agree that no matter how we teach the child, they need some form of education to function in the world when they leave their childhood home."

Grayson took a seat and watched me. Nodded my head at him as I took over.

"Imagine these homeschool kids with Paul.2 in their houses, learning, gaining an education, from a system you created. Not only these homeschool kids, but public schools, schools from low-income neighbourhoods, private schools, even the schools on Mars.

Paul can be that system who could replace teachers or fill in the gaps where schools can't afford new or extra teachers.

That no matter your background, level of education, or your neighbourhood, Paul will teach every kid the same level and understanding of education. We design a tool into Paul that can help measure kids on their levels and know where they need the extra help or the extra care they need, without using the aid of exams or tests, that Paul can measure through curriculum and problem solving."

I peered at Grayson again, then something caught my eye. Paul was standing beside him, waving his hand at me to continue on.

"Our product, combined with your education system, will improve everyone's education!"

"Sooooo….. just like in Ready Player One?" Emmy asked.

I am really not familiar with this Ready Player One at all, but if it gets us over the line, then…. "Yes, just like Ready Player One!" I told her.

I burst out of the office and into the car park, with the rush of adrenaline over me. Our little product was becoming something, especially when Emmy asked to see the business plan.

"Did you hear, Grayson? They are interested in it!"

"Yes, Gwen, I saw it all! I am very impressed by you and your little speech back there. The girl who could barely string two words together when we first met, to a girl who could sell a product to billionaires!" Grayson told me before planting a kiss on my forehead, "But Gwen, just calm down for the moment. They may not be. They want to read our business plan first, then decide. I love how excited you are, but you also need to see the reality of this, too. Just don't get all your hopes up!"

"I'm trying not to, but this is exciting!" I explain, "could you imagine what it would be like to work here?" I point to the building behind me.

Grayson hung off the car door and showed me his perfect, dimple smile. *Oh, I just want to do things to him. Please let me get nasty with you!*

"Good job, Gwen. I am very proud of you too!" Paul said as we walked me to the car.

Chapter 31:
TechCrunch

I sat at my desk studying Emmy's schooling system and how to incorporate this with Paul.2. Reading every article I could find on her, watching her TED talk, and interviews. I also came across her blog and saw how she got started. Each piece of information was interesting. You can feel her internal struggles to get an idea that already exists off the ground, and getting people interested in something as old as time.

I took notes and wrote a plan to build her education system into Paul.2, *Sometimes if you build it the investor will have no choice but to invest!*

I heard a very loud, annoying, *'I need your attention'* cough. Shifting my eyes up to the cough maker, to find

Grayson standing over my desk with his perfect, and yet slightly cheeky, smile.

"What is it?" I asked.

"Sooooo…. When we got started on Paul.2 a few months back, I decided that if we are going to take this seriously, then maybe…. we should enter him into the startup battles at TechCrunch."

I froze in place. *TechCrunch? seriously? One of the biggest tech conventions in the world, and Grayson thought it would be a good idea to enter us in the startup battles?*

"Well, I just got a letter back from them, and it states that they like our product, and we have secured a spot in the startup battles."

"The Fuck?!" was all I could say.

"We're going to TechCrunch!" Grayson answered.

"TechCrunch?" I said back.

"TechCrunch!" Grayson excitedly said.

"TechCrunch?"

"Yes, TechCrunch!"

"Fuck… TechCrunch!"

"Gwen, we got in. We are going to TechCrunch. What is the issue here?" Grayson asked.

"It's TechCrunch, that's the issue. So many people, so many Tech Bros, so many *'I think I'm better than you'* people around!"

"I thought you're over this?"

I sigh, looking around my desk, "Look, if this is important to you, then yes, let's do it!"

Grayson fist pump, "YES!"

"What if we win?" I asked him.

"Great!"

"No, I mean, what if we win? What do we get?"

"Fifty thousand dollars towards our startup."

"When is it?" I asked, going back to typing.

"Tomorrow."

"TOMORROW!" I looked up at him.

"Yeah, we need to pack, don't we?"

Sitting in Grayson's car on our way, I opened my laptop to check the code. Grayson slammed the screen on my hands. "Put that away. Let's just have fun for the moment."

I put my laptop back in my bag when Grayson asks me an important question. "I have been meaning to ask you. Who is Paul?"

"I created Paul.2 as a way for you and Paul to communicate, you know that." I answered.

"No, I mean the real Paul, actually the imaginary Paul. Who is he?" Grayson said as he darted his eyes from the road to me.

"Well…." I gathered the words I need to explain this to Grayson. I know he accepted Paul, but never really asked who he is. "He is blonde, with a path on his left side, so his right side is a bit floppy. He wears wired rimmed glasses, wears a Voltron tee shirt and black skinny jeans with a bright red bomber jacket."

"Interesting?" Grayson said, "So you like blondes?"

"That's going to take a while with my hair!" He continued.

I let out a half chuckle. "That's not fair, Grayson! You did once say; It's not always about looks, it can be about personalities."

"I said that?" Grayson asked.

"Yeah, remember when you were fishing me for my ideal perfect person?"

I look over at him. "Is this why you wear glasses now? I told you my ideal person had to wear glasses!"

"What? NO! I just wear them because my contacts itch my eyes!" Grayson added.

I giggled.

"But you do like them?" Grayson asked.

"Yes, I do. It makes you look hotter." I said, then suddenly covered my mouth.

I can't believe I just said that to Grayson.

"Hotter? Well, then…" Grayson chuckled, "I better be careful this weekend!"

We got to the hotel and waited to check in. As I looked around, there were so many people here, from billionaires to millionaires, tech junkies, tech journalists and bloggers, coders, designers, front and back-end developers. Everyone from Silicon Valley had shown up.

"If everyone is here, who is building the apps? Or who is minding Google?" I whispered to Grayson.

"It's a big one this year." Grayson reminds me.

"I wonder what is drawing everyone here this year?" I said back.

"No idea!" Grayson added as we stepped up to the desk.

"GWEN!?" I heard my name shouted.

I turn towards the voice to find Adam walking over to me. "OH MY GOD, ADAM?!"

Handing my suitcase to Grayson to meet up with Adam. He threw his arms around me and pulled me in for a big squishy hug. "Oh My God, Gwen, it's so good to see you! And look at you, still damn cute as ever!"

"Thanks…" I said, feeling a hot rush to my cheeks.

"So…" Adam shifted his stands. "Why are you here? Selling a product?"

"Well, we got accepted into the Startup battles with Paul.2."

"Why does that sound familiar?" Adam questioned.

"Not sure why? But it's an AI system that Grayson and I have been building."

"Cool, AI… you know that's hot right now. I bet you would win the battles."

I flush cold ran through me, and the sudden realisation of winning came to my head.

"What's the product called?"

"Paul," I told him.

"That makes sense." Adam added.

Grayson joined us, "OH, Grayson, meet Adam, someone I met months ago."

Grayson put his hand out and shook Adam's. "Nice to meet you."

"Why does Paul make sense?" I asked Adam.

He let out a private chuckle, then said, "So, you remember the night we met?"

I nodded.

"I kept getting these messages from some guy named Paul. I don't know any Pauls." Adam pulled out his phone and scrolled through, "It kept telling me about this girl up at the bar."

He turned his phone around to show me the messages. "Each message told me how she'd been stood up, that she was about to leave, and that she was so sad—you know, things like that."

I took Adam's phone and scrolled through each message, with Paul's name up the top.

"I ignored it at first, as if it was someone playing a prank on me. But…." Adam explained, "Curiosity got the better of me and so I went to see if she was okay. I mean, there are guys out there who are just plain assholes, and I want her to know we aren't all assholes. I made the excuse that it was my turn to shout and went to talk to her. Yes, I saw that some asshole did or said something to her."

I handed the phone back, I kept listening to Adam's story, "Gwen, it was you that Paul kept talking about."

"Fuck." I said in one breath.

"Did you set me up?" Adam asked.

"NO!" I had to explain things to him. "We created this dating app called FindMe. It works based on what you are looking for. Once the algorithm finds you a match, it sets you guys up on a date, prompting you guys where to sit, what to ask, and where to go. I'm sorry, but we added a code into the app to search social media and Grayson tested it out on our AI. You were the target."

Adam laughed, "OH MY GOD GWEN! That's brilliant! Glad to be a part of your experiment!" He leans in closer. "See, I knew you were smart!"

Just then, another guy came over to Adam. "Hey, meet Gwen and Grayson, Derek."

My jaw dropped, and my eyes stopped blinking. There stood this tall, silver fox guy, in a Godzilla t-shirt, with arms folded. *HOLY FUCKING SHIT! DEREK GOODWIN?!*

"Nice to meet you," he said with a lisp.

I didn't know he talked with a lisp!

"Wonderful to meet you, sir," Grayson said as he shook his hand.

"Sorry, but I need to steal this one away, business stuff." Derek said, now with his lisp more tuned.

"Hey, see you around, Gwen," Adam added.

Once Adam left, Grayson took his place. "Hey look…" he started while rubbing the back of his head, "... There's been a mixup with the rooms. Somehow or someone, somewhat accidentally ordered the one room, with a king size bed. Just the one bed!"

He dangled the key in front of me. I tried to hide my excitement from him, "Soooo…. I guess this means we might have to share?"

Chapter 32:
King Size Bed

I opened the room and stood gasping at how beautiful the room was.

"Yeah, they only had the Honeymoon suite left." Grayson told me as he pushed past. I left my suitcase in the doorway as I raced through each section of the room, checking out all the details and trinkets left behind.

I returned to the main room and stood in the corner, once again admiring the size of this room.

Suddenly, something pulled behind me, closer to Grayson. Feeling his baby smooth cheek brushed against mine. "Like the room?" he whispered.

Before I could reply to his comment, he was already standing in front of me, his hand around my waist, leaning down slowly kissing me, to passionate kissing. He swung me around and popped me up on the table in the corner. I pulled on his t-shirt, pulling him in closer to me as we continued to make out passionately.

"He is not going to like what he sees, Gwen," that bad voice returns. I haven't heard from it for a long time, *so why now, why pop into my head as I'm about to do something I have been waiting for what feels like an eternity?*

"Come on Gwen, you can't be serious? He is hot as, with washboard abs, and perfect Asian features. And there's you, ugly, plump, four eyed nerd."
I quickly pushed Grayson off of me, placing my hands on his shoulder and my arms stretched out. He took a step back. "Gwen?" he whispered.
 I couldn't find the words to tell him to give me a minute. Then I heard a voice I needed to hear, a voice to let me know everything is okay.

"Gwen, don't listen to those thoughts. They aren't real. You will be okay. It's Grayson. You are playing out one of your fantasies, remember?" I looked over Grayson's shoulder briefly to see Paul standing there giving that *'go ahead'* look. He knew that this, this thing here right now, is something I wanted, something I needed.
"Sorry, I didn't mean to take it too far. If you need more time, I can wait!" Grayson added.
I took a deep breath in and looked over at Paul again. "Do it!" Paul shouted.

A smile came across my face as I grabbed Grayson by the shirt to make out with him again.

Grayson took a quick step back and took off his t-shirt. He looked down at my feet and said, "You have odd socks on."

I took my shoes off before. "I still have a Punky Brewster phase," I told him.

He let out a small chuckle, crawled back over me. He brushed a strand of hair out of my face and kissed me again.

"I like your odd socks," he added.

Grayson pulled me off the table and pushed me up against the wall, interlaced his fingers with mine and then lifted my arms above my head, pushing himself hard onto me. I gasp for air.

I didn't know how exciting this could be!

With one hand, he held my hands in place and with the other; he unbuttoned my pants and slid his hand over the top of my underwear, gently teasing me with each movement. My body loosen as his fingers went deep, and his thumb brushed against my clit, a shiver came over me.

He pulled his fingers out. "What's wrong?" he whispered to me.

I needed to tell him something as reality came back. "You got cold hands."

He placed his fingers in front of his mouth and breathed on them to warm them up. I grabbed his warm hand and leaned into him. "Can we go to bed now?"

I walked over to the bed, turned around to find Grayson had disappeared into the bathroom. I took off my clothes and crawled into bed. I looked over at the armchair in the corner. "Don't mind me…" Paul added, "… I'm just supporting you."

"Go away!" I said through the grit of my teeth, "I'm already nervous. The last thing I need is my imaginary friend watching."

Paul got up. "Okay, I'll leave, but you have to tell me every little dirty, nasty detail afterwards."

I sat up in bed, watching his clothes fly out of the bathroom. The lights in the room dimmed. It was dark, but light enough to see shadows. He popped his head around the corner and said, "are you okay with this?"

I took a deep breath, and a huge smile came over my face. "Yes, Ready!" I sat up in bed, tapped my feet with excitement.

Grayson walked into the room and stood there at the end of the bed. I could make out his shape and his features.

OH NO! Naked Grayson is the ultimate level of hottest!

His perfect shoulders, the muscles on his arms. His slightly perfect line six-pack. Then I couldn't help myself; I looked down at his erect penis, realising what I would get myself into.

He leaned over the bed, grabbed my ankles, and dragged me closer to him, making me fall on my back, then he disappeared under the covers. He crawled over me, nuzzling my legs opening.

A small kiss brushed my inner thighs, slowly moving up, and I jolted again, and then, again and again, the thoughts of him noticing my horrible shave job left me as I moved my body to the rhythm of his tongue. While he continued pleasuring me, I ran my fingers through his perfect hair. I felt my heart race, and my breathing became more rapid. I moaned louder and louder. My back arched up so quickly, and I couldn't breathe. My body just froze there in the spot for a split second. Then suddenly, my whole body relaxed.

Grayson crawled up to me, kissed my neck, and then whispered, "I like it that I can make you cum hard!"

Okay, good to know. Wait... I totally did!

He returned to kissing my neck and biting my ear lobe while holding my breast tight, teasing me. I grabbed his face and moved towards mine. We started kissing again while his erection rubbed my thigh.

He finally whispered to me, "Can I have a turn?"

I reached down and gently wrapped my hand around his penis. He jolted a little. I helped him guide himself into me. He slowly entered.

OH GOD! He feels so big inside of me!

"All Good?" Grayson asked, as he slowly started to thrush.

"Oh, God…" I gaps, "go… a little… Faster!"

"As you wish," Grayson added, as he thrusted a little faster.

My breathing became more rapid. Grayson ripped off his glasses and let out a little moan every now and then, my body became hot.

Then, "Oh God, I think I'm close!" Grayson huffed, "No! Not yet!" I let out. I knew I was getting close, myself. I quickly wrapped my legs around him and pushed on him to go deeper. Grayson got faster, his breath got deeper, then suddenly, my body tense up, "OH MY FUCKING GOD!" as my body came down. With one quick, deep hard thrust inside, suddenly sliding out, Grayson gave himself a few quick jerks, only for him to cum all over my leg.

He dropped himself beside me. Our heavy breathing was in sync as we both tried to catch our breaths, "Suc…cess!" Grayson said.

"What?"

"I did… what…. I promise."

He rolled over, put his glasses back on, "I made you cum twice!"

I burst out laughing.

The Californian sun peeped through the blinds. I slowly woke up to a strange sensation that I was being watched. I quickly turn my head to Paul kneeling beside the bed, watching me with big puppy dog eyes.
"Morning sleepy head!" Paul said as he watched me.
I was about to say something, but Paul covered his lips with his finger. I followed his gaze and saw Grayson lying on his back with one of his arms above his head, still fast asleep. Little whooshing noises were coming out of him. He looks so peaceful lying there.
"Hey you wanna get out of here?" Paul said, trying to get my attention back.
I was about to say something, but Paul interrupted me, "Look, we have battles tomorrow and today is a good chance to make sure everything is perfect."
I nodded.
"Come on, let's sneak out and get a coffee!" He continued, walking his fingers in the air.

Chapter 33:
Social Mobile Local

Well, here we were, backstage at the Startup Battles. There were so many people here. One guy in the corner jumping up and down, another walking around in little circles, *Gross! Someone just vomited*!

I inhale deeply. My head tightens. Grayson and I kept walking closer to the stage, still looking at the competition. Each step we took, the competition looked fierce. Groups of guys sitting in circles hovering over a laptop, another group of guys wearing matching jackets, and another matching t-shirts.

"Knew I forgot something!" Paul said, "Matching t-shirts for the three of us."

"Matching t-shirts will not win us the competition. Besides, they make you look like a sellout!"

One guy lifted his head at me, "Sorry, I don't mean you…. they look good!" I tried to correct myself.

"Okay, no more talking, Paul. I can't focus on correcting myself and this competition."

Grayson pulled himself into a corner and crouched down. He opened my laptop and looked over the PowerPoint I designed. He muttered to himself.

"Talking to Paul I see?" I asked him.

He looked up at me with those beautiful brown eyes of his. "No… I'm just making sure I'm on point. I don't want to miss an opportunity at any point."

"Fair," I added.

"Missed opportunity? He is going to screw this up for you, then back to TroniX for you!" I heard the bad voice again.

Not now, please, Not NOW!

Grayson handed me my laptop, and I noticed my jaw was quivering. I tried to hold it but couldn't. My hand shook, too.

"Gwen, you alright?" Paul asked.

I opened my mouth and my breathing became heavy.

"Gwen?" Paul said.

My eyes darted from one group of people to the next, then to the next. My breathing became heavier.

"Gwen, look at me?" Paul said.

I quickly darted my eyes towards Paul. Eyes widened, *"You're going to fail, your product sucks!"* That horrible voice inside my head is getting to me.

"Gwen, slow down!" Paul added, grabbing my hands, "breathe with me…"

He slowed down his breathing, and I tried to mimic his patterns. *"Seriously, this is what you wore to this thing? You look ugly. No one listens to ugly bitches!"*

Grayson grabbed my hand, said, "Hey, we are needed over there," and started dragging me over.

I lost my hearing, and my placement. I took another deep breath, "just wait here guys. When you hear your name, then proceed on stage."

Wait, I'm in the wings. I darted around to find my bearings. I didn't know we were going on so soon. I don't have time to think, breathe, or… *OH NO!* A sudden chill fell over me. I froze on the spot. I tried to call for Grayson, but my mouth kept shut.

I don't want to do this anymore!

My belly turned over and over, and my mouth was wet and dry at the same time.

"See, told you, you sucked! You're going to vomit on stage. Millions of people are laughing at you!"

OH GOD MILLIONS!!!

"Gwen, listen to me. You are going to nail this!" Paul said, "Please breathe, deep breaths, Gwen."

I started taking deep breaths, *in and out, in and out, in and out.* I started to feel better. I could move again.

"Ladies and gentlemen, please welcome to the stage Grayson Li and Gwen Hooper from Three's company with Paul.2."

Grayson took the first steps out. I went to follow him out, but I quickly said to Paul, 'I got this, I got… this!" Then blew out one more big breath and followed Grayson on stage.

As we walked on the stage, I heard a roar of clapping, followed by chatter. I hooked up our laptop to the cables already on the stand while Grayson stood out the front. "Have you ever wondered what it would be like to have the perfect best friend? Or a wingman that actually helps you get the girl?" There was some giggling from the audience.

Okay, so far, so good!

"Or you need someone to remind you of important dates and times. Or just having company around you. Have you ever been so lonely you just wished you had someone to talk to?"

He looked over at me. I went to click on the PowerPoint; it froze. *Of course it froze! Why would anything work while you're on stage presenting to thousands of people? OH GOD, I really have blown our chances.*

I started to breathe heavily again as I panicked.

"Turn on AI, Gwen." Paul said, standing next to me.

With a quick ALT TAB, I switch over to the AI. Pointed to Grayson. He looked up and nodded.

"…Then, meet Paul.2! We are connecting the world with one lonely person at a time with our So Lo Mo."

"Bullshit! You don't even know what So Lo Mo means!"

"Shut up!" I muttered, "not the time!"

Watching colours bouncing across the screen like a DVD logo on screensaver mode was not that impressive. Grayson had to abandon his speech; he went on talking to Paul.2. "Let me show you how he works. Hey Paul."

"Hello, Grayson," Paul.2 said.

There were some murmurs from the audience. I froze, watching the audience whisper to each other. "Paul.2 will have facial recognition, as it will set it up to recognise the user, but also surrounding people, like if he was part of a meeting, or a dinner party."

More murmurs from the audience. *"They are talking about you Gwen; they know this product is fake. You're going to be found out that both you and Grayson faked your way into Silicon Valley!"*

FUCK THIS VOICE!

"Shush!" I whispered.

Grayson thought a bit and said, "Paul, you are on display at the Startup Battle."

"Oh no, Grayson, why didn't you warn me? I need to put my makeup on." Paul responded.

The audience laughed.

"See, they are laughing at how stupid you are!"

The chill ran up my body again, my hands pulsed into fists, my eyes widen yet again.

"Not now, please not right now!" I muttered to myself.

"We have created a dialogue for Paul to use. We are creating a more human-like feel to this AI," Grayson added.

"Can I introduce you to some important people?" Grayson asked Paul.2

"Go ahead, I'm ready."

"I want you to meet Bill Holmes, Moss Timmons, Betty Ferguson, and Leonard Gilbert," Grayson said.

"Hello, I believe you are today's judges at the Startup Battle," Paul.2 said.

"As you can see, Paul has lightning-speed access to Google and can respond to any question you ask," Grayson explained back to the audience.

I watched the audience taking in everything Grayson was showing.

"My God Gwen, look at them. They are really liking what they see." Paul added.

"What will it take for Max to drag your name through the mud? You are tainted. You stand to lose everything. You deserve none of this!"

My belly flipped again. That sudden rise of sick feeling came over me. I darted my eyes around, looking for the closest exit.

"Hey, thanks for recommending that Netflix series to me too, Paul," Grayson said as he was still showing Paul.2 on stage.

"I told you it was good; did you see the twist at the end of season 2?" Paul.2 said back.

"Oh My God, yes I did!" Grayson answered Paul.2 and turned back to the audience, saying, "As you can see, Paul is equipped with conversations to make it feel like its lunchtime discussion, or dinnertime conversations."

The audience's murmurs became louder. I turned around to dry-reach quickly, then turned back.

"You're going to vomit!"

Grayson turns back to the big screen. "Paul, can you help me out? I need a great place to take my girlfriend on a date?" Grayson continued with his demonstration.

GIRLFRIEND?! Oh GOD NO! I had sex with Grayson, and he has a girlfriend!

I gripped the edge of the podium, and my breathing became rapid. I couldn't catch my breath.

"Gwen, that's you, not someone else. You're the girlfriend, remember?" Paul told me.

"I have found some great places based on your favourite food choices." A list of restaurants popped up on the screen. Then Paul added, "Would you like me to book? Say about seven, as you both finish work at five-thirty p.m.?"

"Nope, it's Iris, he is still seeing Iris. the AI said so!"
I hate this voice!

"Shut…. up" I muttered again.

I slowly looked over at the judges and saw them talking to one another.

"Oh, you know they are saying this product is shit. Mitch told them it's fake!"

"No, it's okay, Paul. But thank you."

"That's okay, Grayson," Paul.2 responded.

"Gwen?" I heard Paul say.

I couldn't move; my body was trembling. I couldn't talk. I just want to run away. That nasty voice kept at me, *'you are such a loser, why would anyone pay attention to you! You can never be successful!'*

I closed my eyes tight, and whispered, *Shush* to myself. I finally hit the peak.

Grayson turned back to the audience. "Paul is the best friend, the wingman, the personal assistant, the perfect—"

"Grayson." Paul.2 interrupted, "Did we win?"

Huge laughter from the audience erupted, snapping me out of my concentration.

Grayson looked at me, chuckling as well. His chuckling stopped suddenly as we locked eyes.

"Please give it up for Grayson Li, Gwen Hooper and Paul.2 with Three's Company!" Moss announced.

Suddenly the roar of cheers, clapping, standing ovation took over the auditorium. I turn to look at everyone cheering us on. *'Look at them, Gwen. All those people are here to take you down. This product sucks!'*

I looked over at the wing. My eyes darted back to Paul; I knew it was now or never. Inhaling deeply, I muttered, "Move!" I looked over at the wing again and quickly left the stage, leaving Grayson there.

I pushed past people. My focus was blurry, until I found an exit, pushing down on the door and ran outside.

I bent over, trying to find as much air outside. When I could, I took one big breath and yelled, "STOP IT!"

"Gwen?" Paul said to me, "Look at me!"

"FUCK OFF PAUL! I NEED TO BREATHE!" I shouted at him.

"Stand up and place your hands on your head. You will get more air that way," Paul said.

'No matter how hard you try, you are still that loser from high school!' the nasty voice added.

"SHUT UP!" I yelled out as I danced around with my hands on my head.

"Gwen, just breathe." Paul added.

'You are nothing but a waste of space. Success doesn't look good on you. You will always be a failure!'

"SHUT IT! SHUT THE FUCK UP!"

With my arms down, I point at Paul. "SHUT THE FUCK UP, FUCKING STOP IT! RIGHT NOW! I am allowed to be successful. I'm not this loser from high school. I'M NOT THE LOSER FROM TRONIX! This is the real world, NO ONE CARES! I am sick and tired of these thoughts, I'M DONE! I'm done with this nasty voice telling me that I'm not allowed to be who I want to be. I want to be successful. I want to be a tech billionaire. I want to run my own company! I WANT TO BE THE NEXT BIG THING HERE! Isn't it my turn? I WANT MY TURN! MY TURN!!!"

I blew out the last bit of air from my lungs, wondering where that came from, and why I pointed this at Paul. I placed my hands on my hips and said one last thing. "It's my turn to be successful! My turn…."

I stood there, staring at Paul. The feeling of dread was gone, replaced with this feeling of calm. I felt better. That nasty voice was gone. Paul stood there staring at me, with his arms crossed, and chuckled, "And… it's about time, Gwen!"

"Gwen?" I heard behind me. I suddenly froze.

"Grayson!" I said, running into his arms, holding him tighter.

"You okay?" he asked.

"I needed some air?" I told him.

"You know you are right? It is your time to be the successful one!" he said, coming down to my eye level. "How about we get a drink?" he continued.

"It's about 10:30 in the morning!" I replied.

"I am aware of the time."

Chapter 34:
The Deal

TechCrunch was ending. Everyone out about, checking out of their rooms, sitting around having their breakfast. The chatter, the laughter in the dining room had this nice peaceful feel to the room. Deals were made, people networked, and relationships of all kinds flourished.

I sat at the table, drinking my glass of juice, while finishing my plate of food. A commotion over one side of the lobby got to me, seeing Emmy Watts talking to some reporters.

"You didn't hear the news?" OJ said as he joined me at my table.

"What news?" I asked him.

Yesterday afternoon, on stage, Moss collapsed, and paramedics transported him to the hospital. Emmy and Jocelyn were at his side all night."

OJ looked over at her. "She looks tired."

"Do they know what happened?" I asked him.

"No, as far as I know, Emmy has been doing most of his work. And damn, she's good at it." He said, taking a bite of his toast.

Grayson put his plate down, looked at his phone, and then threw it on the table.

"We didn't win!"

"Who won?"

"No idea, some fairy tale company!" OJ added, "you should have seen the Weissman Score, amazing!"

The commotion died down, and the ground floor of the hotel went back to normal chatters and murmurs.

"I saw you guys on stage. I didn't realise how interactive this AI was. I'm shocked you guys didn't win," OJ added as he placed his crust on his plate.

"We didn't have a Weissman score," Grayson said.

"It doesn't matter. People will be jumping on you guys!"

OJ picked up a glass of water. "Speak of jumping. Did my trick work?"

"What trick?" I asked.

"The hotel room trick?"

Grayson punched OJ in the arm.

"Wait a minute, did you pretend there was a mixup of our rooms so we can spend time together?"

"Well, it's not a trick, trick…" Grayson said, rubbing the back of his head, "...More like a trick, kind of trick."

I laughed hard.

"Grayson told me you guys are dating now, which, by the way, is awesome. I was rooting for you, Gwen! Iris made me feel uncomfortable." Then he let out a shiver. "I told Grayson, if you guys are going to TechCrunch, then do the room mixup thing. It's the oldest trick in the book, but hey it works!"

I was about to say something else, but someone else came to join us at the table. I watched her climb over the chair, placed herself down on the chair, crossed her legs and stole the watermelon off OJ's plate. She took a bite and said, "Hey OJ, when we get back, I'm going to need your help with some configurations with this app"

"Yep, on it, Emmy!" he answered. "How's Moss?"

"Touch and go at the moment." She said.

"We can put everything aside until he is better."

Emmy shook her head, "No, as long as the company is running, I think he will be happy."

Emmy placed the watermelon rind down, "Speaking of apps and running companies, I saw you guys at the Start Up Battles yesterday. I know I have been sitting on the business plan for a few weeks now. I just had some personal things that came up and needed to sort them out."

She looked around the table. "I want to make an offer to you."

"An Offer?!" Grayson said.

"Shush…. the ladies are talking!" Emmy quieted Grayson.

She took another piece of OJ's watermelon. "Look, I have watched enough Shark Tank and poked Mark Cuban a bit for some tips to understand how these deals work."

She pointed the rind of the watermelon at Gwen, dripping some of the juice on the table, "I am willing to give you two hundred thousand dollars for a ten percent."

I choked on my water, trying to catch my breath, my mind raced, I searched for the right words when I heard a chair scrape, "Don't listen to the Educator." he pronounced each word with his lisp, "I mean, she has no idea how to run a company."

Looking up to see this Silver Fox gamer in a green flannel, leaning on his chair. *Something was about to go down!*

"A school maybe. But you can't run a company like a school. That would never work." He turned and faced her. "Didn't she just admit she had watched enough Shark Tank to figure out how to make a deal?"

Is this for reals? I'm sitting here having breakfast with a billionaire battle happening at my table! And over MY product?

"Oh, fuck off Derek. When was the last time you made a deal?" Emmy added.

"Serious…" Derek placed his hand on Emmy's mouth to shut her up. "See, this AI thing is amazing. Yeah, it sucks you guys didn't win, but I want it. It will work amazingly well in my gaming company."

"Please!" Emmy sarcastically added, as she removed his hand.

"Shush, you!" Derek added. But he turned back to Gwen and Grayson, "I want that product! I'll give you guys 10 million for it."

I quickly grabbed Grayson by the arm, hearing the new offer. *Ten million! Imagine what we can do with that money!*

"Beat that, Emmy!" Derek said with a gleeful grin.

"I'm pretty sure that I just did." She adjusted herself in her seat, straightening her back, holding her head high. She pointed her focus all now on Derek. "You offer them ten million. Now, does this ten come from your company, or your back pocket?"

She poured herself a glass of water, "Derek, my dear sweet mindless billionaire, you know how much I adore you, but right now business is business, and this will be my product." She told him as she patted the side of his face, "Two hundred thousand bucks, for ten percent, is far more profitable for Gwen and Grayson, who might want to invest in their own product."

She took a sip of her water. "These two aren't dumb. They have been in the world of investments, tech and Silicon Valley far longer than myself. These guys will never let go of a perfectly good, well profitable product like this. I might as well take 10 percent into the business and let them continue on building, designing, making this product for themselves!"

She placed the glass down. "You are going to hand over ten million dollars. They hand over the product. This product is, or maybe still, a prototype. This means you will need to strip it down to its bare bones, find out how it ticks, then put it all back together and build from that. See…." she made a thinking face at him to continue to mock his offer, "…I believe this product would cost you more, as you will need to hire new staff to do all that. There's no extended offers, contracts or even T and C's going with this ten million!"

She lifted her head with a smug smile and adjusted her glasses. "And my dear sir… is what we call a checkmate! Or us Aussie's would say, *'Up your Bum, Chum!'*" she added as she waved her two fingers in Derek's face.

My head was swimming. *Do we take the ten million and live our lives? Or start a new company? Or do we take Emmy's deal and work at Innovative Tech, building more to Paul.2, designing him to be the best thing out there.*

I felt a little jab in my back. "What do you want, Gwen?" I heard Paul say behind me, "Both deals sound fantastic. Ten million and retire, or two hundred thousand and build?"

I took a deep breath, thinking about which way to go.

Paul let out a chuckle. "You know what you want, I know what you want. I can see it now." He jabbed me again. "Tell them! Tell them your decision. Remember, whatever you pick will make Grayson happy!"

I watched Derek remove Emmy's fingers from his face. He didn't seem to let go of her hand as he laced his fingers in with hers. *Oh my God, are they back together?*

I turn to face Grayson. Grayson removed my hand off his arm. He looked into my eyes, gave my hand a tight squeeze.

I knew he was as invested as I was, and he devoted himself wholeheartedly. The amount of sacrifice he had done for us to be sitting here, for this company to be let go for a small ten million.

We both nodded at each other, and I turned to say, "Derek, I thank you for your offer, but we have put so much of our lives into this product. I do believe that with Emmy, we will be able to take this further. I see this AI becoming more involved with her education, as well as other aspects it can go."

I turned to Emmy who was on to the next piece of watermelon off OJ's plate, "Emmy, we would like to take your offer, and we are both keen to start as soon as possible."

With a quick fist pump and a YES, she turned to Derek. "No heart feelings, mate!"

Derek shook her hand, then pulled it up to kiss it and added, "come on, let's go and celebrate your victory!"

Chapter 35:
Goodbye, Old Friend

Months have come and gone. The Startup battles feel like a pipe dream now, as both Grayson and I have settled into working at Innovative Tech.

The atmosphere of the company is enlightening, full of cheerful people. The company itself uses the honour system. Come and go when you want, work from home if needed, lunch is there with a 24-hour lunchroom.

Paul.2, or The Paul as the company knew it, became an innovative product of the year, selling on the app store for a profit of $49.99 per year. We decided to make it a cost, to keep it ad free. The number of people who downloaded the

Paul and its plugins surprised us, and to add extra plugins, cost only $1.

Emmy never saw anything wrong with calling it Paul. She thought it was easy to say and easy to spell. "You need a product that everyone can spell easily. Some of these AIs we have out at the moment are hard to pronounce and spell!"

Three's Company has been working on another version of AI and working alongside the engineering department with OJ, creating AI robots.

OH, Yes! My life is good! I can breathe again, no more bad thoughts, no more headaches, no more sitting in my car watching my knuckles turning white. No more dealing with assholes!

My house became a home. I loved how full it was now, that it became one of my favourite places to hang out. Grayson moved in after letting Iris take everything from him. He couldn't care less, he knew he was in a pleasant spot in his life too.

My bookshelves were now full of books, action figures, Lego, old school toys, and picture frames.

I would catch myself staring at each of the pictures on the wall and on the fridge. Remembering the fun times we had, the barbeque in the backyard, the company's trips and gatherings, that amazing trip to New York that Grayson I took, and pretending the hotel screwed up our rooms again, *Oh no! Looks like we have to share a bed again, oh dear!*

After admiring each moment, I would let out a small happy huff and leave the room with a smile, glad to know my house was now complete.

Each Saturday Morning OJ, Grayson, and I now hang out for coffee, gossip and to share ideas.

OJ and Grayson started a new D&D club at our house, with new teammates, Adam included.

Listening to the roars of laughter, cheers, and the bantering that went on through the night. And the excuses we all gave Emmy every Thursday morning on why we were so tired.

I couldn't ask for anything more. Yes, my life turned out to be perfect!

Another D&D night was upon us. I sat on the edge of the table, listening to Grayson direct the gamers. OJ rolled his dice, and another roar filled the room.

"So, what are you going to do?" Grayson asked, trying to hide his smile.

"I will use my sling to slay this monster."

Grayson nodded at him. OJ picked up his dice and gave a hard roll. The room roared again. "You hit the monster in the eye. He is now blind! Adam, what would you do?"

Adam looked at his game sheet, then said, "Magic Spell!"

Adam moved his hands around and said, "cast a fuck off spell, as we need to get in that room!"

Grayson laughed out loud, throwing his head back.

"Fire Ball!" Adam said as he pushed his hand forward. He picked up his dice, rolled and got a critical hit!

"The fire enveloped and blinded the monster. Melting him into a puddle on the floor. You guys can now enter!" Grayson said, wiping a tear from his eye.

As Grayson moved our character on the map, something else caught my eye, a strange figure I haven't seen in a long time.

I got off my seat and followed this figure outside. I saw him sitting there on the step, and I joined him.

"So, I guess my work here is done," Paul said to me.

"What work?"

Paul pointed his head to the front door when I heard another roar of cheers coming from inside the house.

"I did everything I can to help you, Gwen. You got what you wanted." Paul said, "You got your friends, you got your voice, you got your career, you took revenge on Max... even if he doesn't realise this. But most importantly, you got Grayson!"

Paul smiled and let out a small sigh. "I'm not needed anymore."

"NO! Don't say that!" I told him, knowing this could be the last time I talked to Paul. "I still need you! Don't I?"

"Gwen, you know it, and I know it," Paul said, trying to keep the conversation going.

I sat there in silence, pulling my legs closer to me. Placing both my arms on top and resting my head to stare at Paul. A lump formed in my throat, and my bottom lip trembled. *I can't let Paul go! I just can't! what if I need him again? What if...*

"What happens next? Do you become someone else's imaginary friend, or that's it?" I asked him.

"It's a tough question," Paul said, leaning back on the porch.

"I hope you become someone else's imaginary friend. You're very helpful! I'm sure there is another lonely adult out there who needs your help." I tried not to get upset.

"You pretty much fixed that with your AI." Paul answered me.

I let out a chuckle, trying to hide my sadness.

"I can't stop this, can I? What if I need you? What if I find myself in the same predicament again? What if Grayson turns out to be another Max? What if...."

I heard the front door open; "Gwen, you okay?"

"Yeah, just give me a minute. I just needed some air." I told Grayson, as I wiped my eyes.

"Cool, I think we need a break!" he said, then popped his head out again. "I meant with the game, not us... definitely not us!"

Paul stood up and dusted himself off, while chuckling, "See, you're in excellent hands. Grayson is the best. He is not Max! Not one bit. And besides, you can handle yourself. You proved to me time and time again."

I got off the step and dusted off as I joined Paul. "So, this is really goodbye then?"

Paul put his arms out, "come on, bring it in, and give one last kiss!"

I leaped into his arms, grabbed him tight, leaned up to look up at him, placed a kiss on his lips, "Until next time, Snotface!" He whispers to me.

I closed my eyes, tightened my lips, clinched my hand, trying not to let Paul go. I held him tighter, feeling the pressure of my arms round him.

"Gwen, are you sure everything is okay?" Grayson said as he put his jacket on.

I opened my eyes. *Wait, where is Paul? WHERE IS PAUL!!!*

Leaning on the rail, tapping my fingers while looking for Paul. The streetlights beam casting a shadow over the street. My eyes darted all over the front yard, my jaw locked, doing little bounces on my toes, *No, No, No…. NO! Where did he go? Where is Paul? OH NO! NO, NO, NO, NO!*

Grayson wrapped his arm around me. "Gwen, it's cold out here."

A tear escaped from my eye and ran down my cheek. Grayson wiped it off with his thumb. "Gwen, you okay?" he asked, trying to get an answer out of me.

He's gone, he's gone, he's gone! I just lost my imaginary friend! But I can do this! I can do this!

Another tear escaped, and I quickly wiped it myself. I looked up at Grayson. And there it was, I suddenly stopped crying, my head ease from the pressure, I let out a deep breath and a small smile was placed on my face, "Nothing is wrong," I snorted. "I'm just happy. I got what I wanted."

Grayson pulled me in for a hug, and his sweet, icy scent got to me one more time. His hug, his smell calmed me down to that peacefulness I finally got.

Then suddenly, Colin came up the stairs. I picked her up and gave her a scratch on the head, I looked up at Grayson, "Hey, don't we have a dragon to battle in a dungeon somewhere?"

He laughs, "Not yet, Gwen!"

Then he closed the door behind us.

The End.

Acknowledgements:

This has been a journey to create, coming up with ideas and concepts to this book. I always had a love for technology and the idea of Silicon Valley, as it always was a dream of mine to work there one day. I love the idea of StartUp Companies and the myth behind how they get their start (the rags to riches story!) Watching many documentaries,
movies, tv shows, and bio's on many rising and
falling startups (real and fake ones) seeing how each step is taken. Using this idea as a base for this story. My parents always inspired me to work in fields that I enjoy no matter how uniformity they are. Hence the reason for my wonderful career in Learning and Development.

The idea of 'Paul' the imaginary friend came to me when I was at my deepest point in my life. Depression kicked in and I always wished I had someone there to cheer me on or help me when I needed it the most. Someone to help me do the simplest task such as getting out of bed, or talking to people, as therapy was still taboo in my family at that time.
Manifesting an entity to help me pull myself out of a dark place helped me move on with the next steps in my life and encouraged me to become the
person I am today.

There are so many people I need to thank for helping and contributing to this story.

My family has been a great help throughout the journey, encouraging me, and asking me the right questions to keep me motivated in completing the story. Biggest thank you to Justin (the real OJ) and Lincoln.

Justin also encouraged me to join writer groups in our area where I ended up meeting some wonderful people, who read the earlier versions of My friend Paul and taught me how to write, as well as taking me to writing classes. Their expertise and acknowledgements towards writing and storytelling helped me to not only rediscover a new love for writing, but also to improve My friend Paul to its fullest potential. And as promised Thank You to **Petra, Kate, and Sarah.** See, I kept my promise of making your names stick out!!! (LOL)

Lastly there are two people I need to thank. I will not reveal their names for confidential purposes, but the two therapists I spoke to about the idea of imaginary friends in adults. These two professionals explain to me the theory behind why certain adults would have or still continue to have imaginary friends in their lives, and what these friends symbolise to those patients. They also continued to explain the difference between each common type of imaginary friend and also how to end the friendship with these entities.

I hope you have enjoyed this story and look out for my next book.

Thank you kindly.

About the Author:

Michelle Odette Whelan is a Melbourne-based writer, voiceover artist, instructional designer, certified dyslexic and ASD, and full-time nerd passionate about the weird.

A former roller derby player, Michelle channels her energy into creative projects that blend her love of technology, Silicon Valley innovation, and offbeat storytelling.

Her fascination with the paranormal, folklore, and science fiction inspires her unique narratives, which explore the quirky and unexpected.

When she's not writing novels or working on her podcast, Michelle enjoys delving into tech trends, sipping classic coffee, spending time with her family, the local writer groups and celebrating the unconventional.

 Banjocanwrite